MORE THAN 100%

DEAD

A Cortlandt Scott Mystery

Lee Mossel

Lee Mossel

Dedication

More Than 100% Dead is dedicated to Jan. She does it all and supports me in every way.

Thanks, Special!

PROLOGUE

Some ancient philosopher had said, "Success has a thousand fathers; failure is a bastard." I think that old gray beard must have been prophesizing the oil business. No one ever "claimed" credit for a dry hole, but for every successful wildcat, a multitude of people would jump to the front of the line. When a large field, particularly a "giant" like Trumpet Creek was discovered, everybody wanted a piece of the action. Engineers who'd supervised the drilling operations would say they "drilled it;" landmen who'd taken the oil and gas leases from the ranchers or farmers who owned the mineral rights would say they "leased it." The operator, the guy with his name on the permit and who probably put up some or all of the money, would *always* maintain he was responsible for the success. I, of course, was predisposed toward the originating geologist who'd managed to get his idea, his baby, his *prospect* drilled. After all, I'd been there, done that, and had the tee-shirt. It's what I did before becoming a PI. Sometimes I missed it, but not enough to go back.

There was considerable discussion about who had *really* discovered Trumpet Creek. Some of the Denver oil community supported Freddie Pearlman's claim that his company, Big East Oil, had actually discovered the field with a gas well drilled a couple of years previously. Others favored Wildcat Oil because they had produced the first oil.

Big East's well had tested natural gas at a high rate, but with no gas pipelines in the area to transport and sell natural gas, the well was capped. Geologically, the well had been located in an area called the "gas cap" on the east side of the rapidly expanding oil field. In a gas cap, free natural gas "floats" on top of crude oil in the same manner as steam accumulates on top of water when it boils.

The Big East geologists quickly and correctly interpreted the well information to mean there was an oil field immediately west. Their enthusiasm faded rapidly when their land staff found Wildcat Oil held the leases to the west. Big East tried every ploy and proposal they could think of to get the right to drill but nothing worked. It didn't help that Freddie Pearlman and "Wildcat Willie" Davidson shared a mutual dislike for one another.

CHAPTER

ONE

I was on my second cup of coffee when my office phone rang; unusual for a Wednesday morning. It seemed most calls for a private investigator either came early Monday morning or late Friday afternoon. They were designed to screw up the whole week or at least the weekend.

I checked caller ID and was mildly surprised to see my friend Tom Montgomery's name. Tom's a Denver Police Department homicide detective. We shared a craving for Cajun food and really cold beer, two things another friend, Louisiana transplant Andy Thibodeaux, provided in his restaurant.

"Hey Tom, how're you doing? What's up…you don't usually call the office?"

Tom rarely bothered with pleasantries and this time was no different. "What do you know about a Denver oil guy named William Davidson and Wildcat Oil?"

"Quite a bit, everybody knows him as Wildcat Willie. Why?"

"Because somebody put two in the back of his head last night or this morning."

"*Holy shit*! Where'd you find him?"

"In his private parking spot under the Alamo Plaza Building; the security patrol found him about 5:15 a.m. He was halfway in and halfway out of the biggest damn Mercedes I've ever seen."

"*Man-o-man!* This'll be the biggest murder case in Denver in years! You catch the lead?"

"Yep, that's me. I just got briefed by the chief of police himself, and he told me to pull out all the stops on this one--unlimited overtime for all detectives until there's a break. I can use all the manpower I want."

"How come you're wasting time calling me? Shouldn't you be out detecting or something?"

"Screw you, wiseass. You're always telling me how well connected to the oil business you are. Here's your chance to prove that's something more than ancient history. I need you working on this case."

"Are you actually *asking* me to help? Who's going to pay me?"

"You're going to do it out of the goodness of your heart, although the DA, who was in my office with the chief, did mention something about funds being available for *special investigators*. Don't start thinking you're 'special' but I'm pretty sure you'll get paid if that's what's worrying you."

I wasn't worried about it and it was time to cut the banter. "I was just giving you a little shit, Tom. I'll do whatever you need. What do you know so far?"

He sighed heavily. "Not very damn much; we'll be waiting on the ME's report, not that it'll change anything. Two slugs in the head are a pretty obvious cause of death but it'll probably be helpful to get a ballistics report when they dig 'em out. The good news is the report is fast- tracked like everything else. I should have something by late this afternoon. Otherwise, all I've done is take a look at the murder scene and stroll around the garage. It looks like somebody walked up from behind just as he was getting in his car. Like I said, he was kind of half in, half out, the door was open and he got it just behind the left ear. He must have weighed over three hundred so it probably wasn't all that easy for him to get behind the driver's seat. The killer could have walked up on him without much trouble.

"I'll have a search warrant for Davidson's office pretty soon, and that's another thing: the DA said they'll have a handful of warrants all signed and ready to go anytime we need one. We just have to fill in addresses; the ADAs will fill in the probable cause."

"Man, you weren't BS-ing about this being fast tracked. Where do you want me to start?"

"While we're waiting for the search warrant, I want to come over to your office and talk this through. Then, I want you to come to Davidson's office with me. Put on some coffee and I'll be over in fifteen minutes."

"Coffee's made; I'll see you here.

CHAPTER

TWO

Before Tom called, I'd been reading a series of *Rocky
Mountain Oil Journal* stories about Trumpet Creek, a giant
oilfield being developed in southeast Montana. I decided to
finish the articles because Wildcat Willie Davidson was--or
had been--a big part of it. The *Journal* was speculating on the
eventual size of the new "elephant" sized field. Conservative
estimates put it at fifty million barrels; optimists were saying
two hundred million barrels. Regardless, Trumpet Creek
would be the biggest oil discovery in the Rocky Mountains in
over twenty years. No matter how the reserves turned out, it
was a phenomenal amount of oil. At current crude prices, the

gross value might reach twenty billion--with a capital "B"--dollars.

I heard the door open and close, walked out to my tiny reception area with no receptionist, and found my friend Tom. He'd never been the snappiest dresser in Denver and nothing had changed for his biggest case ever. He was wearing gray slacks, a bluish muted plaid sport coat, and an open collared, light blue shirt. The ensemble didn't go together. Tom didn't care.

"Where's the damn coffee?"

"Nice to see you too, buddy. C'mon in, I'll lock the door so we won't be disturbed." I led the way through the conference and work room into my private office, motioned to one of the leather club chairs, and said, "Grab a seat, I'll get the coffee." I noticed he was carrying a small briefcase, which was unusual. He took a seat, opened the briefcase, and removed a notepad and pen. I topped up my cup, poured a fresh one for Tom, and sat in the other chair beside him.

He took a noisy sip, grimaced at the heat, and blew across the top. "Hot, too damned hot!"

I grinned and said, "You should use milk or wait 'til it cools, dummy!"

He set the cup on the side table between us. "Let's get to it, okay? What can you tell me about this Davidson? Who would want to see him dead; who would profit from it? The faster we can come up with a motive, the faster we can probably figure this out. How well did you know him?"

I took a swallow of my slightly cooler coffee and set the cup next to Tom's. "I didn't *know* him personally. I've met him maybe half a dozen times, mostly at charity events or parties. But I've known *of* and *about* him for a long time, ever since I came to Denver. I knew a couple guys who worked for him. According to them, he was a real hard ass--tough to work for and cut every corner he could. It's not going to be difficult to put together a list of people who didn't like him. The bad news for you is it'll be a long list."

I told Tom the history: William Davidson had hit Denver with a fair-sized bankroll and an oversized ego. He took an expansive suite of offices in one of the first high-rise buildings built during the eighties' oil boom, announced he was in the oil business, and set about staffing his new company, Wildcat Oil, with geologists and landmen. He recruited his professionals from the few major oil companies still left in the Rockies, most of which had left in the late sixties and early seventies.

More than the geologists themselves, Davidson wanted
their drilling prospects and ideas. He offered salaries above
industry standard and, of more importance to the geologists,
an overriding royalty which meant they got a percentage of
any production they found. Even a single modest oil well
could earn thousands of dollars a month; a nice field could
make the geologist rich. Soon, Wildcat Oil was approaching
other oil companies with deals to drill "his" geologists' old
prospects. He drilled so many he became known as "Wildcat
Willie."

He also became known for something else: slow paying
his sub-contractors and suppliers. Common practice was
payment in forty-five to sixty days; Wildcat Oil took ninety or
even more. Still, the service companies and suppliers kept
working for him because of the number of wells he drilled.
Those companies may have to wait to be paid, but Wildcat Oil
drilled hundreds of wells. They kept contractors busy through
the periodic booms and busts of the industry. Once a
company got on the Wildcat Oil train, it was hard to step off.

Tom interrupted my narrative to ask, "You're not saying
some drilling contractor or cement company could get so mad
over not getting paid quickly they'd commit murder, are you?"

"No, that's not what I'm saying. I'm just telling you his
way of doing business got under people's skin and made them
mad. He pushed the limits at every turn." I got a bottle of
water from my mini-fridge and said, "In the early days, he also
developed a reputation for selling more than a hundred percent
of his deals and--"

Tom interrupted again, "How the hell do you do
that...sell *more* than a hundred percent of something?"

"It's in the promotion on a wildcat drilling prospect. A
'standard' promotion is what's known as 'a third for a
quarter.' It means selling a twenty-five percent interest, the
'quarter', for thirty-three percent, the 'third', of the cost of
drilling plus the leases. Using that ratio, small operators will
often sell up to seventy-five percent of the interest for a
hundred percent of the cost. In that case, if it's a dry hole, the
operator gets his lease money back and it didn't cost him
anything to drill. If it *is* a discovery, the operator starts paying
twenty-five percent of the costs to complete and operate the
well and gets twenty-five percent of the revenue. You
understand?"

Tom picked up his cup, sipped slowly, and considered
what I'd told him, "I think so, but I'm not sure it sounds on the
up and up. You say it's a 'standard' industry deal. Does that

mean other companies do the same thing…or was Wildcat Oil the only one?"

"No, no…it *is* standard. Practically all independents finance their wildcat drilling that way. I got started the same way. The problems start if an operator *knows* a well is going to be dry, but drills it anyway, and *purposely* tries to make money on it.

"He sells a hundred percent or more of the interest on the same basis. If it's a dry hole, usually no one's the wiser, the shithead pockets the money and goes on to the next deal. *But*, if lightning strikes and he somehow makes a discovery, he's fucked in a couple of ways.

"First, since he sold more interest than he has, it makes him liable for fraud and all kinds of other charges. Second, even if he held it to exactly one hundred percent, but it turns out to be a discovery, he has to pay twenty-five percent of the completion costs. But, he doesn't get *any* income; he's doubly screwed.

"Back in the day, talk was Wildcat Willie 'couldn't afford to drill a discovery' because he'd sold more than a hundred percent. Apparently, though, it happened a few times and he had to scramble. He would go to the investors, hat in hand, and blame his land department for 'fucking up the deal' and 'not paying attention' or some such BS. Then, he would ask the partners to reduce their interest; or he'd offer them more than their money back to get out of the deal. I guess he was able to weasel out every time, but he *really* pissed some people off and made a bunch of enemies."

Tom started to nod. "Yeah, I get it now. I can see how it would make an investor madder than hell…maybe mad enough to kill."

"I'm guessing people have been killed for less, but remember that crap happened a long time ago. After Davidson started finding some legit wells and had a producing field or two, he didn't need to run scams anymore. I haven't heard any of that kinda shit about him lately. If I had to place a bet, I'd put it on an employee or former employee he screwed over."

Tom stood and walked behind my desk to look down on Champa Street. "How was he screwing his employees?"

I knew this would take even more explaining and sometimes Tom wasn't the easiest guy to explain something to, *but* it was important. "Do you know how an overriding royalty works?" Tom shook his head, so I continued. "An overriding royalty is a percentage of the production of a well or wells on a lease. The operator carves out one or two percent and 'assigns' it to anyone he wants, usually an employee or a group of employees, as an incentive--like a bonus. The 'override' comes out of the operator's share of revenue so it doesn't affect the mineral owner, you know, the farmer or rancher.

"The normal way of doing things is to make a written assignment, which is a document that legally assigns the override to the employee. The document is recorded in the county where the well is located, just like a mortgage or a deed. The operator furnishes a copy of the assignment to the crude oil buyer. When the well starts producing and selling oil, the crude buyer then pays the employee directly. The assignment covers *all* the leases in a prospect. That way, as new wells come on, the employee gets his piece on each one--

"*Jesus Christ,* Cort! Cut to the chase, will you? You're putting me to sleep here! What's all this got to do with Davidson screwing his employees?"

I'd known this would be tough. Tom was not a patient person. "Hey…you're the one who asked the question! Hang on, I'm getting there. Wildcat Willie did it a different way with what's called a 'bookkeeper's override.' He collected a hundred percent of the revenue and had his accounting department cut the employee a check for his 'overriding royalty' each month.

"The problem came when somebody wanted to quit working for Wildcat Oil. Davidson would tell accounting to stop paying the guy's override checks. The employee didn't have much recourse because there was no recording or assignment showing he owned anything. If the amount wasn't much, sometimes an employee would just walk away and Willie would pocket the money. Other times, particularly with geologists, they'd get a lawyer and threaten to sue. Usually, Willie'd just laugh it off and have the assignments prepared and recorded. But a time or two, he decided to fight it and went to court. As far as I know, he lost every time. Either way, it left a lot of hard feelings. So, do you get it, and do you understand how he was constantly making enemies, and sometimes it was personal?"

Tom returned to his chair, drained the coffee, rolled his eyes, and said, "Took you long enough to get to the point, but that one's easier to understand than all the rigmarole about selling 'more than a hundred percent' of something. And I get the part about it being 'personal.' I assume you could be talking about big bucks if a guy'd found a lot of wells."

"You got that right. Say a lease has five producers on it and each one makes a hundred barrels a day. That adds up to five hundred barrels a day. Assume the geologist who found the field has a one percent override; that equals five barrels a day or a hundred and fifty barrels a month for the geologist. Multiply by the current crude price of ninety bucks a barrel and it equals, uh, about thirteen grand a month."

Tom looked startled. *"Christ!* I can see how somebody would want revenge if he got cut out of that kind of money. You know anyone who qualifies?"

"Not off the top of my head, but I know the guy who will probably be taking over at Wildcat Oil. I'm sure we can get a printout of everyone who's ever worked there, too. Make sure you get it in your warrant."

"We can get anything he's got." Tom's cell rang; he held up his index finger and answered. "Montgomery…yeah…okay…great…bring it with you." He disconnected.

"I've got a new homicide detective as of this morning, Lee Anne LeBlanc. She'll bring the warrant and meet us at Wildcat Oil's office. You ready to go?"

CHAPTER

THREE

We walked the five blocks to Eighteenth and Market
Street and entered the Alamo Plaza Building. Yellow crime
scene tape was strung across the entrance to the parking
beneath the building. Wildcat Oil leased the top three floors,
including a penthouse suite where Davidson's private office
was located. A uniform cop was standing next to an elevator
door which was blocked off with traffic cones. It was a
dedicated car serving only Wildcat Oil's floors.

Tom badged the cop, "Montgomery, homicide. This
guy's Cort Scott. He's helping on the investigation. You got
a log book down here?"

The uniform shook his head. "They're keeping it upstairs. Your other detective's there; got here about five minutes ago."

Tom glanced at the cop's nameplate, bobbed his head, and said, "Thanks, uh...Martin. Do I need a key or something to run the car?"

"No. Just hit the floor button; the car returns here automatically."

Tom pushed the button marked "PH", the doors slid shut, and we climbed swiftly and silently thirty floors to the penthouse. The doors swooshed open and we stepped out into a lobby that would not have been out of place in the Taj Mahal or Buckingham Palace. The terrazzo floor tiles were three foot squares in a checkerboard of copper and ivory. The glass, double-door entry was at least ten feet high and set inside a white marble arch.

I opened the right hand door for Tom and we stepped onto an emerald green, deep pile carpet that felt like walking on the eighteenth green at Augusta National. The receptionist's desk and counter would have serviced a fairly busy martini bar. As we approached, a very tall--slightly taller than Tom--slender and strikingly beautiful woman rose from the receptionist's chair and smiled at Tom. She was a knockout. On a scale of one to ten she was a seventy-five. Her complexion was smooth and the color of café au lait made with extra milk. She walked toward us carrying a thick document which she handed to Tom. "Hey Lee Anne, you must have run like hell to beat us here. I assume this must be our license to creep the place, huh? This guy is Cort Scott. He's a PI who *used* to call himself a geologist and, ahh hell...I guess I gotta say it, he's a friend of mine. I've asked him to give us a hand on this one since he knows several of the players." He chin-pointed at the woman and said, "Cort, this is Lee Anne LeBlanc. She just made detective and was assigned to Homicide. This is her first case so go easy on her, okay? Don't be pulling your usual BS on a rook."

I would've taken offense if I hadn't seen his slight smile. "Hi Lee Anne, don't believe everything you hear from this guy. I'll help *you* in any way I can--in preference to your fearless leader by the way." I returned Tom's grin with a Cheshire cat smile.

Lee Anne LeBlanc put out her hand and we shook. She had soft hands but a firm grip. "It's nice to meet you, Mr. Scott. Lieutenant Montgomery mentioned you'd be involved. I'm sure we'll all appreciate it." She had a soft, rather sexy, cultured voice with a hint of accent from somewhere down South.

"Please call me Cort. Where are you from, Lee Anne? I detect a little accent...Louisiana, maybe?"

"Wow, good ear, Mr., uh, I mean *Cort.* You're right on. I'm originally from New Orleans. How'd you pick that up?" She pronounced it "New ORE-lans", not "New Ore-LEENS" like Yankees, or "N'Awlins" like wanna-be southerners.

"Oh, I've got friends from there." I thought she was probably of Creole ancestry: The Creoles were a mix of French, Spanish, Caribbean, and Native American heritage. Rather than being a downtrodden minority like the descendants of slaves or even the swamp rat Cajuns, the Creoles were almost considered Louisiana aristocracy. "I assume Tom hasn't taken you to our buddy Andy Thibodeaux's place yet?"

Tom spoke quickly, "No, and furthermore, I don't plan on subjecting such a beautiful and cultured lady as Lee Anne to that dive."

I laughed, "I don't blame you."

Tom said, "We're wasting time. This *is* the warrant, right?"

"Yes sir, the DA's office sent it over about half an hour ago. The DA himself called right after and said it should cover absolutely everything here, including the contents of any safes or lock boxes. He did ask us to call him if we wanted to break into anything. I've already called Davidson's secretary- -oops, *'administrative assistant'* as I was firmly informed--and told her to bring all the file keys. We had cops at the company's main reception two floors down when the employees began arriving this morning. Everybody signed a roster and was told to go about their work. The receptionist for this floor, Davidson's private office, was sent home; the administrative assistant, whose name's Vada Benson by the way, is waiting in the main reception."

Tom nodded in appreciation. "Good start, Lee Anne. Have you been inside?"

"Not really, I just opened the door and glanced in. There's an outer office where Benson sits and then another big-ass door for Davidson's private office." The slight profanity sounded funny coming from such an elegant woman.

Tom said, "Okay, get Benson up here. We need to talk to her and I want her present when we start going through things."

Lee Anne nodded. "They've got an interior stairwell. I'll go get her."

Tom said, "No, don't do that. You're a detective not a messenger. Call down to the cop on the desk and have her sent up. I don't want her thinking she's something special."

Lee Anne flashed him a grateful smile and said, "Thanks, Lieutenant. Good to know."

As Lee Anne made the call, Tom signed the bottom of the warrant, stepped to the side of the counter, and opened the door to Vada Benson's office. The carpet changed from the deep pile of the front to a Chinese silk of reds, greens, blues, and whites. The office was sparsely but expensively furnished. To the left, a secretarial desk sat in front of a wall credenza. Wooden horizontal files were recessed into the walls on each side of the credenza and large paintings were hung on the remaining walls. A small loveseat and an upholstered straight-back chair faced the desk. In the wall straight ahead of us was still another doorway with a large wooden door. It was closed. Tom stopped and eyeballed the door. "I hope it's unlocked. It'd be a shame to have to break it down." He laughed as he tried the door. It wasn't locked.

He stepped inside and I followed. Wildcat Willie's "man cave" office was a study in ostentatiousness. We were facing a wall of windows looking west to the Rockies and, at the end of the room, south along the Front Range. The view encompassed everything from Longs Peak to Pikes Peak. The windows were floor to ceiling with no panes or dividers. It was a clear "Colorado bluebird sky" day and the view was spectacular. Davidson's desk was to our right and looked more like a small conference table. It was oval, open underneath, with gracefully curved legs and ornate wooden "feet" in the shape of a large cat's. The hand-carved leather top also had a cat motif: a crouching feline facing anyone who approached the front of the desk. Tom jerked his thumb toward the desk, "Guy had a thing for cats, didn't he?"

I said, "Well, his nickname *was* Wildcat Willie." Tom rolled his eyes.

Similar to his secretary's office, there was a built-in credenza behind the desk chair. Instead of file cabinets, the rest of this wall was covered in book shelves. The upper ones contained expensive looking vases and mounted, polished slabs of rock with fossils. The lower shelves were full of books of all shapes and sizes; some looked old. I turned around to look at the wall behind me which was covered in framed photos.

I examined pictures of Wildcat Willie Davidson apparently attending every charitable, sporting, grand opening, political, and public event of the past thirty years. He was shaking hands with governors, mayors, city councilmen, Rockies baseball players, Denver Broncos, Avalanche players, coaches, and, apparently, every businessman and woman in Denver and Colorado. There were pictures of Willie standing in front of drilling rigs, pump jacks, oil tank farms, trucks, and stacks of casing.

Tom moved to my side and surveyed the photo wall. "Shy, retiring type wasn't he?"

"You ever meet him?" I asked.

"Nope; looks like I was the only one who didn't. You?"

"Like I said, just at a few events around town; even then he wasn't the most pleasant guy you ever met. He had an ego as big as the rest of him and the money to back it up. He could do most anything he wanted."

We heard voices from the front, and turned to watch as Lee Anne escorted the woman I assumed to be Vada Benson through the door.

Vada was fifty-ish, short, a nice figure, well dressed, and pissed off. "Who the hell do think you are invading Mr. Davidson's private office? Who do you think you are keeping

me out of my own office? What do you mean by making me
stay downstairs and then sending for me like some kind of
lackey? You people are going to have to answer for this kind
of treatment. I'll be filing a complaint with the chief of police
about this!" She ended her little tirade by shaking her finger
at me.

I pointed at Tom, "He's the cop, Mrs. Benson. He's the
one with the warrant."

She continued shaking her finger. "That would be *Ms.*
Benson!"

Tom finally spoke up. "Well *Miz Benson,* I suggest you
take a deep breath and calm yourself. Mr. Scott, here, is right.
I've got a search warrant for these premises and their contents
and we intend to execute that warrant at this time. Now, it's
up to you to decide if you want to assist us in finding who
killed your boss by pointing us in the proper direction within
these offices, *or* if you want us to tear everything apart from
floor to ceiling and waste a bunch of time while his killer
blows town. It's your decision, but you need to make it right
now…and I mean *right now*!" It was one of the longest
speeches I'd ever heard from Tom Montgomery.

Vada Benson staggered as if she'd been punched. Her
entire body seemed to shrink into itself and she began to back

out of Wildcat Willie's office. "I, uh, *Oh My God!* He's dead isn't he? He's *really* dead! Somebody killed him!" She continued to walk backwards around her desk and collapsed into her chair. "Oh my God!"

Lee Anne quickly stepped to her side, put a hand on her shoulder, and quietly said, "The best thing you can do right now, Ms. Benson, is help us. We can use your assistance when we start searching. But first, maybe you could answer some questions to, you know, get us started. Do you think you're up for that, Ms. Benson?"

Benson reached up, grabbed Lee Anne's hand, and clung to it like a lifeline. She nodded a couple of times and finally choked out, "Yes, I'll help. I'm sorry. It's just such a shock to think about, about…you know, his being *murdered.* Please…ask anything you want. Please…take a seat. May I get you anything to drink? I've got water or sodas or tea or coffee---

Tom interrupted. "No, we've got to get started." Tom and Lee Anne took the loveseat and I took the chair. "Ms. Benson, when was the last time you saw Mr. Davidson?"

CHAPTER

FOUR

An hour later we knew a lot more about Wildcat Willie Davidson. For one thing, he didn't like being called Wildcat "Willie;" Vada Benson made that clear at the outset. He hadn't minded "Wildcat" but hated having his given name of William shortened to Willie. We also found out *Mr. Davidson* and his second wife, Janet, maintained separate residences. When Tom asked about their relationship, Vada paused for several moments before answering, "Strained."

Tom followed up with, "Enough for her to want him dead?"

Again, she hesitated before replying. "I wouldn't know about that, but I didn't know everything about their 'arrangement.' I know they had a pre-nup, but I don't know the provisions. I *do* know she has an unlimited budget which he never questioned. I'm sure she'll inherit much of the company, but I'm equally sure she won't want anything to do with running it. *That* would require her learning something about the business and maybe even becoming involved. She wouldn't want to do that; in fact, she abhors anything to do with work."

Tom and Lee Anne asked several more questions about the family. Davidson had two children from his first marriage: a son and a daughter. He'd been divorced from his first wife, Rhonda, in 1986. Janet Davidson also had a daughter from a previous marriage; she'd married Davidson in 2000. They hadn't had any kids together. Benson claimed she didn't know much about any of the children other than there was no love lost among the step-siblings *or* the step-parents on either side. She said the son and daughter lived in the Denver area; Janet's daughter lived in San Francisco. Benson volunteered that each of the children received a substantial income from trusts set up years previously. She gave us a printout with their addresses and phone numbers. I glanced at the sheet and noticed the son was listed as Vincent Freeman. "Ms. Benson, what's the deal with the son's name? How come he's listed as 'Freeman' not Davidson?"

She gave me a cold stare and answered, "Mr. Davidson never talked about him."

I exchanged looks with Lee Anne who shrugged. I made a mental note to follow up.

Finally, Tom got around to asking the most important question of all, "Did Mr. Davidson have any enemies, people who might want him dead?"

Vada Benson answered quickly. "Probably more than most when you get right down to it; neither he nor the company is--uh-- *was,* very well liked."

Tom raised his eyebrows, "That's a pretty strong statement, Ms. Benson. Have either Davidson or the company received threats of any kind?"

Vada Benson nearly burst out laughing. "More than you can count, Lieutenant. Do you see these files behind me? The right side is three drawers of complaints, demands, and threats. It's going to take you weeks to read all of them, let alone get a handle on which ones might be serious."

Tom said, "I would like to think you can help with that. You must have an idea about which are the most serious sounding or repetitive. That would be a good start. Do any come to mind right now?"

"Do you want to start with family, business, or environmental terrorists?"

Tom looked at her carefully before replying, "Ms. Benson, I'm not sure you're taking this seriously. Are you saying he received threats from several different sources?"

Again, she smiled. "Oh, yes, Lieutenant. Like I said, three drawers full, going back to when I began working here and started keeping them in a file."

"How long have you worked for him?"

"Almost thirty years; I was one of his first employees."

"Okay, let's start with recent threats. Who's at the top of the list?"

Benson swiveled her chair and pushed back to access the files. She withdrew a file folder containing several sheets of paper, rolled back to her desk, opened it, and took out the top sheet. She glanced over the page and said, "This is a copy of a fax we received last week. There's no signature or indication of who it's from, just that the fax machine was located in a Fed Ex office in Lakewood." She handed the page to Tom; Lee Anne and I leaned over to read it with him.

Liar, Cheat, Thief...

You stole Trumpet Creek Field. You've been a cheating liar since you came to Denver and everybody knows it. I know your ways and how to get to you. You're going to pay for everything.

The fax had been received on Thursday of the previous week. I pointed at the "From" line which indicated the Fed Ex office. "Can you guys do anything with this?"

Lee Anne shrugged. "I don't know. Unless the outlet keeps a sign-in log or maybe has video surveillance, it'll be hard to figure out who sent it. We'll follow up on it, but I wouldn't hold my breath." She told Benson we'd start a list of everything we took under the search warrant and leave her a receipt.

Benson picked up the next sheet from the folder and said, "This email came in, uh…let me see, two weeks ago. It's just the latest in a long string of the same kind of thing. We've been getting them for several years."

You earth-killing bastard--You and your kind are living on borrowed time. You're killing us with all your fucking drilling and fracking and destruction. You may be killing us slowly but we're better than that…we'll kill you as quick as we can. Forever Green Alliance.

The "From" line said:

FGA@hotmail.com/thebouldercoarsegroundcoffee .

Lee Anne looked at it carefully and slowly shook her head. "I think this was sent from a coffee shop in Boulder. I've been there. It used to be an internet café, but once Wi-Fi took off they put in a wireless connection and concentrated on selling coffee. Unless we're really, really lucky, there's probably no way to tell who sent it, but we'll check it out anyway. Whoever did it probably made up some phony internet credentials and accessed the shop's Hotmail account for a free address."

Vada pulled another folder and extracted a letter stapled to an envelope. She read it carefully before handing it directly to Lee Anne who read it out loud.

Davidson,

You cheated me out of my overrides and I'm going to figure out a way to get even. You won't get away with this anymore. J.D. Pierce

I jerked my head up in surprise. Not only was it signed, it was signed by someone I knew. J.D. Pierce was a geologist I'd met several times. He'd worked for Union Oil in Casper, Wyoming, moved to Denver in the seventies, and had been with several independents until the late 1990s. I remembered he had worked for Wildcat Oil for a short time, but the last I'd heard, he had returned to Casper a few years ago. I hadn't heard anything about him since.

I asked Vada, "When did Pierce work here?"

She retrieved another file, flipped the top couple of pages, looked up, and said, "Ex-employees file; lots of them. I missed by a couple of letters, though; I'm at 'N'." She turned down a page and read, "Pierce, J.D., worked here from January 2001 until April 2002."

I asked, "Why'd he leave? Does it say?"

"Just says 'terminated for cause'; that usually meant somebody got crosswise with Davidson. He could be pretty brutal when it came to firing someone. He would just march in and tell them to pack up their stuff, give them thirty minutes to clean out their desks, and then have Mr. Haight, the accounting manager, look at everything they packed and march them out the door."

"Did Pierce have any overrides coming when he left?"

"I wouldn't know about that. I think Wildcat Oil may have bought some leases on his prospects, but I don't know if anything ever got drilled."

"Why didn't Wildcat assign him the overrides?" Tom was showing off his newly found knowledge.

Vada didn't pick up on it, "It wasn't company policy to assign individual overriding royalties."

Tom couldn't help himself. "So, you guys utilized 'bookkeeper overrides', huh?"

She fixed him with a stare. "I see you've been getting an education from Mr. Scott, Lieutenant. Yes, that's the way we handled incentive pay."

"Did Pierce sue Wildcat Oil for any assignments?"

"No."

I had re-read Pierce's letter and asked, "Why did you put this in the threats file rather than the complaints file? Did you think he was making a physical threat?"

"Yes."

Tom checked his watch. "I think we'll just take all the files dealing with threats and complaints, sort through them, and then get back to you for more information on the ones that look credible. Are you okay with that?"

Vada Benson looked relieved. "Yes, that would probably be better than sitting here going through every letter one by one." She stood, shook hands with each of us, and asked, "Is that all you'll need me for right now? I'd like to go home. This has been a very trying morning. I'm having trouble dealing with the...murder."

Lee Anne asked, "Have you been in contact with the wife? Did you notify her?"

Benson shook her head, "No, I haven't. I don't see how that's my job."

Lee Anne shot a questioning look at Tom who raised his eyebrows and also shook his head "No." "Do you have numbers where she can be reached, Ms. Benson?"

"Of course. My God, haven't you people told her yet? That's totally unacceptable!"

We all silently agreed. Lee Anne said, "If I may have those numbers, we'll make the notification immediately."

Tom looked relieved, nodded in appreciation to Lee Anne and said, "Just one more question, if you don't mind. Did you kill him, Ms. Benson?"

She never blinked when she replied, "No, but I can understand why someone did. Davidson was a son-of-a-bitch in every sense of the word."

40 Lee Mossel

CHAPTER

FIVE

Lee Anne took Janet Davidson's contact numbers into Wildcat Willie's office closing the door behind her. Fifteen minutes later she emerged with a look of chagrin. "She's not in Denver; she's in San Francisco. I called the home number and got a voice mail. I didn't want to leave that kind of message, so left my name and number and a request to call me. Then, I tried her cell number and got her. I identified myself, told her I had some bad news, and asked if she had anyone with her. She said she was with her daughter and wanted to know what the bad news was. I told her where we are and that her husband had been killed…murdered."

I asked, "How'd she react?"

"Well, basically, she didn't. She said, 'Oh' and asked where, when and how; no crying or hysterics. I told her what we knew, asked when she would be returning, and that we'd need to talk to her as soon as possible. That was it; she thanked me for calling and hung up."

Tom considered Lee Anne's report, "Interesting. When's she coming back?"

"That's a good question. She wanted to know if *I* knew when the funeral would be! Can you believe that? I told her it was probably her call or maybe his daughter's. She said she was scheduled back on Wednesday, but would check with the daughter on the funeral. I couldn't believe it!"

It took half an hour to box up the threat files; Benson hadn't been kidding about the number of them. When we finished, Tom checked his watch again, grinned, and said, "As much as I've tried to put this off, I guess it's time we introduced Lee Anne to Andy Thibodeaux. It's 1:30 p.m., so we should miss most of the lunch bunch, but *your* buddies, the oil field trash crowd, will still be hanging around the bar. What do you think, Cort? Think she's ready?"

I laughed and said, "It has to happen sometime; why not now?" We walked over to the Sixteenth Street Mall and caught the mall shuttle to Glenarm and the Sounds of the

South, our friend Andy's Cajun restaurant. Tom was right, the lunch crowd had cleared out, but the bar area was still buzzing and mostly full. We spotted an empty table and claimed it. As we took our seats, Andy came from behind the bar and hurried to greet us. "Ah, bonjour, ma frens, good to see you 'all. You eatin', drinkin' or boat?"

Tom and I shook hands with Andy. I said, "It feels like you washed your hands, so I'll introduce you to Miss Lee Anne LeBlanc. She's a cop and works for Tom. We've kept her away from you for as long as we could."

Andy faked a scowl as he stuck out his hand. "LeBlanc? Hmm, dat sounds like a good Cajun name to me. You from New Orleans, you?" He pronounced the city's name the same way as she had.

Lee Anne nodded and said, "That's right. It's nice to meet you Mr. uh…I guess Cort didn't complete the introduction. I didn't catch your last name."

"Dat's dat damn Cort for you. He jus' ain' no good for nothin', him. My name is Thibodeaux. It's a great pleasure to meet you, Miss LeBlanc. It's always a big t'rill to meet somebody from da swamp." He turned to Tom and me and said in a stage whisper, "Whoo-ee, where you been hidin' dis here girl, you? She's da bes' lookin' woman to come in dis place since you brought in you girl fren Lindsey. Why you been holdin' out on old Andy, me?" In a louder voice he said, Ever' body sits yo-self down. You want some drinks, you?"

Tom shook his head, "Nah, we're still on the clock, Andy. Iced tea for me; what would you like Lee Anne?"

She pursed her lips and answered, "Do you have any lemonade made up, Andy?" When he nodded, she said, "Great, bring me a large glass please."

Andy looked at me and grinned, "You ain' on no damn clock, Cort. You wan' a Bud?"

I said, "No, I want about five of 'em, but I'll settle for one to start, buddy."

Andy turned and headed for the bar service area. Tom frowned and rolled his eyes. "Actually, you *are* working." Then he asked Lee Anne, "What'd you think of Davidson's office and the lovely *Miz* Benson?"

Lee Anne smiled as she answered, "She's kind of a piece of work isn't she? From the looks of his office, he knew how to live the high life. I'm guessing it's going to take us a while to sift through those threat files and sort out the ones that look real. I'm betting most are going to be anonymous."

Andy's waitress returned with our drinks and placed them in front of us. Tom looked at me. "What about you? Did you pick up on anything she said?"

"I can't say I'm surprised by the number of threats he'd received. I *was* surprised that J.D. Pierce had the balls to sign that letter to him."

Tom raised his eyebrows. "How well do you know this Pierce guy?"

"Oh, not that well. He's just a guy who's been around for a long time."

"Is he a guy who's capable of murdering someone?"

"I wouldn't have thought so, but I haven't seen him in a few years, so things might have changed. The last time I heard anything about him, he had moved back to Casper. He sounded pissed in his letter, so maybe it's something that's festered for a long time."

The server returned and asked for our orders. Lee Anne motioned for us to go ahead while she continued to read the menu. Tom ordered the Cajun Combo, Andy's house specialty dish of crawfish etouffee, red beans and rice, and catfish. I opted for catfish filets with a side of red beans and rice. Finally, Lee Anne nodded her head at the server and said, "I haven't seen a menu like this since I left New Orleans!

This is tough. I'll have the petit Cajun Combo, the smaller
portion version of what Tom's having.

"I can't believe I haven't been here before! You really
have been holding out on me, Lieutenant." She smiled
mischievously.

I made a good pull on my beer, set it down, and asked
Tom, "Where do we go from here and what do you want me to
do?"

He said, "I want you to concentrate on the oil business
side; talk to the people you know. Maybe you can look up this
J.D. Pierce guy? Obviously, you can't arrest anybody, but you
can get an 'on the record' statement from him; get an idea of
whether he's mixed up in this or not.

"We'll start working on the threat files and start
interviewing Davidson's kids. The first step will be to try and
track the emails and faxes." He turned to Lee Anne, "You get
our IT guys going on that, okay?" She nodded.

He addressed me again. "When can you start on Pierce?"

I replied, "Any time; is tomorrow too soon?"

Lee Anne grinned and Tom shot me a look. "Always the
wise-ass, aren't you?"

I thought about Davidson's kids and asked Tom, "Did you
pick up on that deal with the *son's* last name being Freeman?"

He nodded. "Yeah, there's gotta be a story there. I'm not sure our dear Miz Benson was telling us everything she knows about that. Another thing--how do you work for somebody for thirty years and end up calling them 'a son-of-a-bitch?' I'm guessing we're going to have several more questions for her."

The server brought our meals and we tucked in. Lee Anne's eyes lit up after her first bite of the etouffee and she punctuated her meal with little pleasure sounds and sighs. We finished quickly and I signaled for the check. "Okay, guys, this one's on me. I'm assuming the DA is giving me an unlimited expense account for this gig. Let's go see."

Back at the Justice Center, Tom asked Lee Anne to get started with the email and fax addresses and took me to ADA Macklin Groves' office. Mack and I went back several years to when he'd been a litigator for one of the leading Seventeenth Street white-collar law firms. As my attorney, Jason Masters, had put it when Groves had joined the Denver DA's office as second in command to DA James Burge, "He crossed over to the dark side."

Mack and I shook hands, "I know you guys are in a hurry, so if you'll sign these papers, you can get out of here."

I gave him a wide-eyed stare and asked, "What am I signing?"

"Don't worry, it's nothing too bad. You're just agreeing not to beat the shit out of anybody when you're asking them questions, acknowledging you're not a cop, and crap like that." Mack shoved three sheets across his desk toward me.

"So what *can* I do?"

Tom broke in, "Anything I tell you to do--sign the goddamn papers!"

Mack put his hand on top of the papers and said, "That's not exactly correct. Officially, you're working for the DA's office, not the cop shop, although Tom will be taking your reports and you'll liaise with him. Cort, you've got a bit of a reputation for bending the rules on interrogations; you need to keep this on the straight and narrow. This is the dictionary definition of a high profile case; we can't afford to have any screw ups that could jeopardize evidence or the case. Are we clear on that?"

I signed in the places marked by red sticky arrows and handed the papers back to Mack. "Yeah, I'm clear, but you guys need to understand I'm not going to set myself up for anything bad to happen either. Some things I'll have to do my own way."

CHAPTER

SIX

I talked to Tom a little longer, said good bye to Lee Anne, and returned to my office. The message light on my desk phone was flashing and I sat through five recorded calls from friends asking about the murder; most wanted to know if I had any ideas about who did it. News of the killing had made the noon newscasts of the Denver TV stations. I didn't return any of the calls, thinking my new status as a "special investigator" probably didn't allow for it, even though it would have been nice to get the callers' ideas.

I looked up J.D. Pierce in my Rocky Mountain Oilfield Directory and was mildly surprised to find he had an office in

Denver and not Casper. I dialed and when he answered said, "J.D., it's Cort Scott calling. How are you doing?"

"Who'd you say it was?" Pierce had a raspy voice that sounded like a lot of unfiltered cigarettes and cheap whisky had gone down the pipe.

"Cort Scott. I met you a few times some years ago. I used to be a petroleum geologist here in Denver."

"Oh yeah, I sorta remember you; that was a long time ago. I'm all right, I guess. Can't complain; no one gives a shit anyway. What can I do for you?"

"I'm sure you've heard the news about Wildcat Willie Davidson. I'm helping the cops on the investigation and would like to talk to you. We're trying to fill in some background; would you have some time tomorrow to get together? I can come to your office."

"It's all over the news somebody killed the prick; tough shit as far as I'm concerned. But, what the hell would I know about it? What you say about *background* sounds like bullshit. And, why you--are you a cop now?"

"No, I'm not a cop, I'm a private investigator. The police thought since I have some connections in the oil business, I might be able to help them. I just want to talk to you about when you worked for Wildcat Oil."

"It's not something I want to talk about, Scott. It was the longest year of my life and the son-of-a-bitch made it that way."

"Exactly the kind of thing I want to discuss. If you weren't alone, there must be others with the same feelings. We're trying to get a handle on who might have wanted him dead."

"Sounds to me like you think I did it. I didn't and I don't see what else there is to talk about."

"Look, J.D., I'm just trying to piece it together. I don't have any idea who killed him. You worked for him and you didn't like him. You might be able to shed some light on who else felt the same way."

Pierce didn't answer for several seconds. "Yeah, all right...I'll talk to you. When do you want to come by?"

I hadn't thought it through so had to hesitate. "Why don't I swing by your office at eleven o'clock tomorrow, will that work?"

Pierce said, "Yeah, what the hell? I'll see you tomorrow."

***

I returned home to Parker at 5:35 p.m. and was pleased to see Lindsey's Ford Edge parked in the third garage slot. My girlfriend, Lindsey Collins, was a crime scene investigator for the Arapahoe County Sheriff's office. We'd met at a murder site. Unfortunately, it was for my first client, after I'd changed careers from petroleum geology to private investigations. That first case had careened from tragedy to tragedy and went totally off the rails with another murder--my longtime girlfriend, Gerri German. With the help of Lindsey's boss, Arapahoe County Sheriff homicide investigator, George Albins, I'd tracked down the gang of killers. My "revenge" had been sending the assholes to prison. All except Gerri's murderer who got the death penalty and was awaiting execution in Wyoming. George and I had become close friends. He 'understood' about my relationship with his employee, Lindsey.

An unwanted consequence of Gerri's death had been inheriting her stock in Mountain West Gas Exploration, a public company I'd helped her start. Her shares, added to mine, gave me the majority interest and control. I hadn't wanted either position. Selling the shares through a secondary stock offering made me millions, but I also hadn't wanted the fortune. I set up an irrevocable trust for her ne'er-do-well brother who had become some sort of modern day Robinson

Crusoe, endowed the geology departments of our respective universities, and funded several deserving charities.

Years earlier, I'd done well enough on my own to buy my house in Parker, indulge myself with Corvettes and a customized 1980 Ford Bronco, maintain a premium wine cellar, and, generally, live well. After struggling with my grief and guilt over Gerri's death, I had reconnected with Lindsey. Now, we lived together in my Parker house. She'd kept her condo in the affluent south Denver suburb of Greenwood Village and, occasionally, would take a few days of "me time" away from Parker. We both enjoyed the homecoming festivities following these brief separations. Today was such an occasion because Lindsey had been gone for three days.

She was standing on the back deck looking at the open space behind the house. A bottle of 2010 Stoneleigh New Zealand Sauvignon Blanc was chilling in an ice bucket on the pantry bar. I poured a glass, walked across the kitchen, and stepped onto the deck.

Lindsey turned at the sound of the door, smiled, and we embraced. It was a good embrace; the kind that warmed me from where our knees touched to where our lips met. The kiss warmed the rest of my body--and my heart.

When we finally pulled back, she sighed, "Mmm...worth the wait! You're home kinda late, what's up?"

I sampled the wine and smiled my appreciation. "CSI Collins, you'll be glad to know PI Cortlandt Scott is now officially 'special investigator' Cortlandt Scott and employed by the Denver DA's office."

"Wow, no kidding? Oh wait, I bet I get it. This has to do with the murder of the oil guy, doesn't it? The story is all over the news."

"Yep, that'd be why. Tom decided he needed a 'go to' guy who knows people in the local oil biz. That's me."

"So why did you say you're working for the DA?"

"Because they're the only ones who can hire special investigators."

"Okay, makes sense. What are you going to do for them, or maybe I should say Tom?"

"First thing I'm doing is talking to a guy named J.D. Pierce who worked for Wildcat Oil a few years ago. He sent Wildcat Willie a threatening note and Tom wants me to check him out. I sort of know him from when I was still doing geology; I'm going by his office tomorrow. Even if he turns out not to be a suspect, he might be able to point me toward other people who had it in for Davidson. From what we heard today, there may be a hell of a bunch of them."

"Hmm, two days in row going downtown, huh? Sounds like an early dinner and a brief reunion for us, sleuth." She gave me the lascivious grin she saved for especially seductive moments. It always got my attention.

"Who said anything about dinner? I think we should start the reunion right now. Even that might not give us enough time." I pulled her back into the embrace.

"Whoa, c'mon buddy! You're going to have to feed me if you want me to keep up my energy level. You're not getting off the hook that easily!"

"Problem is I had a late lunch with Tom and his new lady detective at Andy's place. I'm not very hungry--except for you, of course." That drew the sex-laden grin again. "What would you say to a fruit and cheese plate, a slice of leftover chocolate turtle cheesecake, and another glass or five of wine? After that, we could hit the hot tub and then, you know, see what happens."

Lindsey turned on her heel, slid the door open, looked over her shoulder, winked, and said, "Okay on the food, wine, and hot tub; I already know what's going to happen after that."

***

I turned off the low glow of the bedside lamp; Lindsey sighed, slid down in the bed, and pulled up the single sheet. We held hands as we lay side by side for a few minutes. She whispered, "I love coming home for these little *reunions*. It almost makes being alone a few days worthwhile."

"I *definitely* like it. What do you do when you're gone, Linds? It's not anything I say or do causing you to leave, is it?"

"Oh no, no...nothing like that at all. I don't know, sometimes I just need a little time to myself. That's all. I stay up late and read, drink tea, maybe even watch TV--things we don't do here. Sometimes I call Mom and just talk. She's pretty lonely since Dad died last year. It's absolutely nothing you've ever done, sweetheart. It's just me being me. You'll get used to it."

"You know, Linds, we've never talked much about your life before we met. I've told you about my background; the stuff about being in the Army and then working as a geologist; about getting burnout and trying this PI gig. You know about Gerri's murder and my inheriting her stock, but I don't know much about you."

She was quiet for a moment before replying, "There's not that much to tell, I guess. I was born here in Denver a year after my parents both started as instructors at Colorado School of Mines. My mom was teaching statistical analysis and my dad was in the math department.

"We lived in Golden about halfway up Lookout Mountain and I went to Golden High and then to Colorado State University. I was a pretty good athlete: played everything in high school and then walked on for volleyball at CSU. I made the team and got an athletic scholarship for the next three years. My folks were kinda disappointed I didn't follow in one of their career paths, but I majored in biology and took several courses in criminal justice. I guess it's what got me into the crime scene forensics game. I did an internship with the Arapahoe County sheriff's office between my junior and senior year and they offered me a job when I graduated. I spent a couple of years just doing lab analyses of trace evidence before George Albins got me promoted to crime scene investigations.

"Three years ago my father was diagnosed with ALS, Lou Gehrig's disease, and died eighteen months later. That's been rough on my mom; she's still teaching at Mines, but I can tell her heart's not in it. The person you've met is not the same one who raised me. She's just not "Mom" anymore. I'd like it if we could go see her more; it's not like it's a long trip or anything."

I squeezed her hand and said, "We can do that, babe. It'd be good for all of us. I'd like to know your mother better and I'd like her to know me too." Lindsey squeezed back.

"Makes three of us; thanks. I wish she could meet someone. It's probably too soon after Dad's death, but I think it would be good for her. Anything to get her out of the house and see a change of scenery would help. Could we invite her out here for dinner sometime? She'd love the wildlife and vegetation. I *know* she'd love your wine cellar, especially if you let her have some of the good stuff." Lindsey chuckled and elbowed me lightly in the ribs.

I faked a groan and said, "Wow, you're asking a lot there, girlie. I mean, just because you saved my butt out in California doesn't mean you get to set our whole social agenda." That drew another elbow.

"You know what I mean, jerk! Can we do it?"

I rolled onto my side, she did the same, and we spooned. I spoke into her hair as softly as I could, "Absolutely, babe, we'll have her over as soon as we can. And one more thing-- don't ever stay away too long, Linds. As much as I love it when you return, I miss you like hell when you're gone."

I couldn't make out the words she mumbled as she drifted off. I stayed there for a few minutes before rolling over. I lay awake for a while and wondered what working for the DA--and Tom--was going to be like.

CHAPTER

SEVEN

The next morning I was up early and went for a short run through the open space trails in my neighborhood. It was a beautiful, early summer Colorado morning, signaling another great day. I pounded the last half mile and was winded when I slipped in the patio door on the lower level. I obviously needed to get back to regular running; that little sprint shouldn't have caught me up short.

I could hear Lindsey's music playing as I climbed the stairs to the main level. She liked '70s and '80s rock; I preferred '50s oldies or country and western, creating a nonstop controversy around the house and in the cars. In the bathroom, she was sitting at her vanity putting the finishing touches on her makeup. She looked up as I stripped off my soaking tee shirt, "Whew, hope you're showering, sleuth; must have been a good run."

I replied, "I needed to sweat out all the booze you used to seduce me last night."

"I didn't hear you complaining: before, during, or after." She stood, patted her hair, and went into the closet. "In fact, seems to me you made a bunch of promises about my mom, dinners, wine and, well, lots of stuff."

I laughed, "See? I *was* drunk! You took advantage of me." I opened the door and turned the shower on, slipped off my running shoes, and dropped my shorts.

Lindsey stepped out of the closet wearing silver gray slacks and a burgundy shirt. She looked great. "Pleading intoxication doesn't get you off the hook, big boy; I'm going to call my mom this morning and invite her down on Saturday. I assume that's okay with you?"

I faked like I was going to embrace her with my sweaty body; she jumped back and laughed. I said, "Oh, all right, go ahead and invite her; might as well get it over with."

She laughed, grabbed my towel from the rack, and threw it at me. "You're such a shit! Wash up; you've got work to do and I've got to get to the office. George has the lab working full tilt on all kinds of backlogged evidence, plus we're coordinating a DNA cold case project with Denver, Jefferson, and Douglas counties. We've been trying to process DNA from some really old rapes and assaults and entering it into the CODIS system. Several states have been able to solve some cases with that kind of information; some go back twenty or thirty years. We're supposed to get results on ten or twelve submissions today." She bent at the waist and leaned forward for a kiss where only our lips would touch and I wouldn't soil her outfit. I did the same and we touched lips.

Lindsey asked, "What's Tom's plan of action on the murder investigation?"

"He's got his IT guys trying to run down fax and email addresses from the threat files we took from Davidson's office. We'd have to get real lucky to actually track something to an individual, but you never know. I wish we had some kind of hard evidence like your DNA stuff to go on, but that doesn't look likely. I'll see you tonight, babe."

***

I backed my Corvette out of the garage, waved at the neighbor lady, and cruised out of the subdivision to Parker Road to head downtown. I parked on the third floor of the garage and walked around the corner to my office in the Equitable Building, on the corner of Seventeenth Street and Champa.

I made a cup of coffee in my new single-cup brewing machine and started reading the front page stories in *The Denver Post* about yesterday's murder. The lead story was relatively brief and concluded with the now ubiquitous "police department spokesman" statement about the depth, breadth, and intensity of the investigation; how the department was following several leads but had no suspects or persons of interest at this point.

Apparently, the crime scene photos must have been too graphic as the paper ran a two-year-old full headshot of William "Wildcat Willie" Davidson. A page eight story had pictures of Janet and Jennifer Davidson, carefully mentioning Janet was Davidson's second wife and Jennifer was his daughter from a previous marriage. Interestingly, no mention was made of Vincent Freeman. Obviously, there was a lot to learn about the "son."

I called Tom, but his phone went to voice mail, so I tried Lee Anne LeBlanc. When she answered, "Detective LeBlanc", I was immediately reminded of how striking she was. "Morning, Lee Anne, it's Cort Scott."

"Oh, good morning, Mr. Sc--oops, did it again, didn't I--uh, *Cort*."

"You'll get used to it. I tried Tom, but he's in a meeting so---

She interrupted, "He's been in constant meetings since we returned to the office yesterday. They started again first thing this morning. He's in with the chief right now. I had no idea what a big deal this murder investigation was going to be."

"Yeah, Davidson was a big name in Denver. I'll bet Tom *is* going crazy; I know how much he *enjoys* meetings." I laughed.

"Yeah, right! He's already complaining. Can I help you with anything?"

"No, not really, I just wanted to check in and let you know I've set up a meeting with J.D. Pierce. I'm meeting him at his office at eleven this morning."

"Wow, fast work on your part; did you want one of us to come along?"

"No, I don't think so. Pierce is a prickly character, plus I've told him I'm not a cop; I don't think he'd appreciate it if I brought a real one with me. He doesn't seem too cooperative anyway. I'll let you know what he has to say."

"Okay, I'll tell Lieutenant Montgomery you checked in. He made some comments regarding you yesterday; basically, he said we'd have to call you to find out what you're doing." She laughed; it was a delightful laugh.

"Well, like I said, I look forward to working with *you*. Him? Not so much!" I could hear her laughter when I broke the connection.

I began to put together scenarios, all of which ended with someone putting two slugs in Wildcat Willie Davidson. I thought about what I wanted to ask J.D. Pierce. The times I'd met him, he'd come across as a bit of an ass. My conversation with him yesterday hadn't done much to change my opinion. I would need to get Pierce's alibi for early yesterday morning.

I was also very interested in checking out the environmental terrorist angle. I'd had some experience dealing with those kinds of nutcases when I'd worked a case for the United States Geological Survey. While investigating the death of one of their field geologists, I found out she'd been murdered by a Red Chinese spy masquerading as an environmentalist. The frightening thing was that he had several people willing to do his dirty work, thinking they were protecting the environment. They hadn't known anything about his ulterior, more nefarious, motives. Lindsey had

saved both our lives during that case. It had brought us to the
stage we were in now. Although it was hard for me to say, I
knew I'd finally gotten over Gerri's death; I loved Lindsey.

***

Pierce's office was on the seventh floor of the old
Petroleum Building at Sixteenth and Broadway in central
Denver. It was an executive suite arrangement with ten
individual offices sharing reception, secretarial service, and a
conference room. The perky receptionist directed me to
Pierce's office at the far end of the hall. I walked the length of
the hallway to an opaque glass door with black lettering
reading: J.D. Pierce, Petroleum Geologist. A second line read:
Prospect Evaluations.

I rapped on the glass twice and entered a moderately
sized, one-room office. Pierce was seated behind a battered
wooden desk with two round, upholstered chairs in front of it.
The chairs looked like refugees from a fifties' basement
recreation room. He had two side-by-side drafting tables
arranged along the wall to his left. Both were covered with
colored geologic maps.

Pierce didn't bother to get up or offer to shake hands. "I
see you found it. What do you want?" He looked about the
same as the last time I'd seen him: tall, a little overweight,

dark hair, with a receding hairline. He was casually dressed in khaki slacks and a long sleeved, checkered print shirt.

"Thanks for seeing me, J.D. Like I said, I just want to ask a few questions about Wildcat Willie's murder."

"So, ask your questions. Like *I* said, I don't know anything about it."

"For starters, where were you night before last and early yesterday morning?"

"*Jesus Christ!* Why don't you just ask me if I killed the son-of-a-bitch?"

"Okay. Did you kill him?"

"No."

"All right, now you've established that, why don't you answer my first question and we can move on?"

"C'mon, Scott, what the hell can I say? I was home all night and in here at 8:30 a.m. yesterday; stayed until five o'clock p.m., and went home again after that. Does that get me off the hook?"

"Doesn't do you much good for midnight 'til 8:30 a.m. yesterday, plus it depends on whether you can prove it or not. Can you? You have anybody who can back up your alibi?"

"You know, I should just tell you to fuck off, but it won't get you off my back, will it? Before going home night before last, I was drinking and bullshitting with Bert Jessen and Dennis Marks at the Slant Hole. We left there around 9:00 p.m. and I was home by 9:30. The receptionist can verify what time I came in yesterday. Is that good enough?"

"You wouldn't give me the receptionist if she couldn't confirm it, but it still doesn't cover the actual time Davidson got plugged." In my mind, though, I checked Pierce off the suspect list. He certainly wasn't the brightest bulb on the porch, but even he wouldn't be dumb enough to give me three alibi witnesses who could be checked out so easily. "Who do you think would want to take out Davidson?"

Pierce exploded in sarcastic laughter, "Anybody who ever worked for the bastard…or met him for that matter. C'mon, Scott, you've heard all the stories about him. You can take it from me; they're all true, or maybe even worse than what you heard. He screwed every person who ever worked for him. Even the geologists who finally got their override assignments had to go through hell to do it; some of 'em went to court and it ended up costing them a bundle."

"How come you backed off? The letter you wrote was pretty pointed."

"He hadn't drilled any of the prospects I'd generated. I mean, I should have gotten assignments on the leases he acquired, but it wouldn't have been worth it to sue him."

"Did any of them get drilled after you left?"

"No; at least nothing has ever been staked or permitted. I think he may have just shit-canned the ideas after I left, rather than worry about my suing his ass."

I thought about that for a moment. It was entirely possible Pierce's prospects weren't good enough to drill in the first place. I didn't know if he'd ever found any oil, but now was not the time to bring it up. Instead, I asked, "Can you think of anyone, specifically, he screwed over who might carry a grudge? Someone who *really* would go after him? Someone who would kill him?"

"When you put it like that, probably not; at least not inside Wildcat Oil. Of course, he made lots of enemies outside the company; plenty of people who were jealous of him. There were even rumors he still had guys after him from his days in New York. I heard he'd welshed on some deals he'd made to get his first drilling money and some of those guys were plenty pissed."

"What do you mean by 'welshed'?"

"He sold more than a hundred percent in some wells and then got investors to back out by giving their money back. He didn't tell 'em the wells had already been drilled and were discoveries. When they found out they'd lost millions, the shit hit the fan. Willie just ignored 'em; told 'em what was done was done."

"I used to hear those kinds of stories, but it was years ago. How long ago are you talking about?"

"Way back when he was first getting started. I also heard those old Jews have long memories and they carry grudges."

"Why do you say *Jews*?"

"Shit, you know how he got started. He rode into Denver with a sack full of money, called himself an 'oilman', and then promoted the hell out of a bunch of people from his old neighborhood--all Jews."

I glanced at Pierce's wall clock: 11:43 a.m. "Okay, I appreciate your talking to me. Tell you what; I'll buy your lunch. Where would you like to go?'

"Look, Scott, you don't have to buy my lunch. If I'm off your radar as far as Davidson's murder is concerned, you don't owe me anything."

That suited me. I didn't relish spending another hour or so with Pierce. If he was like I remembered, he would want to spend a lot longer than an hour; he liked to drink beer. "Okay, thanks again. I'll be in touch."

This time, J.D. Pierce stood and walked around his desk. "Listen, Scott, I'm sorry if I came on strong. I've had a stick up my ass ever since I worked for that shithead. As soon as I heard he'd been killed, I *knew* the cops would want to know about a letter I sent him. To tell you the truth, I'm glad it was you instead of them asking the questions. If I can help, let me know." He stuck out his hand and I shook it.

I stopped at the receptionist's desk on my way out and asked if she had logged Mr. Pierce in yesterday morning. She nodded, turned to her monitor, tapped in a few keystrokes, and pointed towards the screen. "Yes sir, I was here yesterday and I show Mr. Pierce checked in at 8:37 a.m. Is that what you need?" I nodded and thanked her.

CHAPTER

EIGHT

Pierce's mention of Wildcat Willie's New York problems was going to open up a whole new can of worms. I wasn't sure how to go about checking out that part of the story, particularly if the story was thirty years old. Maybe Vada Benson would know something.

As I ran down my check list, it also occurred to me I needed to find out which Wildcat Oil geologist could claim credit for Trumpet Creek, and if he'd been suitably rewarded. That would require talking to Ken Iverson, Wildcat Oil's exploration manager. Iverson would probably be running the company now. He should know where most of the bodies were buried. I also needed to call on Freddie Pearlman at Big East Oil and see how envious he really was.

Back at my office, I called Tom. This time he picked up.

"Hey Tom, I just got back from talking to Pierce."

"Yeah? Did you make an arrest?"

"Funny! You're really turning into a comedian, buddy. I don't think he had anything to do with the murder, but he did have one interesting thing to say. He told me Davidson still had enemies dating back to when he first came to Denver."

"Oh yeah? Who?"

"He didn't have any names; just that Willie had stiffed some of his original investors from New York. Remember how I told you about operators selling more than a hundred percent of the working interest in wells?"

"Yeah."

"Apparently that definitely happened with some Jewish guys who were backing him; according to Pierce they're still pissed about it."

"We'll check it out, but if it happened thirty years ago, I think we'll back-burner it for now. New York is a long way to go."

"I figured that'd be your answer. Of course, I'd be glad to volunteer Lindsey's and my services--on your tab."

"Now who's cracking jokes? I'm sure you would, wise-ass. I'll get back to you on that one, but don't hold your breath. Did Pierce have any other ideas?"

"Not really; he said everyone who ever worked at Wildcat Oil should be on the suspect list. Apparently, Davidson ran a sweatshop and stuck it to everybody."

"The more times it comes up, the more I believe it."

"Are you doing any good on your end?"

"Actually, we might have. The IT guys were able to track the tree-hugger's email. It came out of a coffee shop Wi-Fi setup in Boulder. I don't know how much further they can take it, but they're working as hard as they can."

"Sounds like a start; probably not surprising something like that would originate in Boulder. It's a hotbed of environmentalism and preservationists; there's a protest of some kind almost every day."

"No shit, Sherlock. And, what's worse, no one's ever cracked into any of those groups. They're about as tight-knit as they come; suspicious of everybody. Frankly, the Boulder police haven't been a lot of help either; they're actually supportive of some of their homegrown greenies."

I asked, "What are you going to do now? Any follow-up planned?"

"We don't have anything to follow up on, other than to keep pounding on the IT bunch to see if we can trace the emails any further. How about you? Where are you going from here?"

"I want to talk to Freddie Pearlman and maybe some of his staff. I'd like to know how mad they really are about not getting credit for discovering Trumpet Creek field. I'm also going to check out which Wildcat Oil geologist is claiming the discovery; find out if he's getting rich."

He said, "There are a lot of angles to this and they're all going to take time. I think you should keep on it from the oil business side; we'll work the family, forensics, and IT aspects. Give me a call anytime you get something, okay? By the way, you surprised me by calling in this morning. Lee Anne gave me a full report. I didn't think you'd do it."

"Yeah? Well, she's a lot easier to talk to than you, not to mention better looking!"

"Don't push your luck, buddy."

***

I called Wildcat Oil and asked for Ken Iverson. It had been at least two years since I'd talked to him. I was a little surprised when he picked up; he had to be covered up with work following the murder. "Hey, Ken, Cort Scott. It's been quite a while since we've talked."

"Yeah, long time, Cort. What can I do for you? I've got a lot on my plate right at the moment."

"I can imagine; I'll try to make it quick. I'm helping the police and the DA's office on Davidson's murder investigation; I'm working the oil business side and I've got a couple of questions."

Iverson cleared his throat. "I heard you were involved; Vada Benson told me. How can I help?"

"Two things: first, who's getting credit for finding Trumpet Creek?"

"We are, of course. What's that got to do with anything?"

"No, I mean *specifically*. There must be one geologist who came up with the prospect. I know Freddie Pearlman's outfit claims they drilled the gas well that set everything up, but you guys had to have some reason for acquiring your leases to the west. Who drew the lease outline?"

"Okay, I get you. That'd be Gord Levitt. You know him? He came to work here, oh, maybe eighteen months ago. Came from Calgary; he used to work for Pan Canadian before they were merged out of existence."

"No, I don't know him. What's a Canadian doing working the Powder River Basin?"

"Actually, Pan Canadian had a pretty big group working the Rocky Mountain region. Their head office was in Calgary, but they had offices in Billings and Denver. Gord was exploration manager for the U.S. When we hired him, he had prospects scattered all around the Rockies and Trumpet Creek was one of them. We were putting our lease block together at almost the same time as Big East."

"Ken, I need to ask this so don't get pissed off. Has this Gord Levitt received an overriding royalty assignment for the Trumpet Creek leases yet?"

"You know no one gets an assignment from Wildcat. What the hell is it to you?"

"Ah, c'mon, Ken! I asked you not to get mad, didn't I? Look, I know *some* geologists got override assignments when they threatened to sue the company. Obviously, Trumpet Creek is big enough no one's going to walk away without a fight." I hoped Iverson wasn't taking this personally.

He waited several moments before replying with a sigh. "Yeah, I know our reputation. I hope to change it. But, to answer your question, no, Gord hasn't received any assignments."

"Has he mentioned it or do you know if he talked to Davidson about it?"

"He *did* talk to Mr. Davidson; he's asked me too. I told him we were working on it."

"Did that satisfy him?"

"He definitely wants a hard copy assignment, but he's already getting some damn big checks. I don't think he's mad at us, and he sure as hell wasn't mad enough to do something stupid like kill Mr. Davidson."

I liked the way he referred to Wildcat Willie as 'Mister Davidson.' Ken Iverson was "old school" and, regardless of Davidson's dirty tricks, was continuing to treat him with respect. "Again, no disrespect, Ken, but years ago, I used to hear a lot of talk about Wildcat Willie stiffing some of his investors, rumors about his selling too much working interest in prospects and having to get people to back off or buy them out after he'd made a discovery. You know anything about any of that?"

Iverson coughed and cleared his throat obviously giving himself time to formulate a reply. "It hasn't happened since I've been here, I'll tell you that. Doesn't mean it never happened though; we get calls every now and then from somebody who says they were cheated out of a fortune.

Frankly, it used to occur a lot; we actually had some guys in the office a few weeks back who claimed the same thing. They went all the way back to before Mr. Davidson ever left New York."

"Who were they? You got any names?"

"A nasty old bastard named Sol Klein and a younger guy he claimed was his nephew, Manny Greene. Greene didn't look or act like he's anybody's nephew."

That got my attention. "What do you mean?"

"He was real aggressive, if you know what I mean. He kept saying they needed to talk to Mr. Davidson *in person*; how it was important to meet him face to face because his *uncle* didn't seem to be getting his point across. The old man kept looking at him and nodding his head like he agreed."

"Did they get in to see Davidson?"

"Hell no! We weren't about to let that happen. I ducked out for a minute and told my secretary what was going on. We locked off the elevator to the penthouse suite; she phoned Vada to tell Mr. Davidson to leave for the day and to use the freight elevator, which needs a key. My *visitors* kept yelling at me, saying they weren't through. They finally left after an hour or so. I tell you, it was a long goddamned hour, too!"

"Did you talk to Davidson about them?"

"Sure, first thing the next day; he kinda laughed it off and said something about being glad those days were behind him."

"Have you heard any more from this Klein guy?"

"I've got a message slip on my desk with his name on it. He called yesterday at noon our time--two in the afternoon in New York--not long after the news got out. Message says it's urgent, but I don't plan on returning the call. I've got too much other business to attend to."

"Ken, I need to get that telephone number from you. Plus, did they leave a business card or anything with an address on it when they were here before?"

"Yeah, Klein left a card. I'll have my secretary look it up and give you a call."

"Okay, thanks. I may have some more questions later, but you've helped."

"I hope so. Will you do me a favor and kind of keep me in the loop with what's going on?"

"I'll try, but I can't make any promises. The cops are going to be awfully close-mouthed about everything 'til they make an arrest."

I ended the call, dialed Big East Oil, and asked for Fred Pearlman. It must have been my lucky day for getting connected. "Hello Cort! Good to hear from you; I assume you're calling about the murder, aren't you?" I knew Fred Pearlman fairly well; I'd even done a couple of drilling deals with him back in my exploration days. In contrast to Wildcat Willie Davidson, he enjoyed an excellent reputation as a person and an oil operator.

"Hey, Fred, how you getting on? Yeah, you're right about why I'm calling. Crappy deal, huh? I know you weren't a big Wildcat Willie Davidson fan, but that kinda shit shouldn't happen to anybody, him included."

Fred blew out a long breath. "That's a fact. Lord knows I despised the bastard, but he didn't deserve this. What can I do for you?"

"I'm helping the cops, in particular my friend, Tom Montgomery, who's heading up the homicide investigation, by contacting people I know in the oil biz. Because it was pretty well known you and Willie weren't exactly a mutual admiration society, I need to ask you some stuff. Basically, I just want to eliminate you as a suspect."

"Wow, I didn't know I was considered a suspect!"

"Uh, probably a bad choice of terms, Fred. Sorry. We don't have any *suspects*."

He laughed. "It's okay, Cort. Ask your questions; I'll do the best I can."

"Thanks. Okay, first off, where were *you* two nights ago?"

"That's an easy one and ought to put me in the clear. I was at a charity dinner at the Broadmoor Hotel in Colorado Springs; I stayed overnight there. We had cocktails from 5:00 p.m. 'til six, dinner was from six to eight, then a charity auction from eight until 9:30 p.m. After that, I had a couple of drinks with John and Merri O'Conner in the Charles Court bar and went to bed about midnight. I checked out around 8:30 a.m."

I got the same feeling I'd had with J.D. Pierce. This alibi was too specific and easily checked to be a lie. I was glad. I liked 'Fast' Freddie Pearlman. "Sounds good; now who do you think might have wanted to kill Davidson?"

Fred Pearlman laughed loudly. "How much time and paper have you got? That's going to be one hell of a list! Look, I'm not going to name names. I would just say you need to look at all his employees, business deals gone south and partners he screwed. You get the picture?"

"Yeah, unfortunately I do. I've already gotten a start on some of it. You're right about the length of the list; at least I can draw a line through your name. Let me ask you one more thing, I know you and your whole company are plenty pissed about Trumpet Creek. You know what I mean, not getting credit for the discovery well and all. Is there anybody on your staff who was mad enough to want to do something about it? You know, to go after Wildcat Oil or Davidson personally?"

Pearlman snorted, "That's bullshit! Sure, my guys were bent outta shape over it, but frankly, there's not a fucking thing we can do. It's water under the bridge. We had our prospect maps and Wildcat Oil had theirs; theirs were better. We'd like to get a *little* credit somewhere along the line, you know maybe a mention in the journals or something, but nobody here would have committed murder over it."

I hadn't expected anything different. "All right, Freddie, I'll let you go. If I think of something else, I'll give you a call."

Actually, I'd heard Fast Freddie Pearlman was mad as hell about Wildcat Oil getting credit for the discovery. But was it enough for him to commit murder? That seemed like a stretch, although jealousy was a powerful motive.

After I closed the call, I thought back to what I knew or had heard about the troubles between Pearlman and Davidson. The "problem" apparently stemmed from their similar backgrounds: both had immigrated from in New York to

Denver over thirty years ago, both were Jewish and extremely competitive.

Freddie Pearlman had arrived driving a ten year old Chevy, carrying a newly minted business degree from Yale University, and fifty dollars in his wallet. Davidson showed up shortly afterward, following a brief career in the clothing business. He'd inherited a small fortune on the death of his mother; sold the custom suit making shop she and his father had founded, flew to Denver, and announced he was in the oil business.

Pearlman found work as a junior landman with PetPro Production, a large independent oil producer headquartered in Dallas. It didn't take him long to learn how to buy leases, put acreage blocks together, and make deals to get them drilled. PetPro, like a lot of other independents, relied on obtaining "farm-outs" from major oil companies like Shell or Exxon. Those so-called "big oil" companies would acquire thousands of acres of leases and evaluate them by getting smaller companies to drill wildcat wells and earn portions of the leasehold. Fred Pearlman earned his nickname of "Fast Freddie" by getting wells drilled quickly. He was so good at it that within five years of landing in Denver, he struck out on his own to form Big East and was doing the same kinds of deals he'd done for PetPro Production.

Big East drilled over fifty wildcats with no successes and was close to being broke when they finally found a small field in northeastern Wyoming, near the Montana border. Pearlman named it West Yale Field to honor his alma mater. The field held a million barrels of oil and Big East had twenty-five percent of it. Freddie borrowed against his share of future production for enough money to lease the acreage in Montana that turned out to be the east side of Trumpet Creek. He'd nearly run out of drilling dollars again when he drilled the gas well. He knew what he was sitting on but was frustrated trying to figure a way to drill on Davidson's acreage, where the oil field lay.

Even with all that, I was having trouble putting Pearlman in the frame for Davidson's murder. I was going to have to keep digging and hoping for a break.

CHAPTER

NINE

My phone rang and caller ID read Lee Anne LeBlanc. "Good morning, Detective. How're you doing?"

"Hey, if I'm supposed to call you Cort, you should call me Lee Anne, okay? Listen, we may have caught a break. The IT guys started chasing email addresses and have turned up something interesting. They called the coffee shop in Boulder, Coarse Ground Coffee, to ask about their Wi-Fi and found out the store has a two-camera video surveillance system. One takes a full front of the door; the other scans the seating area. What's even better, they keep the discs for thirty days. The time stamp on the email to Wildcat Oil was 8:47 a.m. two weeks ago tomorrow. At that time of day, I'm guessing there will be a bunch of people on it, but we *should* have a picture of whoever sent it."

I acknowledged her excitement. "That does sound like a good lead. How are we going to know who we're looking for? Do you have some kind of facial recognition software we could use to scan all the Wildcat employees' photos for a quick search?"

Lee Anne laughed. "I assume you're kidding? That kinda stuff is only in the movies and TV detective stories! With all the budget restrictions, we'll be lucky to have something like that in ten years. We're going to have to do it the old-fashioned way: we'll have to physically review all the personnel file photos and then watch the tapes over and over hoping to make a connection. It could take weeks."

"Nothing's easy is it?" I couldn't help but think back to when I'd been chasing the Chinese spies from California to Colorado. The FBI and TSA had used a facial recognition system in the major airports and it had helped immensely. "Okay, let me know what I can do to help."

"Well, there might be one thing you could help me with. Tom told me your girlfriend is a CSI for Arapahoe County, is that right?"

I replied cautiously, "Yes, why do you ask?"

"All the metro area cop shops coordinate DNA requests through Arapahoe County; we want to get all the blood evidence DNA from Davidson's murder scene expedited. Since the shooter was probably close, there's a pretty good chance he got some blood spatter. It's a real long shot, oops-- bad pun--but if we are able to make an arrest, there *might* be a chance to get some evidence from his clothes."

"I don't have a clue about Arapahoe County's priority system, but go ahead and give her a call. Her name's Lindsey Collins. I think she's heading up the DNA project you're talking about. You can mention my name, although I don't know if it'll help."

"Thanks, I'll do it. Are you doing any good on your end?"

"Not enough. Like I told you, J.D. Pierce has a reasonably good alibi and Fred Pearlman's is airtight. Pierce did tell me Wildcat Willie screwed some of his early partners and they're still carrying grudges."

"Yeah, Tom mentioned that, so where are you going with it?"

"I'm not sure, but according to Tom, definitely *not* to New York."

Lee Anne chuckled. "I can't get his permission to go to Broomfield and check out this Vincent Freeman guy who's supposed to be Davidson's son, at least not by myself. Tom wants you to go with me. Are you available this afternoon?"

"Sure. Tell you what, I'll drive; I'll pick you up in front of the Justice Center at 1:00 p.m. I'm driving a Corvette."

This time she laughed out loud. "How did I know that?"

* * *

I wheeled into the circular drive in front of Denver's new Justice Center at 12:55 p.m. I'd thrown on a light windbreaker to cover the shoulder holster with my Beretta Px4 Storm nine millimeter automatic. It was cloudy and windy, strange for early summer; the coat wouldn't look out of place. Lee Anne LeBlanc was standing in the passenger loading area. I leaned over and opened the door; she ducked her head and slipped gracefully into the 'Vette...not an easy task.

She was wearing a light blue pants suit with a button down, open-collared, coral shirt. She glanced appreciatively around the interior. "Nice ride, Cort; beats the heck out of taking a cruiser from the motor-pool, although it'll be tough to transport Freeman if he confesses and gives himself up."

I laughed at that. "You'd be surprised how much I can stuff in the trunk of this zipper."

On the forty minute ride to Broomfield, I asked Lee Anne
how she'd come to be a cop and wound up in Denver. She
was a good story teller and I learned a lot. She'd grown up in
New Orleans and, like Lindsey, had been an outstanding high
school athlete. Her sport was softball and she'd played
collegiately for Tulane University. She was even invited to
tryout for the U.S. Olympic team. Her undergraduate degree
was in sociology, but she couldn't find a job to pay the bills,
grew tired of waiting tables, and finally went to work for the
Iberville Parish justice department. She worked a couple
years in the bail and bond division and was actually surprised
when she was accepted into the police academy in New
Orleans. After graduating near the top of her class, she spent
three years on patrol assignments, mostly in shitholes like the
Desire projects. "I'll tell you what, Cort, there's a lot of stuff
goes down in a place like that you won't find in the sociology
text books."

Despite the graft and corruption rampant in the NOPD,
Lee Anne had risen quickly doing things "by the book."
She'd just made plainclothes in Robbery & Homicide when
she saw an internet posting about opportunities in Denver and,
on a whim, sent in an application. Her timing was good as
DPD was complying with a federal court order to diversify

their ranks by hiring more women and minorities. Lee Anne LeBlanc was a perfect candidate; she'd flown to Denver for an interview the previous November and experienced her first-ever snowstorm. Typically, the next day had been clear and cold with a bright blue sky. She was hooked; there wasn't anything like that in Louisiana. Denver gave her a job offer for more pay, better benefits, and, more importantly, a locale out of New Orleans. She accepted on the spot. One month later she went to work.

We drove west on Colfax, jumped on I-25 northbound, and took US 36 to the Broomfield exit where we headed east. Lee Anne had printed out a map and directions to Vince Freeman's address. Three miles east of downtown Broomfield, we entered an area of "McMansions" on big lots spread out on low rolling hillsides. Most of the places had white rail fences; there were lots of horses and llamas in the pastures. Except for the llamas, I was reminded of the horse country around Louisville, Kentucky.

I followed Lee Anne's directions to a place with a high, sculpted cement wall set back from the road. I noted equally tall chain link fences running down the sides of the acreage, but no horses or llamas. I turned into the entry drive and stopped in front of two massive iron gates.

Lee Anne said, "Place looks like a damned fort. I ran the assessor's records before you picked me up; the owner of record is listed as Green Alliance, Ltd., same as on the email from Boulder. I also ran Vincent Freeman. He's got a bunch of misdemeanor arrests for environmental protests, but he's also got two biggies: assault on police officer busts. Both of them were plea bargained down: one to illegal assembly and the second one to resisting arrest. He did twenty five days in Boulder County jail on the resisting. I read the arrest warrants--he beat the crap out of a Boulder cop and put him in the hospital. I'm guessing the cops were really pissed about the plea bargains."

I gave her a sideways glance. "Thanks for letting me know ahead of time. I would've brought my boxing gloves if I'd known."

She pointed at surveillance cameras mounted high on the stone pillars on each side of the entry gate. A call box and card entry screen stood in the center of the driveway. I pulled forward to see if the gates would open automatically; they didn't. I pushed the call button and a few seconds later a male voice crackled over the intercom speaker. "Whadda you need?"

"Cortlandt Scott and Lee Anne LeBlanc to see Vincent Freeman."

"Who the hell are Cortlandt Scott and Lee Anne LeBlanc?"

Lee Anne leaned across me and spoke loudly toward the call box, "Denver PD; open the gate please."

The voice replied, "That doesn't look like a police car; you gotta warrant?"

I looked at Lee Anne and turned back to the speaker, "No warrant yet. This is unofficial. We just want to talk to Vincent about his father's murder."

The voice didn't answer for several moments. "Okay, drive up to the house." The right gate clicked and began to swing inward. I put the seven speed transmission in first, edged forward, and then accelerated up the curving drive.

We could see the house topping a low hill on the back quarter of the property. The entire place was enclosed by the chain link fence we'd spotted from the road; it looked like twenty or thirty acres. The hillside beyond the house was covered with trees and scrub oak thickets. The house did look like a fort. Lee Anne said, "I wonder if that was Freeman?"

"I don't know. The hesitation between answers makes me think it wasn't. I'll bet he was listening and watching though; someone had to have the authority to let us in."

It took four minutes to reach the house. I killed the engine, got out, and walked around to open the door for Lee Anne. She exited as gracefully as she had entered; a more difficult task. A broad set of steps led to a wide, covered porch and a wooden double door. I spotted two more surveillance cameras mounted under the porch roof. "This place has a lot of security."

Lee Anne nodded and asked in a soft whisper, "Are you carrying a gun?"

I nodded back. "Yeah, I'm like an American Express card; never leave home without it." We climbed the steps, crossed the porch to the doors, and I rang the doorbell. Several moments passed before we heard a bolt lock retract and the door was opened by a short guy built like a fireplug. He was wearing stained khaki cargo shorts hanging to his knees and a washed-out, faded tropical shirt several sizes too big. Even with the bed sheet of a shirt, it was hard to miss his muscular, knotted forearms and overdeveloped shoulders. I made him as an Ultra Fighting Challenge type, a cage match fighter where anything goes. Dude's hair was orange, hung to his collar, and looked dirty.

"You the cops?" It wasn't the voice from the callbox.

Lee Anne badged the guy and said, "Yes. Are you Vincent Freeman?"

"Fuck no! Vince's in the back. Follow me."

I couldn't help it. "Nice talk; you greet all the ladies who come to the door like that?"

Orange hair grinned and said, "She ain't no lady; she's a fuckin' cop. You wanna see Vince or not?"

I gritted my teeth. "Yeah, we want to see *Vince*. We can finish *our* conversation later."

"Copy that, dickhead. I'll look forward to it." The mouthy little shit turned on his heel and started walking toward the back of the house.

I reached to grab him but felt Lee Anne's hand on my arm. I looked at her as she shook her head and said softly, "Let it go; I've heard worse. We need to see Freeman."

I didn't like it, but stifled my impulse to grab orange hair and teach him some manners. We hurried to catch up. We passed through a sparsely furnished living room, down a short hall and into a large room extending across the entire back third of the house. It was furnished with mismatched tables

and chairs, recliners, and club chairs. The place looked like
the basement party room of the Deltas from the *Animal House*
movie. Our foul-mouthed guide turned left, stopped, and
pointed to the end of the room. A man was seated at the far
end of a leather couch in the back corner of the room. "That's
Vince; y'all have a nice visit now, ya hear." He smirked as he
turned away.

We walked to the couch. Vincent Freeman didn't bother
to get up and we didn't bother to offer our hands. There were
three straight-back slat chairs facing the couch separated by
six or seven feet. Lee Anne took the chair on the far left; I
took the one on the right leaving the middle spot vacant. From
our seats, we were looking out on a patio behind the house.
Five men, now including orange hair, were seated on various
loungers and lawn chairs. One guy was toking on a torpedo as
big as a Polish sausage. As we watched, he passed the bomb
to orange hair who took in a drag that would've staggered a
Clydesdale.

No one spoke until Lee Anne cleared her throat and said,
"Mr. Freeman? Thanks for seeing us. We're sorry for your
loss."

Even seated, it was easy to see Vincent Freeman was a
big man. I estimated him at well over six feet and two

hundred pounds. Wearing Madras plaid shorts and a maroon golf shirt, he was barefoot. The sole of his right foot, propped over his left knee, was filthy. Staring hard at Lee Anne, he said, "Really? Why should you give a shit; I sure as hell don't." It still wasn't the voice from the callbox.

Lee Anne blinked at the crude response. "He *was* your father. That seems like a rather harsh reaction to his being murdered."

Freeman's gaze shifted to me, although he addressed Lee Anne. "He might have fathered me, but he sure as hell wasn't my *father*. The son-of-a-bitch should be rotting in hell by now and it's a good riddance." He stared directly at me now. "Who the fuck are you? You're not a cop; not driving a car like that." Using foul language must have been a prerequisite for living here. His answer meant he *had* been looking at a monitor for the gate cameras.

I didn't break eye contact. "I'm Cortlandt Scott. I'm a PI helping in the investigation of your *father's* murder." I emphasized "father" to gauge his reaction. There wasn't one. He didn't rise to the bait. "Do you have any idea of who might have wanted to kill him?"

Finally, a reaction: "Who wouldn't want him dead? Everyone hated the despicable bastard. It was just a matter of time until someone had the balls to kill him."

Lee Anne asked, "Does that include you, Mr. Freeman?"

A different reaction: a loud barking laugh. "'Fraid not, honey...I'm a chicken-shit. I admire whoever did it, though."

The pungent, acrid smell of ganja drifted in from the patio. I saw Lee Anne's nostrils flare and she couldn't help looking outside. Freeman laughed again and jerked his chin toward the patio. "Purely medicinal, sweetheart; everybody has script. You wanta see 'em? Of course, the enlightened people of Colorado have legalized it now anyway."

"I'm not a *sweetheart*, Mr. Freeman. I'm sure you do have prescriptions for everyone; it's pretty easy to find a weed doctor in Colorado now. That's not why we're here. We're trying to catch whoever murdered your father. Do you have any interest in helping us do that?"

"None whatsoever, *sweetheart*. What's more, I wouldn't help you even if I could. Like I said, I'm glad the bastard got what was coming to him. He's been the biggest driller in the Rockies for decades, which means he's the biggest polluter. He's ruined the air quality, the water, natural habitat, and everything he's ever touched! The laugh's been on him,

though. I've turned almost every dime he's ever sent me back
on him. I've backed every environmental protest I could find,
filed petitions opposing his drilling permits and leases, I've
probably cost him millions in delays. You name it and I've
done it. Hell, I used his own money to buy this place and I
support all those guys outside. They're soldiers in my war
against the mighty Wildcat Willie Davidson. And you know
what's even sweeter? I'll continue to get money from the trust
even with him dead, and I'll use every last cent of it to destroy
his goddamn company once and for all!"

This guy was either the best actor around or he was a
zealot. I tried to stare him down but couldn't. Finally, I
asked, "Where were you the night he was murdered?"

Freeman grinned and said, "Right here and I've got five
witnesses who'll back that up." Again he used his chin to
point toward the patio.

Lee Anne stood. "One more question, Mr. Freeman: Did
you send an email from Coarse Ground Coffee threatening
your father?"

Still another grin. "Probably, but so what? It's protected
free speech; check it out. Besides, he's dead anyway and, like
I said, I didn't do it; I've got witnesses." He stood this time
and I'd been right about his size. He turned toward the sliding

screen and spoke loudly, "Nate, get your ass in here and show
our *guests* out, would you?" Turning back to us, he said, "I
hope you never find whoever shot the asshole; whoever it was
did us all a huge favor. And another thing, don't ever come
back here again without a fucking warrant. I shouldn't have
let you in this time, but I thought I'd answer your questions
and get you off my back."

Orange-hair Nate slid back the screen and sauntered in.
His eyes were red-rimmed and his mouth was set in a slack
jawed, insipid grin. "Ready to go already, are we? Hope you
had a great time." He reeked of pot.

He'd led us through the short hall into the living room
when I asked, "Ready to finish our conversation, potty-
mouth?"

He tried a reverse spin kick followed with a back hand
chop, but was too close. I moved inside the kick, deflected the
chop, and threw a short right uppercut. It caught him flush
and lifted his feet off the floor. He staggered and I was
surprised he didn't go down. I was on him before he could
regain his balance, but he ducked a left hook, tried a counter
kick and missed. The marijuana had probably slowed his
reflexes; his momentum carried him directly into another good
right. This one caught him high on the cheek and drove him

to his knees. He shot forward for a double leg takedown straight out of a high school wrestling manual. Too bad the manual hadn't warned against a knee lift to the face. In a high school wrestling match it would have drawn a disqualification, but here it caused a splattered nose and a TKO.

Orange-hair Nate rolled onto his side and covered his face with both hands. Blood leaked from beneath his fingers as he groaned. I squatted beside him as his eyes regained focus. "You're a miserable little prick, *Nate*. If I had more time, I'd wash your mouth out with soap, but this will have to do for now."

I looked back toward the hall and saw Vincent Freeman standing just behind Lee Anne. He had a bemused look on his face. "Nate hasn't had his ass kicked in a long time. He must be out of shape…probably too much 'medicine.' Now, get the hell outta my house."

CHAPTER

TEN

Lee Anne didn't say anything until we exited the driveway gate and turned toward Broomfield. "I sure hope that wasn't for my benefit? I told you, I've heard worse."

"Nope, that was for *my* benefit. Everything about that guy tripped my triggers; I just needed an excuse. That's the beauty of *not* being a cop."

"I hope your *chivalry* and concern for my virtue won't cost us an arrest if it ever comes to it."

"I don't know whether Freeman did it, but we need to learn a lot more about him. I just can't see being a rabid environmentalist as being a motive for murder. I'll grant you one thing though; he sure as hell hated Wildcat Willie. Ironic isn't it...using his own father's money against him?"

She agreed, "Yes, I wish we'd had time for one more question though. I'd like to know why and when he changed his name to 'Freeman.'"

"You're right. We probably should have asked right off the bat, although he didn't offer much of a chance."

We rode in silence until Lee Anne said, "I'm going to call the daughter, Jennifer, and set a time to talk to her. You can come along if you promise not to beat the crap out of someone else. Want to?"

"What? Beat the crap out of someone--or come with you? These are tough questions."

She laughed. "Set myself up for that one, wise guy! I'll try for tomorrow. I know it's Saturday, but we need to keep on top of this; it's already been almost four days and we're not much closer than we were the day it happened."

***

I dropped Lee Anne off at the Justice Center and started for home. Traffic was heavy on southbound I-25; it gave me time to think about the murder. The disturbing thing was how many people had apparently wanted Wildcat Willie Davidson dead, or at least weren't disturbed by his murder. For each

person of interest we accounted for, like J.D. Pierce or even
Fred Pearlman, several more seemed to pop up. Although I'd
told Lee Anne I didn't think Vincent Freeman had done it, that
wasn't a sure thing. Zealots are hard to read; that's why
they're zealots. Freeman might not have personally pulled the
trigger, but sycophants like orange-hair Nate couldn't be ruled
out.

It was 5:25 p.m. when I got home; it had taken an hour
and fifteen minutes. I was glad I didn't drive downtown every
day. Lindsey wouldn't be home for a half-hour or so; I had
time for a little research. I decided to start with Wildcat
Willie's first wife.

***

Rhonda Davidson, nee Levitz, had married William
Davidson in New York City about a year before he pulled up
stakes, moved to Denver, and became Wildcat Willie. The
couple had lit up the social scene soon after arriving; the
society pages of both Denver daily newspapers were full of
photos and stories about their lavish parties and events they
attended.

After a couple years, the stories took on a different tone.
Rhonda Davidson attended more and more events alone;
charity fetes were always listed as *her* events. While she

continued to appear on the society page, Wildcat Willie was on the business pages and, with increasing regularity, in the gossip columns. Although it was only insinuated, a careful reader could discern he had "companions." The companions were apparently not Rhonda.

A few weeks after "the happy couple" announced Jennifer's birth, the *Denver* Post reported divorce proceedings had begun between the Davidsons. Lawyers from both sides cited "irreconcilable differences" as cause for the divorce. The stories made headlines because of the potential settlement amounts, with one business editor speculating the Davidsons might be worth a half billion dollars. The case had moved quickly and the decree was granted in August, 1985.

Suddenly, something struck me: I hadn't seen anything about a son being born to the Davidsons. I googled "Jennifer Davidson" and quickly found her birthdate: February 23, 1985; she was now in her late twenties. I switched to Vincent Freeman, and after wading through several accounts of his arrests and convictions, found a birthdate: June 2, 1985, barely three months after Jennifer. There was little additional information about Vincent: no birth certificate, parents, hospitals, or adoption records. It was like he had arrived in Colorado as a full grown environmental activist and

professional asshole. What was wrong with this picture?
Who was Vincent Davidson Freeman's mother? It sure as hell
wasn't Rhonda Levitz Davidson.

***

I looked out to see Lindsey's Edge turning into the
driveway and was amazed at the time: 7:05 p.m. I'd been on
the computer for over an hour. Time goes fast when you're
having fun. I was waiting in the kitchen when Lindsey
entered.

"Hey, sleuth! What's for dinner? Hey, wait a minute--
where's my drink?" She hugged me and we had a long kiss.
"Sorry I'm late; I was trying to help out your new partner, Lee
Anne LeBlanc."

"She must've called you about speeding up the process on
Davidson's DNA?"

"See? That's why you earn the big bucks as a private eye.
She said she needed it ASAP, but that's the same as everyone
else's request. Of course, she has this big advantage; she
'knows somebody.' Actually, I had her send the sample
directly to the lab by courier and I called the lab director with
a special handling request. We can probably get a three-day
turnaround including having the results submitted directly to

CODIS. There's a possibility we could get everything back as early as Monday."

"Thanks, Linds, we've been running down a lot of blind alleys so far. What'd you think of Lee Anne?"

"What's to think? She seems nice enough over the phone; didn't make too big a deal about 'knowing' you or working for Tom. She sure has a great accent."

"Yeah, it's a little more refined than Andy Thibodeaux's isn't it! I think you have a lot in common with her as far as background and education go. You'll like her when you meet."

"I'll look forward to it. Is she as good looking as her voice makes her sound?"

"How am I supposed to answer that? Anything I say gets me in trouble!" I grinned at her.

"That means she is! *God!* You're so transparent! Where's my drink?" She returned the grin, which was a good thing.

"Hey, give me a break! I've been working. I'll get some wine; what would you fancy?"

Lindsey put her index finger to her brow, scrunched up her eyes, and appeared deep in thought. "How 'bout some Washington state Riesling--at least for starters?"

"*Starters?* What have you got planned?" She didn't answer; just gave me the smile. I went down the steps to the wine cellar two at a time.

***

We were both up early Saturday morning; Lindsey started a workout in the exercise room and I returned to my computer research of the Davidson family.

I started with the daughter. I looked up the address we'd gotten from Vada Benson and found she lived in a luxury townhouse development in Greenwood Village, Denver's most affluent suburb. It wasn't far from Lindsey's condo, but in another stratosphere financially. Jennifer Davidson had graduated from the University of Denver with degrees in sociology and finance and seemed to be utilizing both disciplines spending daddy's money on good causes.

On the boards of five charities, she was chairperson for two of them. In addition, she was involved with two hospitals and their outreach programs, the Denver art council, a hospice, and a food bank. Twenty-eight years old and single, she kept a low social profile with no hints of scandal or public romances. The few pictures available showed a tall, slim, rather awkward-looking woman. Although attractive, she wasn't beautiful; the word "plain" came to mind.

Just as I finished reading the last article I'd found on Jennifer, Lee Anne called. "Good morning, Cort. I made contact with Jennifer Davidson and she's agreed to meet us this afternoon at her house. Can you make it at 12:30 p.m.?"

"That'll work for me. Incidentally, I've been researching her this morning. She sure as hell is not her 'brother's keeper.' From what I've been able to find, Jennifer is a regular goody-two-shoes. She supports several charities and causes and none of them are concerned with the environment.

"But, if you want a real shocker, here's one for you: she and Vincent are *NOT* full brother and sister. They were born three months apart. Wildcat Willie may be their father, but Rhonda Davidson is only Jennifer's mother."

"Wow that *is* a game changer! I wonder who Vincent's mother is?"

"Good question; let's ask Jennifer if she knows. I'll meet you at her house at 12:30 p.m."

CHAPTER

ELEVEN

I turned the 'Vette into the guarded entrance of the Bellagio townhouses at 12:23 p.m. The security guard leaned through the window of the gatehouse and asked for my name and ID. I handed him my PI card. He looked at the card, raised his eyebrows, and said, "Never seen one of these before. How do you get one--box of Cracker Jacks?" He laughed at his own joke. I didn't laugh with him.

"I'm meeting DPD detective Lee Anne LeBlanc at Jennifer Davidson's house; check your list."

"Don't need to; the lady dick is already here. Hey, that's funny--'*lady* dick.'" This guy was a riot.

I gave him my best tough guy, PI stare and said, "Look, pards, I don't want to be late. Would you just give me directions to Ms. Davidson's house?" Ten thousand comedians out of work and this guy was telling jokes.

He got the message. "Go straight to the 'T', take a right, then a left at the next street; it's on the left side, two places down." He handed me my card and opened the gate.

Following the aspiring comedian's directions, I spotted a plain-Jane Ford sedan parked on the street in front of an attractive, end unit townhouse. I stopped behind the nondescript police car, walked up the front sidewalk, and was reaching for the bell when the door opened. Jennifer Davidson was better looking in person than in newspaper photos. She was easily five eight, slim, and didn't appear as awkward as I'd thought. She was wearing a Denver University tee shirt, cut-off jean shorts, and tan sandals. She looked a lot like Celine Dion.

"Hi, you must be Cortlandt Scott. Detective LeBlanc is inside; please come in." She had a slightly high voice, smiled as she spoke, and gave a good first impression.

"Thank you, and please call me Cort; Cortlandt sounds too formal."

"Certainly, uh, *Cort*, and you may call me Jenn; everyone does." Jenn stood aside as I entered. "Right this way, we're in the family room in the back."

I'd spent a lot of money furnishing and decorating my house; Jenn Davidson had spent a lot more on hers. The hallway leading to the back was lined with western art and a quick glance suggested the paintings weren't prints. I spotted two James Bama portraits, a Stephenson horse soldier's scene, and a Turpening mountain man. She either had a very good eye or an excellent buyer; probably both. There were two doors along the hall: one, I assumed, was a coat closet; the other, which was open, a small guest bathroom.

The hallway led to a cozy family room with picture windows and French doors opening onto a flagstone patio, a small patch of lawn, and a backyard garden area. The garden looked Oriental: Japanese maples, potted bonsai trees, and a couple of small, delicate water features. Everything was enclosed by decorative fences and the wall of what I assumed was a detached garage. The entire tableau suggested refinement. And money.

Lee Anne was seated in a large wingback chair, across a wooden coffee table from a loveseat done in the same fabric. Another wingback in a contrasting, but complementary, color stood at the end of the table facing a fireplace on the end of the room.

"Please have a seat, Cort. Lee Anne is having lemonade; may I get you something?"

"Lemonade sounds good, thank you." I sat on the loveseat across from Lee Anne so our hostess would be seated between us.

"Certainly, excuse me for a moment." Jennifer strode to the far end of room and through a swinging door into what I assumed was the kitchen.

I looked around, admiring the room and furnishings. "Little different than Vincent's dump, isn't it?"

Lee Anne agreed. "No kidding! This is really nice; so is she."

Jenn returned carrying a tray with a crystal pitcher full of lemonade, three large glasses, coasters, and napkins. She set a coaster and glass in front of each of us, handed us a napkin, and poured the drinks. Leaving the tray and pitcher on the table, she took a seat in the remaining chair. "Now, I understand you have some questions concerning my father's murder. I'll help any way I can." She sat back in the chair and sipped from her glass.

Lee Anne swiveled slightly to face her. "Jenn, first of all, we're sorry for your loss. It's a terrible thing to lose a parent at any time, and especially to a murder. Our questions may be uncomfortable for you, but they're important."

Jenn waved her hand dismissively. "Thank you. Please don't worry about it. I understand."

"All right, we appreciate your cooperation. First, have the funeral arrangements been made?"

"Yes, the funeral will be Monday. Actually, the medical examiner didn't release the body until yesterday; something about the autopsy. My father was Jewish, but he didn't adhere strictly, didn't attend synagogue, so there was no need to have the funeral and burial quickly."

"I understand. Did you discuss the funeral arrangements with your stepmother, we under---

Jenn interrupted sharply, "Janet is *not* my stepmother! I was never adopted by her; never lived in her home. My mother raised me."

Lee Anne flushed and said, "I'm very sorry; I didn't mean to offend you. Technically, although it's probably a very fine point, you automatically became Janet's 'stepdaughter' when she married your father. It's just that we understood Mrs.

Davidson, Janet, was in California and would have to travel back here for the funeral."

Jenn's face also colored. "I'm sorry. I shouldn't have snapped at you like that. Janet and I are not close. In fact, we don't have a relationship of any kind; I don't want to be considered *any* kind of daughter to her.

"I did speak to her on the day my father was killed. Since she was out of town, I volunteered to take care of the arrangements; I think she was happy about that. Anyway, I called her again yesterday, after I heard from the medical examiner's office and the funeral home. To tell you the truth, I'm not sure she's going to come back by Monday."

I exchanged looks with Lee Anne which I'm sure Jenn observed. She said, "Although, as I said, I'm not close to Janet, I'm not offended by her attitude. I think her relationship with my father was not a good one. I think he treated her poorly."

Lee Anne gave her an understanding look and plunged into the interview. "Jenn, can you tell us where you were when your father was killed?"

"Yes, of course. I was attending a dinner and auction fund raiser for the art council. It was being held in the great hall of the art museum; I was there from around 6:30 p.m. until about midnight. I returned home about 12:30 a.m."

Lee Anne nodded, but continued, "That covers the evening before. Can you account for the time between 12:30 a.m. and seven the next morning?"

Jenn looked a little annoyed but answered, "Well, no, but the gate guard should be able to tell you I didn't leave."

"Did you drive yourself to and from the charity event?"

"No, the art council president, Jeremy Brennan, had arranged a limo for me. I'm sure the gatehouse records can give you the exact times for that too."

"When did you find out about your father's murder?"

"The guard called about 8:45 a.m. to say the Denver police were at the gate and needed to see me. Two officers came to the door and asked to come in. They told me they had some bad news and proceeded to tell me about my father. They were very, uh, 'gracious.'"

"What was your reaction?" I could tell Lee Anne had struggled with the question. How the hell do you ask someone what they think about their father being murdered?

"I was stunned; I had to sit down for a moment. To be entirely truthful, though, I wasn't totally surprised. Truth be told, my father wasn't a very nice man. He'd made a lot of enemies; he didn't treat people very well."

I hadn't said anything until now. "Jenn, how was your relationship with your father?"

She considered my question for a few seconds. "I'd describe it as being as good as could be expected."

I drank some lemonade to gain time; it was very good probably homemade I thought. "That's a bit obtuse. Would you explain what you mean?"

She smiled sadly. "As I mentioned, my father wasn't a very nice man. He thought most problems in life could be solved by throwing money at them. If the problem wasn't resolved, he would throw more money. That's how he dealt with my mother and me. He simply 'paid us off.' To our detriment and shame, we accepted it and, for the most part, let him slide. Essentially, I suppose you'd describe us as 'enablers.' He could go his own way and we didn't create any obstacles...as long as the money kept flowing. I'm not very proud of it, but I didn't do anything to change the circumstances. I believe that knowledge--knowing we were trading our consciences for money--is what killed my mother."

I raised an eyebrow at that. "When did your mother die?"

"It'll be three years in December."

Lee Anne asked, "How did she die?"

Jennifer Davidson took a very deep breath and exhaled in a long shudder. "She drank herself to death. The actual diagnosis was cirrhosis of the liver, but we all know what causes that." A tear slid down Jenn's right cheek. "Basically, my mother never recovered from their divorce. She'd never found anyone new, someone to share her life; actually, she didn't try. She devoted herself to me and to being bitter. It was the bitterness that drove her to drink."

Lee Anne asked, "Do you know why your parents divorced? And when?"

"I wasn't even a year old, so almost twenty-eight years ago. Officially, both sides said 'irreconcilable differences,' but the real reason was because my father was unfaithful. He cheated on my mother, flaunted his girlfriends, and even had a child out of wedlock: Vincent Freeman."

I needed to get some things straight. "So, obviously, you know about Vincent? Do you have a relationship with him?"

Jenn didn't hesitate. "I know he exists, but no, I don't know anything *about* him."

"Have you ever met him?"

"No."

"When did you first learn of him? Did your father tell you?"

She shook her head slowly and paused before replying. "My mother told me about Vincent ten years ago, when I turned eighteen. The conditions of her alimony and child support were going to change and she wanted me to know why. She said she wanted me to know what she'd been living with all those years."

Lee Anne considered her next question carefully, "Did your father dispute the alimony and child support or did they fight about it?"

Again, Jenn shook her head. "No, not really. He always paid on time and, when I was eighteen, a trust he had created for me kicked in and I began receiving income from it. He didn't even stop the child support payments to my mother, although he could have. It was her idea to tell me about Vincent; he also has a trust, and my father was taking responsibility for him. My mother said she hated my father for doing what he'd done, but she couldn't blame Vincent. She felt sorry for him."

I stood and walked over to the French doors and looked out to the garden. "Did your mother ever meet Vincent?"

"I certainly don't think so. Why would she want to?"

I nodded; it had been a rhetorical question anyway. "Do you know what Vincent is involved in?"

"Sort of. I know he's really into environmental causes; particularly concerning the oil business; things my father did. I know he's been arrested at some protests."

"Do you share his feelings?"

This time she waited for several long moments before answering while she slowly sipped lemonade. She seemed to be weighing her response carefully. "I don't believe in violence of any kind regardless of how righteous the cause. I *do* have concerns about the environment, but I'm a conservationist, not a preservationist. They are different you know. I suppose I could be considered a hypocrite because I continue to accept the payments from my trust which is, of course, funded from oil and gas production. I haven't tried to turn the money around and fight my father like Vincent. Frankly, I'd be lying if I told you I don't enjoy my lifestyle because I do. I *have* tried to put much of the money to good use. I give loads to charity and I support several different non-profit organizations."

I returned to my seat, "Jenn, do you know why Vincent's last name is 'Freeman?'"

She shook her head, "I don't. And it'll probably seem strange, but I've never really thought about it. I suppose it was his mother's name."

"Does that mean you know who his mother is?"

"Oh no, I didn't mean to imply that! I have no idea."

I caught Lee Anne's eye, "Do you have any more questions for Ms. Davidson?"

She thought for an instant and said, "Just one: Jenn, do you have any idea who would want to murder your father?"

Jennifer Davidson gave us the same answer as many others, "I guess a lot of people. I don't know who, specifically, would do it, but apparently, the list is pretty long."

We thanked her for her time and she showed us out. As we walked between our cars, Lee Anne said, "What do you think? She's a far cry from good old Vincent, isn't she?"

"To make a poor analogy, as different as oil from water. It sounds to me like our best suspect would have been Rhonda Davidson. But, since she's been dead for three years, I think we're almost back to square one. We're going to have to catch a break of some kind."

Lee Anne nodded. "You've got that right. I'm going home and sit down with the case file and start from scratch.

Maybe I can come up with something new. Thanks for
coming; I'll tag bases with you on Monday."

124 Lee Mossel

CHAPTER

TWELVE

That evening, Lindsey and I went to dinner at a new Italian restaurant in Castle Rock. The place was located in 'Old Town,' which was a misnomer because the area was rapidly becoming entirely 'new' with restaurants, bars, boutique shopping, and even an outdoor rink for roller skating in summer and ice skating in winter. On the twenty minute drive from Parker, I brought her up to speed on our interview with Jenn Davidson. Lindsey was a good listener.

After we took a patio table and ordered glasses of Prosecco, Lindsey asked, "So, do you think you're getting any closer to identifying any viable suspects?"

"Not really. What's worse, I don't think we've totally eliminated *any* possible suspects. We've made the odds pretty long on people like J.D. Pierce and Freddie Pearlman, but we sure as hell haven't developed any leads on the actual killer."

She sipped her wine, perused the menu, and said, "What about this Vincent Freeman guy's mother? Any ideas on who she is?"

"Nope, and I don't know how we're going to find out either. Vincent isn't going to volunteer anything."

"You think it's important?"

"I don't know. We sure as hell don't need more suspects, but knowing would add some to the list--the woman, her family--who knows?"

"You might want to check with Boulder police and the state crime lab; they might have DNA for Vincent. If you'd like, I can do it for you."

I toasted her and said, "You're okay, you know. Regardless of what it says in there on the bathroom wall."

She gave me a look and flipped me the bird.

We ordered a couple of antipasto salads and our entrees: Tuscan chicken for Lindsey and veal Marsala for me. From the best wine list I'd seen in a long time, we agreed on a 2008 Drouhin Oregon Pinot Noir.

"What's your next step?" Lindsey asked.

"I'm going to do the same thing as Lee Anne: review the entire case file and see if I've missed something. Honestly, I feel like I'm spinning my wheels waiting for something to happen."

The server brought our dinners and we tucked in. The food matched the wine list; it was excellent.

***

Our first break came Monday morning. I was in a recliner on the back deck finishing the newspaper when Lindsey called. "Hey sleuth, you better be sitting down! I've got something that'll knock your socks off!"

"Oh yeah? It must be big; you've only been at work for two hours."

"Remember what I told you about *maybe* getting those cold case DNA reports today?"

"Sure, what happened? Did you get a hit on something?"

"No, we got a home run, man, a grand slam!"

"Oh yeah? How's that?"

"We got several different results back this morning, including the crime scene stuff for your murder vic, Davidson. So, guess what? He was already in the system, but probably not in the way you'd think."

"C'mon, Linds, what's going on? You're baiting me here."

"Like I said, we've been working on cold case files; some of 'em going back twenty, thirty years or more. One of those cases was a rape from Denver. The victim had an old-fashioned rape kit run and then disappeared. She told the cops she didn't know who had raped her; she didn't even give them a description. The police couldn't follow up because she moved and didn't leave an address which, apparently, isn't unusual in rape cases, particularly back then. She never returned any phone calls and shut down her telephone account a few days after the incident. DPD had her name but nothing else, and after a couple weeks pretty much quit trying to find her. Again, not unusual twenty-five years ago."

"You still haven't told me how all this connects?"

"*Because the DNA hit came back as a match for your murder victim!* William Davidson! The rape 'victim' was Vada Benson!"

That brought me out of my deck chair. "You've gotta be shittin' me! Wildcat Willie Davidson raped Vada Benson?"

Lindsey said, "That's what the evidence says."

I was having trouble processing everything. "When did the rape occur?"

"September twenty-first, 1984. Almost twenty-nine years ago."

I did the math and it hit me like a sledge hammer. Vada Benson was Vincent Freeman's mother and Wildcat Willie Davidson had raped her. The phone pinged indicating another call. Caller ID said it was Tom Montgomery. "Linds, I gotta go; Tom's calling. Does he have this information?"

"He should. I called Lee Anne before I called you. It was her request. Call me back when you can."

"Will do, babe, thanks!"

"Christ, Tom, what took you so long to call? Linds just told me about the DNA hit on Wildcat Willie!"

Tom was almost shouting into the phone. "I had our techs go over it twice to make sure! Kinda puts a different slant on things doesn't it?"

"No shit, Sherlock! What are you going to do now?"

"I'm going to wait for you to get your ass downtown and then you, Lee Anne, and I are going to have another talk with the lovely *Ms.* Vada Benson."

***

Tom and I bracketed Lee Anne as we walked up the sidewalk to the Glass Spire, Denver's new high-end condo residence across the South Platte River from Union Station, the neo-classical train depot undergoing renovation as a hotel and glitzy shopping arcade. At the security counter in the elegant lobby, Tom told the woman monitoring the closed circuit TVs that Vada Benson was expecting us. During the short drive from the Justice Center, he said he'd called Vada and she'd agreed to meet us.

The guard directed us to the penthouse elevator across the lobby. We rode up the forty-three floors in silence; it was amazingly quick. The doors quietly swooshed open and we stepped out into a world of fine appointments and anteroom furnishings. There were four penthouses, 4300 A through D, each occupying a quarter of the floor. Discreet, gold-lettered signage indicated units 4300 C and D were located to our left and right, respectively. Units 4300 A and B were accessed from a wide hallway directly in front of us that lead to the west side of the building. Vada Benson's address, 4300 A, was the entire southwest corner of the floor, the premier location. As we started down the hall, Lee Anne softly said, "Big time bucks; her *administrative assistant* position must pay pretty well."

I rang the bell and the eight-foot, solid oak door clicked and opened. We walked in and found ourselves in a spacious entryway furnished with upholstered chairs on either side of end tables at each end of the room. Immediately, the white and gold double doors in front of us opened and Vada Benson stood in the doorway.

I don't know why it was surprising to me, but she was dressed in worn jeans, leather strap sandals, and a pink polo shirt. The logo for Silver Oak Winery, one of my favorite California cabernets, was emblazoned across the left breast of her shirt. "I was beginning to wonder how long it would take you to run your traps and follow up on our earlier interview." She wasn't smiling, but didn't seem particularly mad either. "Come in; we'll be more comfortable inside." She opened the door fully and stepped aside.

The condo was stunning. I had expected an outstanding view and wasn't disappointed. My eyes were pulled directly to the south and west exterior walls which were entirely glass. The Bronco's football stadium was in the immediate foreground and we were high enough to actually see a portion of the field; Mt. Evans was directly in front of us on the skyline; Pikes Peak dominated the view farther south along the Front Range. I could pick out several landmarks in west Denver and Lakewood: Sloan's Lake, Green Mountain, North and South Table Mountains, and the Federal Center.

Benson pointed to the loveseats and chairs scattered around the living area, all arranged to take advantage of the views. "Have a seat; do you want anything to drink?"

Tom shook his head, "No. We've got several questions."

"Okay, it's all business then. Ask away." She sat in the only chair facing away from the windows.

Tom took a white leather club chair directly in front of her. "Why didn't you tell us about Wildcat Willie Davidson raping you, Ms. Benson?"

"Because it wasn't any of your business."

I watched Tom's neck and face turn red as he tried to control his temper. "That's bullshit! It *WAS* our business! It puts you at the very goddamn top of the list of who would want to see him dead for Christ sake."

Benson's facial expression mirrored Tom's anger. "No, *that's* bullshit! Look around you. Do you think I wanted him dead when he provided me with this? I don't care what you think about me. So what if I 'sold out' and let him buy me off? Who got hurt? Sure, he got away with it, but the longer time went by, the less it seemed like a rape."

Lee Anne looked uncomfortable. "Rape is rape, Ms. Benson; why would you say something like that?"

Vada Benson fixed her with a stare. "Because I was young and dumb, led him on, and then got scared when he didn't stop when I wanted him to."

Lee Anne shook her head. "If you wanted him to stop and said 'No', he raped you. There aren't shades of gray here and it doesn't matter when or where it happened."

Benson jumped up and walked to the chrome and glass bar tucked into the wall on the east side of the room. She dropped two ice cubes into an oversized tumbler and poured enough Grey Goose vodka to cover the ice. She returned to the chair, air toasted us, and took a drink. "Maybe you guys can't have a drink, but I can. And, what's more, I'm damn sure going to!" She took another sip. "Okay, here's the whole story, for what it's worth.

CHAPTER

THIRTEEN

"I moved to Denver from Oklahoma City in February, 1984. It was right after my parents were killed in a car accident. I was twenty-three years old, single, and had a degree in business administration from OU, but it was during one of the down cycles in the oil business and I couldn't find a job of any kind in Oklahoma. I ended up applying at over thirty oil and gas outfits in Denver because I'd worked some summer jobs in oil company offices back home. I got *one* damned interview, with Wildcat Oil. I was down to my last few dollars and was going to have to give up my apartment, move back to Oklahoma, and live with my sister, when I got called in for a second interview. I'd been applying for production accounting or land department positions, but they told me Mr. Davidson's administrative assistant had left and asked if I would consider the position, although they recognized I was over qualified.

"I coulda cared less about 'over qualifications.' I was out of options and desperate, so I agreed and was immediately taken in to interview with the big man himself. He was very businesslike, seemed impressed with my resume, and offered me the job on the spot. I went to work June 1st, which was weird because it was a Friday.

"Even though the rest of the oil business was in the toilet, Wildcat Oil was super busy. They had the money and the backing to take advantage of all the companies who were cutting back. Everybody needed to get their acreage evaluated and were giving good deals to anyone who could drill wells. We were drilling three or four wildcats a week all over the Rockies and, amazingly enough, lots of them were finding oil. All the employees were getting in on the override pools and receiving bonuses. I couldn't believe it, but I got my first bonus, twenty-five hundred dollars, only two weeks after starting work. Twenty-five hundred bucks was equal to a month's salary!"

Benson took another heavy hit of the vodka before continuing. "I could tell Davidson was attracted to me right away, I mean physically. He'd come out of his office and stand by my desk three or four times a day and just talk. He was always complimenting me even when I knew I didn't look my best. He started inviting me into his office for a drink after work every Friday and I accepted."

Lee Anne interrupted the story. "You *did* know he was married, didn't you?"

Benson gave her the hard stare again. "Of course I knew; I didn't care. We weren't doing anything wrong."

Lee Anne shrugged, "Go ahead."

"Sometime in August, he asked me out for dinner. I couldn't believe he took me to the Brown Palace Club. I mean, it doesn't get much more public than that. We must have met five people he knew, but he didn't seem to care. Over dinner, he told me he and his wife weren't getting along, but he was in a 'bind' because she was pregnant."

Benson looked at each of us like she was gauging our reactions. "Oh, go ahead and say it! I know what you're thinking. It's the world's oldest line for a married man trying to seduce a young woman. You think I didn't know that? Well, guess what? I didn't give a damn! I was making more money than I would have thought possible, I was on the arm of one of the most powerful men in Denver, and I'd already made up my mind to let the string play out. So, does that make me a whore? Depends on your definition, I guess. I chose to think I was playing the game according to my own rules."

I was thinking about the calendar events of 1984 and 1985. "Tell us what led up to September twenty-first, 1984."

She drained her glass, took a deep breath, and said, "We'd started having sex the week after our dinner at the Brown Palace. The first time was in his office. You know he made the professional staff, the geologists and landmen and engineers, work Saturday mornings? He used to say you never knew which Saturday morning would lead to the biggest discovery in the Rockies. He wasn't hypocritical about it because he came in too.

"The week after our dinner, he asked me to come in on Saturday, but not until noon. When I got there, everyone else was leaving; just like now, his office was on the floor above everyone else's. Anyway, when I got there, I knocked on his door and stepped into his private office. He was sitting on the couch and had an open bottle of '76 Jordan Cabernet with two glasses on the coffee table. He said, 'I'm glad you're here,

Vada. Come join me.' I sat down, he poured some wine, and ten minutes later we were having sex.

"On the twenty-first of September, which was a Friday, he was in a big meeting with some of his investors from New York. At about 5:45 p.m., he came out of his office and said it was going to run late, probably at least a couple more hours. He said he wanted to come to my apartment when it was over, but I told him I was meeting a couple of girlfriends for pizza and drinks and probably wouldn't be home until late. He got kinda pissed off and stomped back into the meeting.

"I met my friends at Pietro's Pizzeria around 7:00 p.m. and we had pizzas and a bunch of drinks. Pietro's was walking distance from my apartment and I got home about eleven o'clock. I lived on the second floor of the building. It was one of those two story, open-balcony designs, so each apartment has an outside door. I'd no more than gotten inside when someone knocked on the door; pounded on the door would have been more like it. I had it on a chain and opened it just enough to see who was there. It was him.

"He said, 'Let me in; I didn't think you were ever going to get home.' I could tell he'd had some drinks and so had I, so I said, 'I don't think that's a good idea.' He started yelling, 'Goddamn it, I said let me in!' and started pounding on the door again. I didn't want to attract my neighbors' attention so I said, 'Okay, okay, quit making noise.' I closed the door enough to get the chain off, started to open it, and he rushed in, almost knocking me over. He grabbed me and started kissing me until I pushed him away. I told him, again, it wasn't a good idea; we were both drunk and we should wait for a better time and place. I even told him we could 'do it' tomorrow at the office. No matter what I said, he just kept grabbing me and finally got me into the bedroom. I thought he was going to tear my clothes so I said 'Wait' and took them off myself."

Tom shook his head and his face clouded over. I knew what he was thinking: there's no way she was going to be able to claim rape.

"This time it wasn't 'making love' or even casual sex--he was rough and was hurting me. I actually don't know why I didn't scream or yell or something. He'd never been like that before. I guess I just kept thinking he wasn't himself and what was happening was partially my fault because I'd let him go too far before. I'd never said 'No.' Still, I was mad and instantly thought about making him pay, you know what I mean? Get even. That's why, after he left, I called the police and told them I'd been raped.

"Although I wanted to get it on record, I didn't tell them who it was. I said I didn't know who did it. I even wiped down the door and then smudged my knuckles on it so it'd look like someone had pushed their way in. I told the cops whoever it was had pushed me through the door as soon as I'd unlocked it. I almost bolted when they put me in their medical examination room and some nurse brought in the goddamn rape kit. I mean, no one had ever heard of DNA, let alone using it to tie people to crimes. All I was thinking about was getting proof that *someone* had raped me. In my own mind, I was already planning on using everything I could come up with to make him pay."

It was Lee Anne's turn to get up and walk around the room. She was obviously in distress. She marched to the bar, got out a water glass, filled it to the rim, and drank it down. When she returned to her seat, she said, "So, you were already planning on blackmailing Davidson? Was that the idea?"

It was apparent Vada Benson didn't like Lee Anne and from the look in Lee Anne's eyes, the feeling was mutual. Benson replied in a flat voice, "The son-of-a-bitch raped me. Now days, even wives can accuse their husbands of rape, but it was different then. Why should I have tried to get him arrested and thrown in jail when he was my ticket to ride? If you want me to give you an answer to your question, I'll say, 'No'. I didn't have the whole plan figured out, but I had a damn good outline."

Tom hadn't said much; now he asked Benson, "When did you tell Davidson what you were doing?"

She didn't have to think about her answer. "First thing Monday morning. If I'd have gotten out of the police station and exam room quicker, I would have gone in Saturday morning. As it was, I'm glad I had two days to think everything through. By Monday, I *did* have a plan.

"I was waiting for him in his private office when he arrived. At first, he looked surprised to see me, then relieved, and then he started apologizing. I cut him off and told him I'd called the cops after he left."

Tom asked, "How'd he react?"

Benson gave a derisive laugh and said, "Looked like someone had slugged him in the gut; I thought he was going to faint."

"What'd you do then?" Tom asked.

"I was shaking like a damn leaf in a hurricane, but as calmly as I could, I told him everything I'd done: about going to the police station, having the rape kit, making a statement, the cops checking out my apartment...all of it. But then I dropped the bomb and told him I *hadn't* told the police about him. I hadn't given them his name.

"He staggered around, sat on the couch, and, literally, started to bawl. I let him go for a minute or so and then yelled at him to snap out of it. I told him if he did everything I said, I wouldn't tell the cops, *but* I'd written everything down, including his name, and hidden it in a place he could never find it. Even more importantly, I told him I'd sent a letter to several different people telling them where they could find the story if *anything* ever happened to me."

Tom glanced first at Lee Anne and then me. "So what did you ask him to do?"

Benson smiled but flared. "I didn't *ask* him. I *told* him what he was *going* to do! I'd thought everything through and laid it out for him. I told him, starting immediately, he needed to create a whole new company that would have a one percent working interest in every well Wildcat Oil drilled from then on; that he would fund the company's expenses from his personal accounts *and* use his personal accountants, not Wildcat Oil's, to handle the paperwork and finances. All oil and gas revenues would be paid into accounts to which he and I were the only signatories, and, most important of all, I couldn't be fired as long as he ran Wildcat Oil.

"I knew there was really nothing but my threat to tell all that would force him to do anything, especially the no firing part. I just figured he'd be so paranoid about everything that he'd go along with it.

"I let him have a moment to think about everything and then softened up a little. I told him if he played by my rules, I would never ask for anything else, plus I'd never interfere in his private life in any way."

Tom couldn't help himself. "Jesus, how *very* kind of you."

"*Fuck You, Lieutenant!* Like I said, the bastard *RAPED* me! He *OWED* me and I intended to make him pay!"

I'd been doing some mental calculations, but wasn't sure I was getting the decimal point in the right place because the numbers were too big. "I'm guessing you made a lot of money over the years, Vada. Was it worth having to look at Wildcat Willie every day?"

She gave me a shark's grin: all teeth and no humor, "You're goddamned right it was worth it! Even with oil at twelve bucks a barrel, by the end of '85 I was receiving over ten thousand dollars a month. I see your brain grinding, oilman; here are some more numbers for you. Wildcat Oil was adding twenty-five hundred to three thousand barrels of oil *a day* each year, and even with production declines they're producing close to twenty million barrels a year now. And crude price is $90.00 a barrel! My stinking little one percent is worth between fifteen and twenty million bucks a year!"

My decimal hadn't been misplaced. Tom looked at me and raised his eyebrows in an unspoken question. I just nodded.

Lee Anne asked, "When did you find out you were pregnant? Did that change your deal with Davidson?"

Benson's expression changed to something between sorrow and anger; mad at Lee Anne for asking. "I suspected when I missed my next period, so I went to the doctor. I was six or seven weeks pregnant. My first thought was to get an abortion and I probably should have, but--and I know this sounds crazy after everything I've done--I'm Catholic. I couldn't make myself do it. I haven't been in a church since I was fifteen years old, but those old teachings---

"I told Davidson about it as soon as I found out. He wanted me to get the abortion, offered to pay for it and everything, and then got mad when I said I wouldn't. I had to go back to threatening him to calm him down.

"My plan was to work until I was about four or five months along, figuring I could hide it pretty easily since our offices were separate from the rest of the company and we didn't have many visitors. I planned to conjure up a story about going on a vacation and getting sick with something I couldn't shake. I'd continue 'being sick' for a few months and then come back to work part time. I would get my sister to move up from Oklahoma to take care of the baby. I wouldn't tell her about the rape, just that I'd 'made a mistake' and got pregnant. I'd tell her I was too embarrassed to tell her who the father was. She'd buy into that, no problem.

"I told Davidson he'd have to pay me enough so I could give her a 'salary' of some kind. My sister didn't know how much I was making, but I'd told her I was starting to get some big bonuses; she wasn't going to question where the money was coming from. He had a big household account which was run through the office; I paid most of his personal bills from it so that was no problem either. I knew his wife was expecting in February and he was setting up trust funds and things for their kid. I wanted him to set up something for my baby, something that would kick in at age eighteen. I told him he wouldn't have anything to do with the baby, never see it. Nothing."

Tom repeated an earlier question, "What did he say to that?"

Again, the shark's grin, "What could he say? I had all the trump cards. He either paid up or I'd ruin his whole life."

Tom asked, "So, is that how things have been since? For twenty-eight years?"

She nodded. "Pretty much. We had to have another 'talk' when his first wife, Rhonda, figured everything out and divorced him. It was just about the time Vincent was born and the dumb ass must've let it slip he had fathered a kid. I don't know how the hell he got away without telling her who the mother was, but apparently he did. He even kept it out of the papers somehow.

"Anyway, I was good to my word and didn't interfere in his private life. Not even when he remarried, which was a mistake, by the way. And, in case you're wondering, I never had sex with him again either. He never asked and I never offered." She waved her hand around to show off her home as if to say 'see, here's what it got me and I'm not sorry.'

I asked, "What were the living arrangements for you, Vincent, and your sister? How did all that play out?"

"It was actually smooth. I bought a house in the north Cherry Creek area and had it all fixed up with sort of a 'separate but connected' annex so my sister essentially had her own place. She moved in, decorated it the way she wanted, and we had about a month before I was due.

"After Vincent was born, I stayed home about a month; I had that 'illness' I couldn't shake, remember? Myra, that's my sister, took care of him full time. I paid her just like she was a nanny or nurse, which she was. Vincent was never confused about his mother, we made sure of that from the start. From the time he was old enough to understand, we told him his father and I had separated before he was born and 'Aunt' Myra had come to live with us and take care of him. He never asked about his father until he was in high school. Myra and I both sat down with him and told him mostly a true story about how I had 'made a mistake' by becoming involved with a man who was married and, therefore, could never be a father to him. I didn't tell him about the rape; I had never told Myra that part either. I just said I was very lucky to have a great job where I made lots of money and could afford to support the family."

Lee Anne interrupted her story to ask, "When did Vincent find out his father was William Davidson?"

"When he turned eighteen, a couple of things happened. He was getting ready to leave for college, Willamette University in Oregon, and the trust I'd made Davidson create was going to kick in. I took Vincent and Myra to dinner at Morton's, explained the trust, and then told them about Davidson. I still didn't talk about the rape, though, only the fact Davidson was Vincent's father."

"That must have been rough," I said.

Vada tried to suck a couple more drops of vodka from her empty glass. "It wasn't as bad as I'd expected. Vincent just kinda shook his head and asked how I could have continued to work there. I told him the same thing I just told you: it gave us the life style we enjoyed. Myra said she had suspected from the beginning. I don't know if that was true or not; if it was, she's a lot better actress than I gave her credit for.

"After Vincent left for college, Myra and I talked everything over and decided to make some changes. She stayed in the house and I bought this place. I continue to pay her a salary to take care of the house and cover her expenses; she's happy with the arrangement and has started to travel and enjoy herself."

Tom said, "What happened with Vincent from the time he left for college and now?"

"He did okay at Willamette and got a degree in sociology, whatever the hell that is. When he finished his degree, he came back to Denver and lived with Myra in the house. He's never liked coming here. I'm not sure what all they talked about, but it was during that time he started getting involved in these demonstrations and protests. It wasn't long until he started targeting Wildcat Oil. He found the place in Broomfield three or four years ago and I helped him with the down payment, but he's made all the payments since then using his trust."

Tom rose and looked at Vada Benson. "That's quite a story. I'm not sure I believe every single part of it, especially about continuing to work together for over twenty-five years after, according to you, he raped you. Regardless, it doesn't take you off the suspect list. In my way of thinking, you still had a motive: pure hate. I admit it would be like killing the goose who laid the golden egg, but hate can trump even greed and revenge, which were the only other things you had going.

"You've lived a life of luxury, your kid is taken care of; maybe you'd just had enough of looking at him every day and remembering what he did. Is that what happened?"

Vada set her empty glass on the coffee table, rose to her feet, and motioned toward the entry hall, "Frankly, I don't give a shit about what you think. Unless you brought an arrest warrant, Lieutenant, I suggest it's time for you to leave. The next time we have one of these *talks*, I'll have my lawyer present. I assume you can find your way out."

152 Lee Mossel

CHAPTER

FOURTEEN

Back at Tom's office, the three of us crowded around his desk sipping bottled water. It dawned on me THAT we hadn't asked Vada Benson an important question. "We should have asked her what she thinks of her kid's fight against his old man."

Lee Anne and Tom both nodded their acknowledgement. Tom said, "Why don't you call her and ask? Tell her it's 'unofficial;' she might talk to you."

"I'll give it a try, but I'll probably wait 'til tomorrow to give her some time to cool off. What are you thinking about her now? Do you really believe she's still a suspect?"

Tom drained his water bottle before answering. "I don't know. She'd have been crazy to kill Davidson from a money standpoint. Although, I guess her money's coming directly to her and not through Wildcat Oil. If that's true, it'll continue despite his being dead." I nodded my approval, Tom *had* been listening.

He asked, "Do you have any idea what he was worth?"

I'd anticipated the question, "Over a billion, with a capital 'B'."

Lee Anne blew a low whistle. "That means the current Mrs. Davidson, Jennifer, and the stepdaughter are probably all going to inherit some major fortunes. I didn't get the impression Vincent was going to get anything from the estate, but I think we need to dig a little deeper into each of them. Thing is, the same things apply to them as Vada: it woulda been killing the golden goose."

I pondered that for moment before saying, "Makes you wonder how much is enough, though. Maybe, like Tom said, hate might have overtaken greed as a motive; maybe one or more of them doesn't care about getting any more money."

Tom glanced at Lee Anne before fixing me with a stare. "You're the only one I know who might have an idea about that. You walked away from a boatload of money when you sold or gave away all your stock in Mountain West. When *is* enough enough?"

I bolted to my feet and glared back. "Different circumstances, Tom. I didn't operate on the same plane as Wildcat Willie or, apparently, his family. Plus, I felt guilty about Gerri's death. I didn't want *her* money." I turned to leave.

Tom said, "No offense intended, Cort. I'm sorry."

"I'll be in touch." Actually, I *was* offended; more than offended. I was pissed! Tom knew how I'd felt at the time and he knew the circumstances. He shouldn't have raised the issue in front of Lee Anne.

***

I left the Justice Center and decided to go by my office. I drove the seven blocks to the parking garage and walked to the Equitable Building. Stopping in the ground floor mailroom, I emptied my mailbox and took the stairs to my office. I got a Bud from the 'fridge, sorted the mail, and opened the first class. I couldn't get the other question for Vada Benson out of my mind: What did Vada think about Vincent's involvement in environmental terrorism and trying to monkey-wrench Wildcat Oil's operations? I decided not to wait until tomorrow.

She picked up after a couple rings, "Hello? This is Vada." She slurred 'this' and 'is'; she hadn't stopped after the double vodka.

"Hi Vada, Cort Scott. I wanted---

"Wait a minute; I thought I just kicked your ass out! What the hell are you doin' callin' me?" It wasn't a promising start.

"I'm not calling from the cop shop, Vada. This is unofficial, you know, off the record. I wanted to ask a few more questions...some things we didn't get to earlier."

"Why the hell should I talk to you? I told you guys I wanted my lawyer the next time we talked. You're trying to pin his fuckin' murder on me and I didn't do it!" She was slurring her words.

I tried my most conciliatory voice. "Like I said, this is unofficial. I believe your story about Davidson and I don't think you killed him. If I can help find out who really did it, it'll put you in the clear. You won't be under a microscope; it'll make your life easier. I'd like to do this without having to get the cops and the DA more involved than they already are."

She didn't answer for a moment and I heard the tinkle of ice being swirled in a glass. I pictured her sitting on the loveseat, facing west, and twirling the oversized tumbler.

"This is against my better judgment. But go ahead and ask your questions. I'm only agreeing because you're not a cop, got that?"

"Yes, I get it. Thanks, I appreciate it. First of all, I wanted to know what you think of Vincent's involvement in the environmental protest movement."

"I don't think anything about it. What difference does that make? Vincent is his own man; he does what he wants."

"Did Davidson know who Vincent was and what he was up to?"

"If you're asking if *we,* I mean Davidson and me, ever talked about it, the answer is 'No.' He knew Vincent's last name was Freeman, he read the newspapers, and watched the TV news; I'm sure he knew."

"Where did the name Freeman come from?"

"It was my mother's maiden name. It's on Vincent's birth certificate. I filled it in under 'father's name' and listed mine as Freeman also."

"How'd you do that? Didn't the doctor or hospital know your real name?"

She answered with a boozy chuckle, "You can cause some amazing things to happen with enough cash in hand. And, back then, it didn't take much. I took care of it."

"But Davidson never brought up what Vincent was doing?"

"No. It's like I told you and the cops, the last time Vincent's name ever came up was when I forced Davidson to set up a trust. He did that entirely separate from his other estate stuff--different lawyer; different bank. Obviously, he didn't want Vincent's name coming up, at least while he was alive. I don't think he cared about his 'legacy' or reputation after he died. How's this gonna clear me?"

"Honestly, I don't know. It's just more information I can use.

"Okay, just a couple more things. Did you ever talk to Vincent to discourage him or talk him into targeting another company?"

"No. I actually thought it quite amusing--using Davidson's own money against him like that."

"But what if he'd really done some harm, like shutting down the company; maybe you'd have lost your job?"

"For Chrissakes, Scott! I told you to do the math! What difference would it make to me? I've got more money than I can ever spend!"

Hmm, maybe for her, "enough *was* enough." "All right, just one final thing; when you told us about the night of the rape, you said he was meeting with some investors from New York. Did you know any of their names?"

"Only one, a real creep by the name of Klein; he used to call all the time and drove me nuts. He was the rudest person I ever talked to, including Davidson."

"Thanks for talking to me, Vada."

"Yeah, well, don't make it a habit. Now, I want you to do what you said: clear me."

One thing was obvious: we were going to have to look more carefully at Vincent Freeman. It was 5:45 p.m. and time to go home. I drained my beer, locked up, and left. As I exited the building on Seventeenth Street, I nearly collided with Ken Iverson, Wildcat Oil's acting leader.

"Hey Ken, how's it going? You still swamped?"

Iverson extended his hand and we shook. "It's pretty hectic all right. Of course, it actually might be a little more streamlined without Mr. Davidson around, the buck stops with me now. You figure out who killed him yet?"

"Not yet; we're working on it. Do you have time for a drink? A couple of things have come up and I'd like to ask you some more questions."

Iverson checked his watch and nodded, "If we make it a quick one, sure." We crossed diagonally to Panzano Italian

Grille and took a booth. The bar was full and lots of the
patrons were oil-business types. I ordered a glass of 'J'
Winery Pinot Noir and Ken had the same.

We made small talk about the price of crude oil and
natural gas until the wines arrived. "So what can I do for you,
Cort?"

"What can you tell me about Vada Benson?"

He sipped before replying. "I don't know what I can or
more correctly, *should* say. Why, is she a suspect in Mr.
Davidson's death?"

"Everybody's a suspect at this point. The cops and I are
mostly trying to eliminate names from the list at this point."

"Is my name on the list?"

"Like I said, *everybody* is on it, but, truthfully, I'm not
considering you."

Iverson looked at me intently for a moment. "Vada was
working at Wildcat Oil long before I got there fifteen years
ago. Mr. Davidson told me one time she'd been there
'forever' and then said he couldn't run his part of the company
without her. She basically took care of all his personal
business, including his direct investments in the company. I
think she even did his household expenses."

"That seems like a lot of power for an 'administrative assistant.'"

Ken laughed, "You think so? She intimidates everybody on the staff...including me."

"Anything going on between her and Davidson?"

"You mean romantically? Nah, no way! I think ol' Vada is almost asexual. I've never seen her with anybody, even at the Christmas parties and stuff. And certainly not with Mr. Davidson."

"Do you know what kind of salary she's making?"

"No. Like I said, she worked for him personally and was paid from his personal books. He's always been careful about keeping his business separate from the company's. At any rate, she's not on Wildcat Oil's payroll. I'd bet it's a bundle though; she's always dressed to the nines and I heard she has a condo in the Glass Spire. That can't be cheap."

"Have you ever heard of guy named Vincent Freeman?"

Iverson's face darkened and he exclaimed, "Wow, that's outta left field! Yeah, I've heard plenty about him. The bastard has been all over the oil biz making trouble. I think he's been targeting Wildcat Oil specifically. He's caused a lot of grief on some of our federal and state lease applications. He files demands for environmental assessments and impact statements then ties up the process with requests for public hearings and that kinda shit.

"We've got an application up in the northern Green River Basin in Wyoming that's been *pending* for over five years now. It's cost us over two hundred thousand already and it's never even come up for bid. It's funny you should bring him up because he was the subject of the last discussion I had with Mr. Davidson. He hated that guy; he was looking for ways to shut him down. We actually have a permanent restraining order to keep him off any of our locations."

So, Wildcat Willie *had* been up to speed on the activities of his "son." "It's ironic you called him a 'bastard', Ken. Because he is, in fact, a bastard; *and*, what's more, he happened to be Wildcat Willie's bastard."

Ken Iverson looked like a five pound rainbow trout that'd been gut hooked. His eyes seemed to protrude from their sockets and his face went white, then red. He opened and closed his mouth without saying anything for several moments. Finally, he gasped, "You're shittin' me, right? There's no fucking way! Davidson hated him!" He hadn't called him 'Mr.' "Where the hell did you hear that anyway? It's gotta be bullshit!" He drained his wine and waved his hand at the server for two more--so much for a quick drink.

I let him regain his breath before saying, "There's no doubt about it, Ken. I can't tell you how I know, but it's a fact. And what makes it even more ironic is Willie's own money is financing Freeman. He's the beneficiary of a trust Davidson set up years ago."

The new glasses arrived; Iverson grabbed his and gulped heavily. "I don't believe it, Cort! Oh, I believe what you're telling me, but I can't get it through my head. You're saying Mr. Davidson was paying for his own son to sabotage him? Oh my God, did Freeman kill his own father?"

"We don't know yet; we're investigating him along with several others. Did Willie do anything recently that could have set Freeman off?"

"Not that I know about, or at least not through Wildcat Oil. Like I said, we have a restraining order against him, but it's been in effect for eighteen months or so."

"Would Davidson try to take something into his own hands, you know…do something stupid?"

"You mean like threatening something *physical*?"

"Yep, that's what I mean."

"It's no secret he had a bad temper, but I don't think he'd try anything like that. I've never heard of him physically threatening anybody."

"Okay, thanks Ken. It's a big help knowing Davidson was aware of what Freeman was up to. It raises some new leads for me."

Ken still looked as if he'd suffered a stroke. "Let me ask you something: Am I going to have to deal with Freeman now? I mean, *in* the company?"

"I don't have any idea, but I'd bet you haven't heard the last of him--unless he murdered Willie. If we could prove *that*, he'd be out of your hair permanently."

Ken drained his glass and muttered, "Just one more goddamned log on the fire; pile's getting pretty high."

I finished my wine too, "You sound a little overwhelmed. What else is happening?"

"Not that it's any of your business, but I'm in the process of a divorce. Like I said, "just one more thing."

"I'm sorry to hear it; hope everything straightens out for you."

"Thanks Cort, I'll keep plugging away at it."

CHAPTER

FIFTEEN

The next morning, I saw Lindsey off to work before calling my friend, Brenda Gatlin, an ADA for Boulder County. After some small talk, I asked her if the DA's office had any files on Vincent Freeman. Brenda wanted to know why I was asking. I told her what I was doing and what we had so far. After a couple more questions, she agreed to pull the files on Freeman and meet me for lunch at an upscale burger bar on the Pearl Street Mall. The weather forecast called for midday thunderstorms and violent winds, so I drove my souped-up, restored Ford Bronco. It looked out of place among the Subaru Outbacks, Volvos, and BMWs in the mall parking lot.

I'd known Brenda forever; she'd been a first year in the law firm handling legal matters for The Crude Company, my start-up IPO oil company. After a couple years at the firm, she crossed to "the dark side"--at least according to my attorney, Jason Masters, by moving from corporate to criminal law and joining the Boulder DA's office. She'd risen rapidly through the ranks and was now lead prosecutor. She handled the biggest and highest publicity cases.

Choosing an inside window booth instead of the patio because of the weather forecast, I'd just taken a seat when I spotted Brenda crossing the mall. The wind had risen and was whipping dirt and papers around the street, clawing at her dress, and buffeting the legal briefcase she was carrying. I waved at her through the window; she acknowledged the wave and approached the entrance, crashing through the doors as a gust hit her in the back.

She slid into the booth across from me and gave me a dirty look. "Why didn't you tell me it was going to be such crappy weather? I'd have made you come to my office. This had better be a damn good lunch!"

"Nice to see you too, Bren! You should catch the morning news sometime--they predicted this."

She grinned and said, "Never one to give up the last word are you, Cort?"

"Can you have a drink?"

"Nope, I've got a pre-trial conference on a murder case at 2:00 p.m. But I'll take a rain check and cash it in from your wine cellar."

"That's a deal. Lindsey says 'Hi.'"

"'Hi' back at her; how's she doing?"

"Good. In fact, *we're* doing great."

"That's wonderful to hear. It's been a long haul for you, and for her, since Gerri was murdered. Now, what's up with Vincent Freeman, Boulder and Broomfield's rich bad boy? The shit-bird!"

"Like I told you, I'm helping Tom Montgomery and the DA's office on a murder investigation and Freeman's name has come up. Tom's new, get this--*lady*--homicide detective, said Freeman has a record from Boulder County. But, apparently he plea bargained everything down, including some assault charges against cops. Can that be right?"

"Yeah, unfortunately you're correct." Then she laughed out loud. "So old hidebound Montgomery has a woman homicide detective, huh? That must be a game changer!"

The server brought water and menus; we scanned them quickly and ordered lunch: a gut-bomb burger for me and a bison, lettuce wrap for Brenda. She reached inside her briefcase and produced two thick files. "You must be working the Wildcat Oil murder? It would be too big a coincidence to be asking about Freeman otherwise. What have you got?"

"Well, speaking of game changers, Freeman turns out to be Wildcat Willie Davidson's illegitimate kid. He was the by-product of a 'date rape.' But, instead of fingering him, the woman actually ended up blackmailing Davidson into paying her off for the last twenty-eight years. Plus, she made him set up a trust fund for Vincent Freeman."

Brenda popped her eyes and stared at me incredulously. "You mean she didn't have Davidson arrested or charged?"

"Nope, she's a cool customer. She made an instant decision to report the rape and get it on record, *but* she didn't tell the cops who did it. She had a game plan all worked out, confronted Davidson, and got herself and the kid set up for life. She's made millions since."

"Christ, I admire her balls! Probably worked out better than if she'd have reported him. Still, I don't like the thought of a rapist running around unpunished for thirty years."

"Yeah, it's a tough call. I don't think Freeman knew about the rape, although he knows Davidson was his father. What I don't know is whether all his environmental activism crap is a true calling or if it's some kind of revenge. He's definitely targeted Wildcat Oil and, ironically, has used his trust money to fund the protests. He's cost them a wad of dough with his tactics. We've talked to him and he comes across as a jerk. He's got a bunch of assholes living with him in his Broomfield place and they're all providing alibis for one another. I'm looking for a way to break through to see if their stories hold up."

Brenda set the top file to the side and flipped open the second one. "You've come to the right place, buddy. We've got sheets on several guys in Freeman's coyote pack. Some of this stuff is a couple of years old though; the cast may have changed."

"That's great, Bren! Have you got anything on a guy named Nate?"

She smiled, "Ooh, *yeaaah,* we've got 'Nate!' His name is Nathan Plum by the way; and here he is right in the 'very front row'." Brenda undid the binder clasps and removed about five pages from the top of the file. "Nathan Plum is thirty-five, born in Goodland, Kansas, attended Oklahoma State

University for two years on a wrestling scholarship, and was kicked out for using steroids. He roughnecked on oil rigs for a few years, mostly in western Kansas and eastern Colorado, until he got busted for running drugs. He did two years' probation out of Weld County, Colorado, but was allowed to keep working on drilling rigs. He hit our radar at the same time as Freeman, about four years ago, with an assault on an officer beef.

"Apparently, Plum held a cop from behind while Freeman pounded him. Freeman brought in some high priced legal talent from Denver who represented both of them and it got bargained all the way down to a misdemeanor 'illegal assembly' charge. They each paid two hundred dollar fines and were turned loose.

"Eight months later, the same thing happened, although Freeman did the holding and Nate Plum did the slugging. Almost the same result, too: plea-bargained to resisting arrest. But resisting is a felony, so the judge took a look at the record and sentenced each of them to a hundred and eighty days in county jail.

"It was a non-jury trial and my first solo prosecution. I was silently celebrating until the judge suspended a hundred and seventy-three days, gave the turds credit for one day each, and they ended up serving five with another day off for 'good behavior.' How fucking sad is that?

"Here it was my first case and I ended up getting a contempt citation from the judge for protesting the sentencing in open court!"

The food arrived and we ate in silence for a while. The burger was great. "How the hell did they get off so easily?" I asked.

Brenda raised her index finger signaling for time as she chewed down a portion of the lettuce wrap. "Probably had something to do with the fact the judge resigned a year later after being investigated for taking money in return for light sentences. We knew the son-of-a-bitch was doing it, but we couldn't get rock-solid proof. We managed to force him off the bench, but without something concrete, we couldn't reopen all his sentencing hearings."

"So who else do you know in Freeman's rat's nest?"

She flipped another page in the file and read for a few moments. "We've got information on three others. First is Robert Maxwell, aka 'Rob.' He has a long list of misdemeanor violations for unlawful assembly, trespassing, and the like. Nothing too violent shows up. Next: Charles 'Chuckie' Amundsen. He's a transplant from California and has the same rap sheet as Maxwell, except for a felony assault charge in Bakersfield. He did eight months in Kern County with four months off for good behavior." She looked across the table at me, "Does it seem like a theme here? These guys are bad-asses on the street, but teddy bears inside; they keep getting out early with good behavior."

I nodded, "Yeah, I guess. Who's the last one?"

"This guy's a little different. Name's James Builder; he's been involved in every kind of demonstration since the first Gulf War. You name it and he's protested against it: Iraq invasion, Afghanistan, Guantanamo, Occupy Wall Street, oil and gas leasing on federal and state lands, fracking...I could go on and on. He's got over a hundred arrests and citations going back to the early nineties. He's been arrested in California, Oregon, Washington D.C., New York, Texas, and recently, in Colorado. As far as we know, he's never been involved in violence. Most everything has been a civil disobedience beef and he just gets fined. He's done a few short jail sentences, usually five or six days." She pulled a photo from the file and slid it across the table. The guy in the picture had been one of the guys on Freeman's patio, although he had aged considerably from the photo.

I finished off the last bite of burger, "If his record is that long, how old is this guy?"

Brenda ran her finger to the top of the page, "A little older than the others; he's forty-two."

I asked, "Have you had Freeman's compound under surveillance? I need a way to *talk* to some of these guys, but I wore out my welcome last time."

"I shouldn't share this with you, but, yes, we've been watching the place. How's that help?"

"Do you know if they come and go individually or travel in a bunch?"

"Both. Builder and Freeman usually move around alone, but all of 'em go to a bar out on the east side of Broomfield a couple, three times a week."

"What's the name of the bar?"

"The Rock House. It's pretty eclectic with everything from bikers to tree huggers; lots of kids from the CU campus go there."

"Where do Freeman and Builder go when they're out on their own?"

"Oh, kinda the usual: restaurants, other bars, grocery stores, places like that. Builder goes to a coffee shop almost every morning."

That got my attention. "Coarse Ground Coffee here in Boulder?"

She looked at me suspiciously. "Yep, it must be his favorite too. He's there three or four times a week. How do you know about it?"

I said, "The name came up when we were going through Davidson's 'threat file.' He received an email threat sent from there." The server brought the check which I grabbed. "That's probably the answer to getting a face-to-face with Builder. I'll check out Coarse Ground Coffee starting tomorrow. When he comes in, I'll buy him a cup and see what he might have to say."

"Good luck with that. I can guarantee this guy has been questioned more times than a Taliban jihadist. I doubt if he'll tell you the time of day."

"Maybe people just weren't asking the right questions, Bren. Thanks for everything. Come down and cash that rain check; Linds will be glad to see you." We walked out onto the mall where the wind had let up a little; scattered, large drops of rain had started. We hugged and Brenda headed across the mall toward her office. I walked to the corner and back to the parking lot. It was pouring by the time I got to the Bronco and I was soaked when I climbed inside.

As I made the fifty-mile drive back to Parker, I was thinking about a plan to stake out the Coarse Ground Coffee shop. If it turned out to take several days, I hoped they had a good restroom.

CHAPTER

SIXTEEN

I was up early and on the way to Boulder before 7:00 a.m. and I walked in the front door of Coarse Ground Coffee at 8:07 a.m. There were several people in line at the counter; however, only two of the six booths were occupied. I hadn't had my morning caffeine jolt so I ordered a large Americano, added a little vanilla-flavored creamer, and a dash of cinnamon.

I'd brought *The Denver Post*, a couple of back issues of the *Rocky Mountain Oil Journal,* and a new Robert Crais novel. (I always enjoyed reading about Elvis Cole and his vintage Corvette; I could relate.) I was prepared for a lengthy stay and thought I'd give it until 1:00 p.m. for three days in a row. An open booth near the back of the shop afforded a view of the entry and an excellent place to see people who approached the counter. When the barista handed me the coffee, I quickly claimed the booth I wanted.

I started with sports and found the pitiful Colorado Rockies were mired in a seven game losing streak. The paper was trying to take their readers' minds off the Rocks by concentrating on the opening of Broncos' training camp. Nursing my coffee, I'd read the sports section cover to cover before taking my first bathroom break. The restroom was directly across from my booth so I wasn't away for long. The coffee lasted through the financial section before I headed back to the counter. The shop offered fifty cents off the second order in the same cup, so I opted for mocha with an extra shot of vanilla. Back at the booth, I set the cup down and was turning toward the restroom when I spotted James Builder entering the front door. I sat down, picked up the paper, and held it just below eye level to mask most of my face as I watched him. I didn't think he would recognize me from the visit to Freeman's.

He strolled to the ordering station and took a spot third in line. I could see a folded *Boulder Daily Camera* newspaper under his arm and he was carrying an oversized thermal cup from Coarse Ground Coffee. Up close, Builder looked older than forty-two; protests and demonstrations must have aged him. He placed his order, slid down the counter to pay, and glanced around. He focused on an empty booth two rows in front of mine. He picked up the coffee, walked to the booth, and sat down facing the front of the shop with his back to me.

I stepped across the aisle, used the restroom, picked up my cup and papers, and took the seat across from James Builder. There was a slight flicker of recognition in his eyes when I sat, but he didn't say anything.

"Builder, I'm Cort Scott. I'm a private investigator helping the Denver Police on the murder of Vincent Freeman's father, Wildcat Willie Davidson."

He sipped carefully from his coffee before saying, "I know who you are. You and some woman cop were at the house a few days ago. What're you doing here?" So much for going unrecognized; but now I had a face and a name to match the voice on the intercom at Freeman's gate.

"I wanted to talk to you without the cops *or* Freeman around. One of the email threats sent to Wildcat Oil came from here, so I figured this place was as good as any. I took a chance you'd show."

Builder seemed to consider what I'd said for several moments. He must have been wondering how I'd connected the email to the coffee shop. "Must be your lucky day; you should go buy a lottery ticket. However, I don't want to *talk* to you with or without the cops. Why don't you just slide your ass outta my booth and hit the bricks?"

I decided to press the issue. "Look, we can do this the easy way or the hard way. Talking to me now is the easy way; the hard way is for the cops to get a warrant charging you with possession, bust down the gates of Freeman's damned fort, tear everything apart and roust *your* ass. They'll find your stash, haul every one of you to the station and question you for hours. We both know the medical weed prescriptions Freeman says you have are bogus; even if they're not, they'll bust you for exceeding the legal amounts. That bomb I saw you smoking was big enough to break the rules all by itself."

"Ask me if I give a shit, man! I've been hassled before."

"Okay by me, Builder; I'll go get the warrant, but I doubt if Freeman is going to appreciate it." I slid out of the booth and turned to go.

Builder said, "Hang on a minute. What the hell do you want? Maybe we can get something settled without having the cops involved."

I sat back down. "I just want to find out about Davidson's murder; if you've got any ideas on who might have done it."

He took a big swig of coffee, set the cup on the table, and began rotating it between his palms. "Let's get something straight, okay? I don't know shit about the murder. I never even met the guy; all I know was what Vincent told me, and that wasn't much. I've been in the protest game forever. I've been arrested or issued citations more times than you can count, but I've *never* been arrested for any kind of violent act. I'm the original 'peaceful demonstrator.'"

I looked at him closely. "What about the assaults on policemen that Freeman and Nate Plum were charged with?"

"I wasn't involved in those. I was there all right, but when they started that shit I backed off. I didn't like what was happening."

"How come Freeman keeps you around if you don't want to do things his way?"

"Because I know how to run a *real* protest; I know how to get press coverage to publicize a cause. I know how to get people's attention. Vincent is new to the game, so he came to me."

I thought about that before saying, "Is he committed to a *cause* or is he only focused on making things tough for Wildcat Oil?"

Builder nodded knowingly, "A question I've started asking myself. At first, I thought he was really into it: keeping oil companies off federal and state lands. I helped him set up all kinds of ways to make that happen. We started protesting every lease sale and application to drill, organized marches in Boulder and Denver, and we even outbid some oil companies at lease auctions without any intention of paying for anything. We were just gumming up the works. I thought we were doing some good until I noticed most of the things we did targeted Wildcat Oil. He was ignoring everybody else even when the shit they were doing was a whole lot worse than Wildcat Oil. When I finally asked about it, he got really pissed off; told me if he was paying for everything, he would pick the targets. I kept jawing at him until he told me what the real deal was--about Davidson being his father."

I asked, "So why'd you stay around?"

"He told me if I'd stick it out with him for a few more months, he'd fund me for anything I wanted."

"Did you read anything into him saying 'a few more months'? Did you think he had a calendar of some kind?"

Builder shook his head, "No, I never even thought about it."

"Obviously, you stuck around. What'd you have in mind?"

"I wanted to go to Pennsylvania and New York and get involved in the protests against fracking and horizontal drilling. I needed money to do it, you know, to make a difference; Vincent said he'd help, but he wanted to keep the pressure on Wildcat Oil here."

"When did you have that discussion?"

"About two months ago."

"How did Vincent react when the news about Wildcat Willie came out?"

Builder paused for a moment before saying, "He acted kinda shocked. We were watching the morning news on one of the local TV channels because we'd been protesting in downtown Denver the day before and wanted to see if it made the news. When the story about the murder came on, Vincent just kinda flopped back in his chair and started running his hands over his face. He didn't say anything for a minute or so and then said, 'Well, shit, now it's a whole new ballgame. You can probably go back east before you'd planned.' After that, he went out on the patio by himself and just sat there for over an hour."

"Did he seem sad, or mad, or worried, nervous? Anything?"

"Not really. I mean, like, he'd said he hated Davidson and the company and stuff like that, but he didn't react much to the murder."

"Did you ever see or hear of him talking with his sister?"

Builder opened his eyes wide, "I didn't even know he had a sister. No. I've never seen anything like that. What's her name?"

"Jennifer Davidson. She's actually a half-sister and about the same age as Freeman. She lives in south Denver and is big on the charity circuit; her name's in the paper quite a bit."

He shook his head. "Nope, I've never seen or heard anything about her. Besides, I don't read those sections in the paper."

I tried another tack. "Who's Freeman closest to among the bunch living at the house?"

"I don't think you know much about Vincent; he's not *close* to anybody. He talks to Plum quite a bit, but other than the two of 'em pounding on the cops, I can't see what they have in common. Nate Plum is a first-degree asshole. To tell you the truth, it made me grin when you kicked his ass; I think even Vincent enjoyed it. Plum is an intimidating son-of-a-bitch. He bullies everyone he meets and I wouldn't put anything past him."

"What about murder?"

"Like I said, I wouldn't put anything past him."

"So, have you made plans to leave?"

"Yes. Vincent and I talked about it this morning. He's bought me a one-way plane ticket to Pittsburgh and he's giving me twenty-five thousand dollars. I'm flying out Saturday. There are a bunch of guys I know already there and involved in the protests; I'm hooking up with them."

I couldn't help myself, "You know most of the stuff you're reading about fracking being the cause of burning water taps and water wells blowing up is a crock, don't you? You should do your homework before you run off half-cocked on this stuff! But thanks for what you've told me. I still don't know who killed Wildcat Willie, but you've given me some new ideas."

I hadn't found out much from Builder, although the story about Vincent Freeman's reaction to his father's murder was interesting. Yesterday Lee Anne had told me she'd finally gotten an appointment with Janet Davidson, Wildcat Willie's widow, and expected to talk to her today. I hoped Lee Anne would find out more than I had.

CHAPTER

SEVENTEEN

Lee Anne called at 3:35 p.m. and said she'd just returned from meeting with Janet Davidson. "Cort, you wouldn't believe her place! We thought Vada Benson had some nice digs; you could put her whole penthouse in Janet's living room!"

"Oh yeah? So where's she located?"

"Absolute top of the hill in the middle of Castle Pines Country Club. From her patio you can see from Longs Peak to Pikes Peak and then turn around and see most of the country club golf course as well as the International course. There are *seven* garage doors in the place!"

"So, what'd she have to say for herself? Is she a grief-stricken widow?"

"I think that question was answered when she didn't even attend the funeral. She didn't return until yesterday, at least she didn't try summoning up any crocodile tears. She said they hadn't *really* had a marriage in years; she was sorry he'd been murdered, but it didn't come as a great surprise. It was almost the same story we heard from Benson and then Jennifer, *including* how many people probably wanted him dead. I feel like we're spinning our wheels again. Unless something breaks big time, this thing is going to go cold in a hurry."

I agreed, "I know the feeling. What kind of alibi did Janet have for the time of the murder?"

"The rock solid kind: she was at the Top of the Mark in San Francisco meeting her daughter for lunch. She's got a time and date-stamped credit card receipt to prove it, so both she and her daughter were out of town when Davidson was shot. I asked her why she hadn't come home immediately when she heard the news. She looked at me like I was from Mars or something. She said, and I quote, 'He was already dead; I had business in California, I didn't know anything

about the murder, I didn't *want* to come back to Denver.'
How's that for cool?"

"Bone chilling, but I get it. Sounds like we can scratch
her name off the suspect list; that's progress of some kind, I
guess. What are you going to do now?"

"I honestly don't know. Tom's getting a ton of pressure
from the brass *and* the DA's office, so he's really grinding on
everything. I asked him about interviewing Janet's daughter,
but he laughed and said I was just trying to finesse a trip to
San Francisco. He said we'd go with Janet's story of having
lunch with her."

"Did you ask Janet how the daughter got along with
Davidson?"

"Yes, and she said the girl hated him. So what else is
new, right? Have you met *anybody* who actually liked this
guy?"

I laughed at that, "I don't think so. Look, I don't know if
it'll lead us anyplace, but I'm going to keep on Vincent and
his bunch. He's the only one who was actively striking out at
Davidson and, in some respects, had the most to gain from his
death. I got the impression he might not be a guaranteed, one
hundred percent, tree-hugger, so if you take away the
environmental activism stuff, he seems to have the best

motive. It might be a blind alley, but it's about all I've got at the moment."

Lee Anne was quiet for a moment before replying, "Okay, I'm going to talk to Tom first thing in the morning about trying to dig a little deeper into the money, you know, the wills and trusts and stuff. I keep thinking this may be like politics; 'follow the money.'"

"That's a good idea and it makes me think about something Ken Iverson, who's running Wildcat Oil now, told me. He said a couple guys from New York had been in Denver a little while before the murder and they'd seemed real intent on seeing Wildcat Willie. They were trying to settle some old money grudges from years ago. One of 'em was Sol Klein, the guy Vada Benson told me about. The interesting part was they called Iverson the day after the murder. He didn't return the call, but said it was marked urgent. I might have to quiz Tom again about that trip to New York he turned me down on."

Lee Anne sighed, "As high profile as this is, Tom, or more precisely the DA, isn't going to spring for you to travel to New York; besides, how're you going to find those guys?"

"Ken Iverson gave me an address and phone number for Sol Klein. I'm into this thing now, Lee Anne. I've been

promising Lindsey a trip to New York City for several months
anyway so I'll just go on my own dime. If anything comes of
it, I'll send the DA a bill for expenses." I laughed at my own
joke, but I'd already made my decision.

She sounded skeptical, "Good luck with that."

***

We departed Denver International Airport at 11:18 a.m.
on Wednesday between storms and spent the first half-hour of
the flight dodging thunderheads. The pilot announced he was
increasing altitude to thirty-six thousand feet to get above the
clouds. After that, the ride smoothed out and we were able to
enjoy our airline wine. I'd made reservations at The Palace
and called my good friend, Ed Giles, who snagged a couple
tickets to *Book of Mormon* for Thursday. Ed was an
investment banker who was *very* well connected and even on
such short notice also managed dinner reservations at Sardi's
for after the show, the Plaza on Friday, and Le Cirque for
Saturday. I figured by Sunday we'd be wined, dined, broke,
and ready for a Times Square hotdog.

Once we arrived at La Guardia, claimed our bags, and
caught a rogue limo to The Palace, it was nearly nine-thirty.
The street was still full of people; a big change from Denver.
At 9:30 p.m. on a Wednesday night in Denver, cannons full of

grapeshot fired down 17th Street wouldn't hit anyone. We checked in and went to our room on the thirty-eighth floor; our bags arrived five minutes later. It was better service than the last time I'd stayed there, but that'd been almost twenty years ago.

Although we were both a little tired from the flight, we decided to have a nightcap in the "55", the top floor bar with a fantastic view of the city. We grabbed a high-top by the window on the northwest corner and ordered wine: a Prosecco for Lindsey and a good Australian Barossa Valley Shiraz for me.

"This must be costing you a fortune, sleuth!" Linds sipped the sparkler and grinned at me across the top of the flute glass. "I didn't really expect The Palace, you know. You really know how to impress a girl."

I returned the grin and said, "I expect full repayment in trade goods, babe. Remember, Manhattan Island was purchased for a few blankets and beads. There's a long history of trade and bartering here."

The grin changed from charming to lascivious and Lindsey said, "Hmm, but have you considered if we 'consummate' a trade, you might be liable for transporting me across state lines for immoral purposes?"

"I'll risk it."

She laughed loudly enough to attract a couple of glances from the bar. "Good! I was hoping you'd say that. Let's finish these and head for the trading floor--or the bedroom--whichever comes first."

I couldn't remember my regional geology well enough to say whether or not Manhattan was in an active seismic zone, but I'd swear I felt the earth move.

* * *

We had a room service breakfast delivered at 7:45 a.m. the next morning and tarried over the lingonberry crepes, crisp bacon, and oatmeal. We'd ordered two pots of coffee: a hotel special breakfast blend and a French roast. They were both good, although we had to use our leftover milk to make café au lait with the French roast. I wouldn't need any more caffeine later.

"What are you going to do while I go over to Brooklyn and check out Wildcat Willie's old partners?" I moved from the tiny serving table to the loveseat.

A smile spread across Lindsey's face like a kid in a candy store. "I've only been to New York once before, when I was twelve years old, so I want to walk down 5th Avenue, go to

Rockefeller Center, and maybe have tea at the Waldorf. I've got a bucket list a mile long! Thanks for this!"

"You're welcome! Have fun, country girl. I reserved a town car to take me to Crown Heights over in Brooklyn. I'll see if I can sort out one Mr. Sol Klein. I should be back in plenty of time to grab a bite and get ready for the theater.

Laughing, I said, "Don't walk too much; I wouldn't want you snoring through the show. It's going to be a late night after we have dinner at Sardi's."

Lindsey gave me a fish eye look before saying, "Don't worry about me, you're the one who needs to be careful. I don't think the streets of New York are going to be like the wide open spaces of Colorado. These creeps are on their home turf and you're not."

I put on some tan slacks, a dark red Pinery Country Club golf shirt, and my Ecco low-cut hiking shoes. I had my Beretta 9 mm PX4 Storm in a clip-on holster in the middle of my back and slipped on a light windbreaker shell to cover everything. Lindsey watched silently as I got rigged up then said, "I hope you don't need that."

"I hope I don't either, but after going to the trouble of checking it through on the plane, I'm taking it with me." She stood, wrapped her arms around me and kissed me hard on the mouth.

The Palace doorman swung the doors for me as I exited the hotel. A silver-gray town car was parked in the pickup zone a few yards down the street. A very large black man in a dark blue suit was standing near the car's rear passenger door holding a small, neatly printed sign that read "Scott." I approached him and said, "I'm Cort Scott. You must be my driver, Richard, right?"

The big man nodded and replied, "Yes sir, I'm Richard. Good morning. Where are we headed today, Mr. Scott?" He opened the door for me and I climbed in. The car, an older model, was well maintained, clean, and polished to a high sheen. Richard closed the door behind me, walked around the front, and got behind the wheel.

"You'll be driving me and my girlfriend around for a few days, Richard, so call me Cort, okay? Right now, we're heading for Williamsburg, or it might be Crown Heights, 1086 Broadway anyway. You know where that is?"

Richard gave me a look and said, "Matter of fact, I do." His voice was well modulated and deep, with no trace of an accent or ghetto influence. He looked over his shoulder at me. "It's an easy one; we'll cross on the Williamsburg Bridge and it's a couple of miles." He started the Lincoln, edged away from the curb, caught the traffic, and we were off. After okaying the comfort settings with me, he said, "According to my job sheet, I'm supposed to pick you up again at 6:45 tonight, drop you in the theater district, and then retrieve you at Sardi's for a return to the hotel at midnight. Is that correct?"

"Yep, you've got it. Makes a long day for you, huh?"

"More money in the bank, plus I'm used to it. I don't mind."

"Been in New York long, Richard?"

"My whole life; I was born here."

"How come you don't have a New York accent?"

Richard glanced in the mirror and replied, "You mean a *black* accent? If that's what you're asking, it's because my parents wouldn't allow it. My mom's an English teacher at PS 134 and my dad's an IT guy for Westchester community college. There are no 'accents' in my family; weren't allowed if we wanted to have dinner." He laughed, which made me feel better.

"Sorry, man, I didn't mean to offend you. That's a refreshing story."

"No offense taken. Most people don't have the courage to inquire."

We started across the bridge and I caught some good views upriver as well as out toward the harbor. It took another ten minutes before we pulled up in front of the building. Richard said, "I'll drop you and go to a parking space a half block ahead. Can you walk up when you're finished?"

"Sure, I don't have an appointment and don't know if the guy I want to talk to is here or not. If he isn't in, I might be right back and we'll try again tomorrow; regardless, I won't be too long. If I'm gone more than hour, you can come get me. I'll be in suite 610."

"That's not really in the job description, but it's okay by me. I'll see you in an hour one way or another."

I hopped out and watched Richard drive forward to his parking spot. The entrance to the building was a single glass door directly across the sidewalk. A metal storefront roll-up was on the right and a mailbox store on the left. I crossed the sidewalk, opened the door, and entered a combination stairwell and elevator lobby. A directory board was posted next to the elevator with the occupants in alphabetical order; Klein Investments was listed in Suite 610. So far, so good.

I pushed the elevator button and the door slid open immediately. Inside, the car was dimly lit with a cork tile floor and fake wood paneling. It smelled faintly of some kind of cleaning fluid, like a dry cleaner's store. I pushed six and had to catch my balance as the elevator lurched into motion. The ride was jerky, halting, and noisy, but nonstop. At the sixth floor, the car ground to a halt and the door slid open with a squeal. The occupants of the floor wouldn't need a doorbell to announce the arrival of a visitor.

Arrow directories indicated Suite 610 was to my right. I reached behind me, slid the holster around to my hip, and let the wind breaker fall loosely over it. The door to 610 was an opaque, ribbed, water glass with "Klein Investments" painted in a Gothic script below the suite number. The lights were on so I tried the door. It was locked, so I knocked on the frame. A few seconds later, a shadow dimmed the light and I could make out a man's shape in the glass. The door opened slightly and a voice said, "Yeah? Who is it? Whadda ya want?" This voice *was* accented. It was every Brooklyn Jewish gangster who'd ever appeared in a TV movie.

"My name's Cort Scott; I'm from Denver and need to speak to Sol Klein."

"Whadda ya want to talk to him about?"

"Wildcat Willie Davidson."

"Oh, yeah? Who da hell is Wildcat Willie Davidson?"

I assumed the voice belonged to "the nephew", Manny Greene, so I took a chance. "C'mon, Manny, I haven't got time to fuck around with you; I need to see Klein."

Manny Greene ripped the door open and scowled at me. He was a big guy, a little bigger than me, but he looked more meaty than strong. I guessed him in his mid-thirties, with black hair starting to recede at the forehead and temples, bushy eyebrows, and a hooked nose that looked like it had been broken more than once. He was wearing a shiny, dark green warm up suit, black referees' trainers, and a white tee shirt. The warm up jacket was zipped half-way up but didn't conceal the strap to a shoulder holster and the bulge under his left arm.

Before Greene could make a move, I stepped inside, grabbed his right wrist with my left hand, and pulled him forward. He lost his balance and staggered toward me. I reached inside the jacket and pulled his gun, a Glock 33 .357 auto, and spun him into the hall. "Thanks for the waltz, Manny. Now, let's go back inside and I can have my talk with Sol."

A sullen look passed over his face and he muttered, "Dis ain't over, smart-ass. Next time I'll be ready. Youse surprised me."

"Next time, I'll just shoot you in the balls, Manny."

He stepped around me and reentered the office. The place wasn't set up to receive visitors: it had a single uncomfortable looking round chair and a coffee table with a Starbucks cup sitting on it. It must have been Manny's "office." A closed door was centered in the wall across from the table and chair.

I pointed at the door and said, "Is Sol inside?" Greene nodded so I said, "Okay, lead the way; you don't have to announce me." Greene looked at me like I was nuts.

He took two steps across the tiny entryway, knocked twice on the door, and opened it. I motioned with his Glock and he stepped inside with me on his heels. Sol Klein was sitting in front of a dirt-encrusted, narrow window behind a cheap looking metal desk that was probably Army surplus. One wall was covered with "matching" three-drawer file cabinets.

"What the fuck's going on? Who da hell are you?" Sol looked accusingly at Manny as if Greene had failed the one job he'd been assigned: guarding the door. Sol had a scratchy, nasal voice that made me mad just hearing him.

"My name's Cort Scott, Klein. I'm a PI from Denver. I'm looking into Wildcat Willie Davidson's murder. Your name's at the top of a short list of people who had a beefs with him so you're automatically a suspect in his killing." I purposely didn't mention the cops in hopes Klein might think I was working this on my own and I wouldn't necessarily have to follow the rules.

Klein stood, although it didn't make much difference. The guy was practically a midget; a midget with a pot gut. He was wearing gray-green, sharkskin suit pants that might have been new during the Reagan administration, a white shirt with the sleeves rolled above his elbows, a loose olive tie, and suspenders. He was mostly bald with a fringe of greasy looking gray hair. The suit jacket was draped over the back of his desk chair. The office smelled of sweat and old paper. "Where da fuck do you get off, whatever the hell you said your name is. I ain't killed nobody! And, why're you coming to see me? What makes you even think I know somebody named Davidson?"

"Proper grammar is '*knew*', Sol. Like I said, Davidson is dead but of course, you *knew* that. You left your name and number with Wildcat Oil when you called *after* the murder. Now, sit your ass down and let's have a talk. Manny, turn the other chair around and straddle it." I pointed at a straight-backed office chair beside Klein's desk. Greene did as I said and Sol Klein sat down. I took the remaining chair, placed it in front of the desk, and sat across from Klein. I made sure they both saw me check the chamber of the Glock. "Okay, Sol, let's have it. Why were you so hot to see Davidson when you were in Denver? What kind of deal were you accusing him of welshing on?"

Klein looked at me making no attempt to conceal the hatred in his eyes. "I ain't sayin' shit to you, asshole. If you got a brain in your thick skull, you'll get da fuck outta here. I got guys here who'll put you in da goddamn ground!"

I casually inspected Greene's gun before leveling it and sighting down the barrel directly between Klein's eyes. "Yeah, I can see you've got some real top-flight muscle around you. Guys like Manny here; he's a tough customer, all right. Hey, Manny, why don't you tell your boss how I got your gun? Ah, never mind, he's probably easily bored. Right, Sol?" I jumped up and pushed the Glock into Klein's chest. "Probably won't be too loud in here, Klein. Just one shot; hell, nobody'll even bother to call 9-1-1 in this neighborhood." His eyes widened and uncertainty replaced the hate I'd seen earlier. "Now, let's get this over with. I don't give a shit about you one way or another; I'd just as soon cancel your ticket as not. I want a couple of answers and I'll be out of here. What was your deal with Davidson?"

Klein made a decision. "Me and some other guys put some money with him when he went out to Denver. It was a way to clean up some cash; he had a scam running to sell more than a hundred percent of his drilling deals. When he'd drill-- whadda ya call it, a 'dry hole'--he'd pocket da excess cash and buck some of it back to us. We might only make twenty, thirty cents on a dollar, but it was clean. We could use it immediately. Trouble was the goofy bastard started finding oil and when he couldn't cover his suckers, we had to bite da fucking bullet. But den he got greedy; he wanted to 'go straight' and quit using our money. He wouldn't let us invest with him, and we were da ones who gave him the start. And, I ain't da only one he stiffed, I'm just da biggest. I've been trying to get even for years."

I gestured with the Glock. "When did all this start?"

Klein said, "You do da fuckin' math, Sherlock. How long's dat shithead been in Denver?"

I jabbed him hard enough to leave a bruise. "Give me a time frame, you little prick!"

He winced from the jab, "Close ta forty years ago."

"You must hold a grudge for a long time."

The old mobster let a small grin tug at the corners of his mouth. "I've got grudges dat go back thousands of years; forty years ain't nothin'!"

"So, did you get tired of waiting or what? You hire somebody to snuff him, Sol?"

"I ain't done nothin', Scott. If he'd still been in New York, I'd have settled with him years ago, but him being in Denver made things tough. I ain't connected there. I went to see him 'cause I thought I might scare him a little; took Manny with me, but we didn't do any good. We didn't even see da asshole." He turned to look at Greene, "Not dat dis *pussy* would have done anything." Manny Greene took on a baleful look as he glanced at Klein and then the floor.

I got out of Klein's face and returned to the chair. "So are you telling me you're just letting it go? Doesn't sound like a guy who carries grudges for thousands of years?"

"I didn't say dat; I'm still working some angles. It might be easier now dat da welshing prick is dead." The old man's voice was venomous. "I'll deal with the family."

That caught my attention. "Who do you know in the family?"

Klein realized he'd made a mistake. "It's just a figure of speech. I don't know nobody. I knew his wife before she died, dat's all."

I yelled, "*C'mon, you slimy turd! Who've you talked to?*"

He was starting to look like a guy who was tired of talking and just wanted to get rid of me. "Like I said, I knew his first wife and I've talked to da daughter. That's it."

"When did you talk to the daughter?"

"When I was in Denver. I don't know exactly, 'bout a couple of months ago."

"Not since?"

"No."

"What did you talk about?"

"I just wanted to find out if she knew anybody who could get us inside da company. She told us about Davidson having another kid, a son who hated his guts. Of course, da daughter despised him too." Klein laughed, "Nobody liked da son-of-a-bitch."

I was trying to process all he was telling me: he knew about Jennifer, he knew about Vincent, he knew they weren't the only ones who might have a motive for killing Wildcat Willie. Obviously, we needed to talk to Jennifer and Vincent again and maybe a little more forcefully. I stood, dropped the clip from the Glock, and ejected the chambered round. I stared at Manny Greene, "Don't try to follow me; if I see you around I'll drop you like a bad habit. Don't leave this office for five minutes. I'm going to wait in the hall just to see if you know how to follow orders." I pulled my own gun, turned back to Klein, and said, "Stay the hell out of Denver; if you come to town, I'll tell the cops about it and I'll tell 'em you've met with Davidson's daughter. You're not off the hook for this, Klein, not by a long shot."

I backed out, flipped the cartridge and clip into the far corner of Klein's office, threw Greene's gun on the table in the entry, and walked out the door. I pushed the elevator call and stared at the door to suite 610 until the bell chimed. Nobody came out.

Downstairs, Richard was standing next to the rear door of the limo half a block up the street where I'd seen him park. When I approached, he opened the door and I climbed inside. As he pulled away from the curb, he said, "You know, in the bad old days, this was a pretty tough neighborhood. This area was grand central station for the Jewish mob. They were just as bad or even worse than the Italians."

"I'm not sure things have changed much, Richard. The guys I was just talking to may be mixed up in a Denver murder and I guarantee you they're full time crooks."

Richard glanced in his mirror, caught my eye, and said, "Hmm, what kind of business are you doing, anyway? How come you're messing around with those kinds?"

"I'm a PI from Denver; I'm investigating a murder for the DA's office. Does that make any difference to you? Are you nervous about driving me around?"

He smiled in the mirror, "Not much makes me nervous, Cort. I used to drive for a guy by the name of Bernie Chomsky. Ever hear of him? Nicest guy you ever met, always well dressed, well spoken, and funny as hell. Turned out he was a button man for Herman Edelstein's crew! I finally put it together after a couple of killings here in Williamsburg--addresses where I'd driven him.

"After he was arrested, the police came around and questioned me at length. I didn't know anything about the murders and, eventually, they believed me. By the time everything came out in court, Bernie cut a deal for life without parole by confessing to thirteen murders. Part of the deal was he also pleaded guilty to federal racketeering charges so he could be put in a federal pen. I heard he's in Illinois and spends twenty-three hours a day in isolation. Like I said, not much makes me nervous."

"I get it. You know anything about a mutt by the name of Sol Klein? That's who I was talking to."

Richard checked my eyes in his mirror again. "I know the name. I think he worked for Edelstein, but I don't think Klein was muscle. I never met him."

I laughed, "You'd be right about him not being a hitter. Guy looks like an old, paunchy garden gnome, plus he's got a guy with him who's supposed to be his body guard."

Richard did the check one more time. "Oh, yeah? How'd you get around that?"

"Oh, just the power of persuasion--I'm a smooth talker."

***

The Book of Mormon was "interesting" to say the least. Biting satire, obscene lyrics, good costuming, and probably a few things that cut a little too close to the bone. It all made for quite an evening. It was Lindsey's first-ever Broadway show and she liked it...a lot. We made the short hike to Sardi's, claimed our reservation, and were seated under caricatures of Milton Berle, Carol Channing, and James Earl Jones. I had to explain who many of the old Broadway stars were to Lindsey, which bothered me a great deal. Is she *really* that much younger than I am?

We ordered a bottle of 2010 Columbia Crest Dry Riesling and a melon and prosciutto plate while we studied the post-theater menu, finally deciding on appetizer-sized crab cakes for Lindsey and shrimp scampi for me. The wine arrived perfectly chilled, not ice cold like some places.

Lindsey had a bite of the ham and melon and a sip of wine. "You haven't said a thing about your *meeting* this morning. Either you didn't learn anything or you're mad as hell. Which is it?"

She was getting to know me well. "The latter, I guess. This Sol Klein guy is a real creep. I gather he's an old-time Jewish mobster who financed Wildcat Willie and then got blown off when Davidson started finding oil. That was almost forty years ago and he's still pissed off. He implied he would've offed Willie if he'd gotten the chance. The disconcerting thing is he met with Jennifer and she told him about Vincent and his operation. This murder investigation is developing more arms and legs than an octopus."

Our entrees arrived and we dug in. Lindsey sighed in satisfaction as she tried a small bite of the crab cake, "Oh God, this is *fabulous*! It's even better than what we had in San Francisco! How's your shrimp?"

"Good."

"So, anyway, it sounds like the daughter is an even bigger suspect than before. What're you going to do?"

"I called Tom after I got back to the hotel and told him and Lee Anne what I found out. He doesn't think they have enough for a warrant, but they're going to drop by Jennifer's house and '*ask*' her to come downtown for a talk."

The weekend was a fabulous success. We checked out Central Park, some funky art shops, Greenwich Village, and had our dinners at the Plaza and Le Cirque. We were several pounds heavier and a few thousand dollars lighter when Richard dropped us in the departing passenger area at La Guardia on Sunday. The return flight was smoother than our outbound and, more importantly, on time. We collected our bags, picked up the Bronco, and were home in Parker at 8:45 p.m.

CHAPTER

EIGHTEEN

Monday morning I was up early and went for a run, hoping to burn off a few thousand New York calories while Lindsey showered and got ready for work. I was pouring my coffee when the phone rang: caller ID read "Tom Montgomery." "Hey, Tom, kinda early for you, isn't it?"

"No time to bullshit. Do you think your New York slimeball might have called Jennifer Davidson?"

"How would I know? I told him to stay the hell out of Denver but not much else, why?"

"Because she might be in the wind. Lee Anne went by her place to pay a surprise visit but just called in and said no one's home. The gate guard ran his sheet and says no one has seen her since Friday."

"*Shit!* We shoulda thought of that possibility! What's next?"

"We're getting a search warrant for her house and called the airlines to check on any reservations she might have made. You wanna be at her house when we go in?"

"Sure, I'll leave right now. You have anybody checking on Vincent Freeman?"

"We'll get to that next; I want to get a look at her place first."

I raced into the bedroom as Lindsey was exiting, dressed for work. I said, "Hey, babe, I gotta run. Tom just called to say Jennifer Davidson is not at her house and he's getting a search warrant. There's coffee made if you want a go cup. I'll see you tonight or call if something comes up."

She caught my arm and landed a brushing kiss on my cheek on her way out. "Okay, be careful. And Cort, it was a wonderful weekend...thanks!"

I shrugged out of my running clothes, threw on some jeans and a golf shirt, slipped into a pair of loafers, and ran for the garage. Lindsey had left the garage door up and hadn't even rounded the corner as I backed the Corvette into the street. I caught her by the time we reached Parker Road; we drove north side by side for the six miles until I turned off to catch the E-470 expressway that would take me to Greenwood Village and Jennifer Davidson's house.

When I pulled to a stop at the gated entrance, I was glad to see a different rent-a-cop than my previous visit. I gave the new guy my name and told him I was meeting the police at Jennifer's place. He wrote down my plate number, raised the gate, and motioned me through. I sped to the house and spotted a cruiser, two unmarked cars, and a DPD crime scene van parked in front. Tom and Lee Anne were standing on the sidewalk talking to a couple of suited-up technicians. I parked at the end of the line of police cars and walked quickly to join them.

"Took your sweet time getting here. Little groggy after a few days in the Big Apple, are you?" Tom never cut anyone any slack.

"Morning to you too, *buddy*. Hi, Lee Anne, I hope you haven't been waiting on me."

Lee Anne scowled at Tom and said, "No, these guys just got here with the warrant. We're getting ready to go in."

When we stepped onto the porch, Tom motioned to one of the techs and said, "Okay, the DA's office delivered the warrant. Open it up."

The door had been dusted for prints; the handle, latch, and lock were covered with print powder. The tech knelt, opened a fold-out case, and selected a tool like a miniature cam shaft. He inserted the pick in the lock, turned it back and forth a couple of times, and tried the latch. It was unlocked. He looked at Tom, "So much for home security, Lieutenant. It's all yours."

Tom pushed the door open with his foot, and carefully stepped inside. Lee Anne followed and I brought up the rear. I was afraid of what we might find; I didn't want to find Jennifer Davidson's body. Another crime tech gave each of us latex gloves and with Tom and Lee Anne leading the way, we went room to room. We didn't find any bodies and I was glad about that. On a second pass, we opened the closet doors in the bedrooms and hall, but didn't find anything unusual. The clothes in Jennifer's master bedroom closet appeared undisturbed; nothing was out of place in the drawers or in the bathrooms. There were no signs of a struggle anywhere.

"It doesn't look like anybody grabbed her," I said. "It just looks like she left."

Tom said, "Yeah, maybe somebody called and warned her or something." He gave me an accusatory look. "You should have known better than to bust Sol Klein's balls. You should've cleared it with me."

"You'd have told me not to go and we--or maybe I should say *I*--wouldn't have found out Klein knew her." I wasn't in a mood to take more of Tom's shit.

Tom bristled, but Lee Anne stepped in, "He's right, Tom. We wouldn't have even been here if he hadn't told us about Klein. The important thing is to find out where she's gone. We need to check out Vincent's place."

I could see Tom fighting for control of his emotions. He finally took a deep breath and shook his head. "Yeah, you're right. This damn case is getting to me; there's lots of pressure from up the line."

I nodded in sympathy, "I can only imagine. You want me to check out Vincent's?"

"A police cruiser will give you a little more clout than your toy car. You can ride with Lee Anne this time."

We returned to the sidewalk as the CSI team set up shop and began to process Jennifer's house. I followed Lee Anne and Tom downtown to the justice center. The morning rush had subsided and we made the trip in half an hour.

I climbed in with Lee Anne and we retraced our route back toward Broomfield and Vincent Freeman's house. As we exited I-25 onto US 36 to Boulder, Lee Anne said, "It's a good thing you and Tom are friends. I'd hate to see how he would act around enemies."

I laughed, "You'll learn he's more bark than bite. How are you planning to get past Vincent's gate? You don't have a warrant do you?"

"No, but I'm going to tell him it's going to be a lot rougher if we have to get one, that we'll haul him in if we get a warrant. Cort, can I ask a favor?"

"You can ask." I had a good idea of what she wanted.

"If we run into that guy, Nate, will you back off? It's only going to make our job tougher."

"I'll do the best I can. But I'm not making any absolute promises. He makes me mad just looking at him."

"I understand, but let's not make it any more difficult than we have to."

She turned into the drive, pulled forward to the intercom, and pushed the call button. It was several seconds before a voice said, "Yeah? Looks like a pig mobile; what do you want?" It was the same voice as before: it was James Builder.

I assumed Freeman was listening and Builder was covering his ass for talking to me at the coffee house.

Lee Anne leaned out the window and said, "Denver police, Detective LeBlanc and Cort Scott to see Vincent Freeman. Open the gate, please."

A few more moments passed before the voice replied, "All right, come on up."

I looked at Lee Anne who shrugged, put the cruiser in gear, and drove through the gate as it swung open. "That was easier than I thought; must mean something."

We repeated our earlier trip, stopped in front of the steps leading to the front door, got out, and climbed to the entrance. As I reached for the bell, the door opened and Vincent Freeman stood in the doorway. "What the hell do you want this time? I had to think twice about letting you through the gate. I should have asked for a warrant."

Lee Anne said, "We appreciate your seeing us, Mr. Freeman. We have a few more questions and something new has come up."

Freeman stared at her for several seconds before dipping his head, "All right, let's get it over with." He opened the door the rest of the way and made a gesture indicating we should enter. This time, he led the way into a small, formal living room furnished with leather chairs, rustic tables, and Tiffany-shade floor lamps. It looked like an English gentleman's club.

He motioned toward two chairs while he took a seat on a small loveseat. "What kinda 'new' shit has come up?"

"First of all, have you seen or heard from Jennifer Davidson?"

"I told you last time you were here, I've never met her or talked to her. Nothing's changed about that. Why?"

Lee Anne said, "No one's seen her since Friday. We thought she might have come to see you."

Freeman looked puzzled, "Why would you think that? And, furthermore, why should it concern me one way or another? You guys fitting her up for murdering our shithead father or something?"

His answer surprised me. "What makes you say that? You think she had something to do with it?"

He laughed scornfully, "I don't think anything about it--or her. You guys are wasting your time. Like I said, there's a whole world of people who aren't crying a single goddamn tear over Davidson getting killed. What else you got?"

Lee Anne said, "Do you know any of Davidson's business associates? We're particularly interested in some of his very first investors, people he knew from New York."

Vincent seemed to consider the question carefully. "No, I don't know anybody who did business with the bastard. I'm only interested in getting Wildcat Oil shut down or, at the very least, forcing them to start paying attention to the environment and all the harm they're doing. Now, unless you've got something more than this fishing expedition, I've got things to do."

We both rose and Lee Anne said, "Thanks for your time, Mr. Freeman. We'll be in touch as the investigation continues. Until we find Jennifer, it might be a good idea for you to watch yourself. There's a possibility that someone is targeting the entire family."

He looked at her closely, "I'm not part of the family and I basically don't care about the investigation, but let me know when you figure out who killed him. I'll probably want to shake the guy's hand. You know the way out." He didn't bother to stand.

We retraced our steps to the front, exited, and climbed back into the cruiser. Lee Anne started down the drive before

she spoke, "Well, that was a waste of time. He's the coldest
son-of-a-bitch I've met in a long time."

"I agree; I wish we could find Jennifer and ask her some
tough questions. You have any good ideas for going
forward?"

She sighed, "Not really. There are a few loose ends to
work, like checking out Janet Davidson's alibi. I plan on
calling the Top of the Mark this afternoon and speaking to the
waiter who served her. I don't know what it'll prove, just one
more thing to cross off the list."

I said, "We don't know diddly about Janet's daughter, do
we? What's her name? We just have Janet's statement about
her hating Wildcat Willie. Think there's something we could
do there?"

Lee Anne glanced at me and, for the second time in an
hour, shrugged. "Her name is Rachel Bender, and I'm
assuming it's her maiden name because she's single. Her
mother said she's a 'performance artist,' whatever that's
supposed to be. I don't know what we can do right now.
Unless we get a compelling reason, Tom's not going to okay a
trip to question her.

CHAPTER

NINETEEN

That evening, I was making a marinade for some ribs and sampling a bottle of 2006 Eberle Barbera when the phone rang. "Scott? This is James Builder. You remember at the coffee shop when you asked me about Freeman's sister, and I said I didn't even know he had one? Well, something just came up and I thought you'd be interested."

I was surprised to hear from Builder. "Of course I remember, what 'just came up?'"

"After you and the woman cop left Freeman's today, I packed up my shit, made some calls, and went outside to talk to the other guys. Vincent wasn't there; he'd left to go hiking on Longs Peak and won't be back until later in the week.

Anyway, Nate Plum was drinking and smoking weed and was pretty much out of it. Outta the blue, he started talking about meeting Vincent's sister and how it was a big secret and how we shouldn't mention it around Vincent. I about choked because the first I'd ever heard about a sister was from you at Coarse Ground. Anyway, Plum was all puffed up, talking like it was a love affair or something, which didn't make any sense because you'd said she was some sort of high society dame. Obviously, Plum doesn't fit--he's an asshole. I just listened and didn't say anything. Then he said they were going to meet up tonight."

My mind started racing. That meant Jennifer was either back in Denver or was coming back today from wherever she'd gone. "Did he say where they were meeting?"

"Yeah, the Rock House. He said she was going to be there around nine."

"Do you know if any of the other guys are going with him?"

"He as much as told 'em to stay away."

"This is big; thanks for letting me know. Builder, can I ask you something?"

He hesitated answering, "Yeah, go ahead. What is it?"

"How come you called me? Why'd you let me know?"

"I'm not real sure. Probably because you didn't treat me like some scumbag criminal. Look, man, whether you believe it or not, I'm committed to making a difference. I don't care whether it's for the environment or the military or whatever. But I don't think Vincent cares about anything except screwing up Wildcat Oil and old Davidson. An even bigger reason is Plum; the only thing he's committed to is getting high and raising hell. He's just a hired thug, and guys like him are bad news for the environmental activists who really care."

"Okay, thanks again. I think I get it. Good luck in Pennsylvania."

I hung up, put the marinade in the fridge, and went to my office. I Googled the Rock House, found their website, and opened it. I saw what Brenda Gatlin meant about the place being "eclectic." Tonight was country, tomorrow was classic rock and roll, and the next night was contemporary rock; something for everybody. I hoped Lindsey would be willing to trade the promised ribs and red wine for line dancing and long-neck Buds.

CHAPTER

TWENTY

I called Tom to tell him what Builder had said. We decided I should go to the Rock House to watch Plum and to see if he was really meeting Jennifer. We'd probably learn more from watching than questioning them directly, although we were all dying to know where she'd been.

I drove the Bronco figuring it wouldn't draw as much attention as a Corvette in the Rock House parking lot. We arrived about 7:30 p.m., a half-hour before the band was supposed to start. I wanted to get a table where I could watch the door without being noticed. Lindsey was wearing tight fitting Lady Wranglers, a checked cowgirl shirt, Tony Lama boots, and a straw Charlie Two Horses hat. I had dug out a worn pair of Levis and thrown on a new Clinch western shirt. My cowboy boots had seen better days but were still serviceable. The wear hadn't come from riding horses, something I didn't do. I didn't like wearing western hats either, they got in the way.

We strolled through the entrance and I paid the eight dollar cover charge. We were plenty early; there were fewer than twenty people inside the cavernous bar. The place was set up for the dance crowd, with a center bar surrounded by a racetrack-style dance floor enclosed by a split-rail fence. Tables were placed all around the outside and there were service bars in all four corners. The fire department sign inside the front entrance said maximum capacity was two hundred and seventy-eight. It was a big place.

We let our eyes adjust to the darkness, turned left, and took a table at the corner of the dance floor, six or seven tables from the main entrance aisle. Unless everyone who entered clustered in front of the door, I would have a good view. I went to the nearest service bar and bought a couple of long necks; Lindsey liked Budweiser too.

I filled her in on what we'd found out and what Builder had told me. She said it sounded to her like I was adding a suspect every time I scratched one off. Unfortunately, I had to agree. We sipped the beers as I watched the people filing in. The traffic picked up just before eight, and by quarter after the place was half full, although there'd been no sign of the band. At eight-thirty, a five-piece band called the High Country Ramblers took the stage at the far end of the building. They launched into a good cover of the Eagles' *Take It Easy,* followed by a George Strait song. A few couples began dancing the Texas Two-step.

A few minutes before nine, Nate Plum walked in. Not bothering with "country" night, he was wearing wrinkled khakis, another faded Hawaiian shirt, and tennis shoes. He took a right and pushed his way through the crowd to the service bar. He reappeared with a drink near one of the corner entrances to the dance floor. As I watched, he kept turning to look at the entrance, obviously looking for someone.

He didn't have long to wait: Jennifer Davidson entered, glanced around, spotted Plum, and quickly joined him. They took an empty table halfway down the side and diagonally across from us. Jennifer was not dressed in western clothes either. She was wearing the same jeans and Denver University sweatshirt she'd had on when Lee Anne and I interviewed her. As soon as she was seated, Plum went to the bar and returned with a tall drink of some variety. It had a lot of fruit garnish, but didn't look out of place with his shirt. He set it in front of her and took the chair across the table, not the one next to her. This looked more like a business meeting than a tryst.

Lindsey said she'd get us two more beers so I wouldn't have to stand. I watched as the ultimate odd couple talked; it was distressing to think about what they were discussing. The fact they even knew one another was going to complicate the investigation even more. Jennifer did most of the talking as Plum either nodded or shook his head. Lindsey returned with the beers and said, "They don't look like lovers to me."

"I'm thinking the same thing. This is going to open a whole new can of worms. It means she was lying through her teeth about not knowing Vincent and what he was up to. She would pretty much have to know him to make contact with that orange-haired scumbag. Damn it! This puts her right in the middle of everything!" I'd liked Jennifer Davidson. She hadn't come across as a liar and possible murderer.

We nursed the beers while they continued to talk. At ten-fifty, Jennifer stood and made her way to the toilets, which were halfway down the side wall. Plum drained most of his drink and started looking around. I kept my head down, ducking behind the fence rail. When Jennifer returned, she didn't sit down, only stopped to say a few more words and headed toward the exit. I said, "Linds, follow her out and see what she's driving. I don't want to attract Plum's attention. Here, take the Bronco keys. I'll be there as soon as I can either slip past him or follow him out." Lindsey pursued Jennifer while I kept an eye on Plum.

He waited a few moments, finished the rest of his drink, and started toward the door. When he was outside, I followed. I paused inside the open entrance and watched him walk across the parking lot. I stepped outside after he cut through the first row of cars and approached a Chevy pickup parked near the end of the second row. He got in and the headlights flicked on as he pulled forward and drove up the aisle to the main exit. I ran to the Bronco, jumped in, and turned the key Lindsey had already inserted. I had to back out of my spot, drive to the end of the aisle, and turn right before I spotted Plum's rapidly fading tail lights. We sped toward the main road. I wished more people were leaving the club to give us some cover, but we were by ourselves.

"Did you see what Jennifer was driving?"

Lindsey said, "She wasn't *driving* anything. She came out, raised her hand, and a limo pulled up. She got in the back and they took off. I got the plate number if you want it. I wasn't turned in the right direction to see Plum or you come out. Is that him in the pickup we're following?"

"Yeah, he was only about a minute behind Jennifer. I hung back and saw him get in the Chevy."

We gained on the truck so I slowed to follow and watch. Plum drove the speed limit back toward Broomfield and took the county road I knew fronted Vincent Freeman's place. Even though he hadn't seen the Bronco, I didn't want to press my luck, so Lindsey and I turned the other way, toward Denver and home.

***

After we caught the Northwest Parkway, crossed under I-25, and entered E-470, Lindsey asked, "Well, did you learn anything?"

"I guess I learned not to be deceived by young women who seem too good to be true. Jennifer must've lied about knowing Vincent. I don't know what the hell she was doing with Nate Plum, but I'm guessing it doesn't have anything to do with a love affair."

"What are you going to do now?"

"First thing is to compare notes with Tom and Lee Anne. This means more people to put under surveillance as well as more analysis to figure out what connects them."

We drove in silence for several miles before Lindsey reached across and put her hand on my thigh. "Listening to cheatin' and lyin' and cryin' music makes me want to show you why none of it applies to us, sleuth. I haven't picked up a guy in a country and western bar in years; wanna go home and have our own kinda two-step, cowboy?"

I punched the Bronco up to the seventy-five mph limit and made record time back to Parker. The next morning I laughed as I walked through the living room and saw the trail of cowboy boots, jeans, western shirts, and underwear from the kitchen door to the bedroom. It looked like the aftermath of a strip poker game with no losers.

CHAPTER
TWENTY-ONE

First thing next morning, I called Lee Anne and gave her a full accounting of the Rock House meeting. I told her it looked more like a business meeting than a lovers' tryst; they'd never embraced, kissed, or even touched one another.

Lee Anne sounded exasperated. "What in the *hell* would those two have to talk about? And, more importantly, why did Jennifer lie about not knowing Freeman or what he was up to?"

I had to think about that for a moment. "Meeting Plum doesn't mean she knows Freeman." It sounded farfetched even to me. "You guys come up with anything new?"

"We need to visit Janet Davidson, which we can do now."

"You must have gotten something from the restaurant."

"I talked with the waiter who served Janet Davidson and he said there were *two* people with her that day. One was a young--he called her 'hippie' looking--woman and the other was a man. He said the man was 'youngish', maybe thirties, well dressed, and it looked like a business meeting. Almost like you just described with Jennifer and Nate Plum."

"Give me Janet's address again; I'm on my way."

Driving the 'Vette, it was difficult to convince the guard at the gated entrance that I was on "police business" until I asked if Detective Le Blanc had arrived. He checked his list, found her name, and reluctantly waved me through. When I found Janet Davidson's address, I remembered what Lee Anne had told me about the location and view: it was awe inspiring. I parked behind Lee Anne's cruiser and took a moment just to gawk. From the south-facing driveway, I felt like I could reach out and touch Pikes Peak, forty miles south, as well as the mountains of the Front Range to the west. I could only imagine what the views would be like from the living room and decks.

I wasn't disappointed. Janet Davidson answered the bell and led me into the living area situated in the northwest corner of the house. The room had a raised ceiling, twelve-foot-high windows, and offered an unobstructed view of the foothills and mountains from Pikes Peak all the way north to Longs Peak. I could even see the tall buildings of downtown Denver.

Janet was "medium" in every sense: height, weight, figure, clothing style, and brown hair. She motioned us to chairs that, unfortunately, put our backs to the view while she took a seat in the middle of a huge, butter-colored leather couch. Her voice, like everything else about her, was "medium" with no discernible accent or inflection. She addressed Lee Anne, "I certainly didn't expect to see you again, Detective, at least not quite so soon."

Lee Anne withdrew a notebook from the inside pocket of her blazer, flipped over several pages, and stared at the recently-widowed woman. Her voice seemed lower and her words more clipped than usual when she spoke. "Mrs. Davidson, you weren't exactly forthcoming with your answers when I questioned you last week. I've followed up on your alibi about being at lunch with your daughter in San Francisco at the time your husband was murdered and it checks out as

far as it goes, *but* you *didn't* bother to mention you had
another guest…a man. Why didn't you tell me about him?"

Janet Davidson stared off into the view for a few seconds.
"I, uh, I guess I didn't think it was important. I---

Lee Anne exploded, *"For Christ sake!* You didn't think it
was *important?* It was your husband's murder we were
talking about! What could be more important than that? It's
time for you to start talking and telling the truth. We can
either do it here or we can do it downtown. It's your choice."

The woman blanched, and then slowly regained her color
before saying anything. "I probably should have an attorney,
shouldn't I? Can I have my attorney come here?"

Lee Anne shook her head, "Like I said, we can do this
either way, but if you want to stay here, we're talking *right
now* and no attorney. If you want your lawyer, we'll take you
downtown."

A tear slid down Davidson's cheek and she bent forward
covering her face with her hands. "I want to stay here; I didn't
have anything to do with the murder. I'll answer your
questions."

I looked at Lee Anne, gave her a raised eyebrow shrug,
and dipped my head to indicate she should do the questioning.

She nodded, took a deep breath, and started. "Mrs. Davidson, who was the man you met in San Francisco?"

"His name is Troy Adams."

"Had you ever met him before?"

"No."

"Okay, had you ever talked to him before?"

"I hadn't, but Rachel had."

"So who set up the meeting, you or Rachel?"

"It was Rachel's idea. We'd had the luncheon planned for a month and then the day before, she told me she was bringing a 'guest.'"

"Did she tell you who it was or why she wanted to bring him?"

"Not really, she just said it was somebody who had business with my husband and wanted to meet with us."

Lee Anne took a note, seemed to consider it for a moment, and said, "Last time, you told me your daughter hated your husband. Didn't it strike you as strange she would want to include one of his 'business associates' in a luncheon?"

"Of course, but I thought maybe she was changing her mind or something; maybe she wanted to become more involved in the family. I don't know, I guess I didn't think about it."

Lee Anne stared at her. "Had your relationship with your husband changed recently?"

Janet shook her head, "No, it hadn't changed. We hadn't been close for a very long time. We lived separate lives."

"So, you must not have *really* considered that your daughter wanted a change. This is all very strange to me, Mrs. Davidson. What did Adams talk about at lunch?"

Davidson's demeanor cracked a little. She took a jagged breath to compose herself before replying, "He told us about working with a man in New York who felt my husband had cheated him out of lots of money. He said his man wanted the money back and was willing to do almost anything to collect. He said they had information that could put William in prison, but they'd rather have the money. He wanted to know if we'd help him collect."

"Why did he think you'd be willing to help him? And, more importantly, how did he even know how to contact you?"

Janet Davidson rolled her eyes and seemed to lose focus. "I don't know the answer to either of those questions. I *think* he may have gotten our names from my husband's daughter,

Jennifer. A year or so ago, she called Rachel out of the blue and asked to see her. Rachel was surprised but agreed; Jennifer flew to California and they had dinner together.

"Rachel called me the following day to say it was a really strange meeting, but, as it turned out, she liked Jennifer. She said all Jennifer wanted to talk about was how much in common they had in disliking William; she blamed him for her mother's death. Rachel was so astounded she just kept nodding her head and agreeing."

I asked, "Did Jennifer and Rachel discuss killing your husband?"

She gasped, "Of course not! Rachel would never be involved in murder!"

I had a question, "Did Adams mention a murder?"

"No, absolutely *not!* He just kept asking if we would help in getting their money and about how it would be a form of payback for all we'd been through."

"What did you tell him?"

"We told him we had no interest in any kind of payback or revenge and didn't want to be party to any scheme to extort money. I even said neither he nor his associates should ever contact us again; if they did, we would call the police. As soon as I said that, he left."

Lee Anne asked, "After he left, what did you and your daughter talk about?"

"About how weird it all was; how scary and disturbing."

"Did Rachel mention how Adams had approached her?"

"He had called her and talked about knowing her step-father, and that he had a business proposition for her. She said he didn't mention wanting to collect money or cause trouble for my husband."

I asked her, "Do you know Vincent Freeman or Nate Plum?"

She shook her head, "I've never heard either of those names."

Lee Anne stood and said, "Mrs. Davidson, I need to talk to Mr. Scott privately for a moment. We'll go out on the deck." She motioned for me to follow and we let ourselves out. At the north end of the deck, out of hearing range, Lee Anne said, "That's the craziest story I've ever heard! It's *so* crazy I believe it. Who is this Adams guy? You got any ideas?"

We watched as a member of a foursome hit an approach shot to the sixth green almost directly below us; I wondered if Janet Davidson even played golf. "No, I'm kinda fresh out. I'll start running my traps around the oil community and

investment business to see if someone knows this Adams guy.
"Every time I start believing I'm getting a handle on this,
something changes.

"There are so damn many assumptions and suppositions
involved, I'm not sure we've got anything solid. We *think* Sol
Klein *probably* met with Jennifer, and Jennifer *may* have
given him Rachel's name, and then somebody named Adams
contacted her. Whoever this Adams is, he's apparently
working with, or for, Klein. At a minimum he knows about
the history with Wildcat Willie. We *know* Jennifer has met
with Nate Plum, but we don't know if it involves Vincent
Freeman, and my guess is it doesn't. Klein may have
orchestrated everything.

"I don't believe we're going to get much more from Janet.
You should scare the hell out of her. You know what I mean,
tell her all the stuff about not leaving town, calling with
anything she remembers, and that you'll be back asking more
questions."

We returned to the living room. Janet hadn't moved from
her seat on the couch. Lee Anne said, "Mrs. Davidson, we
don't know whether you've been completely honest with us or
not; we suspect you haven't. At this point, we're not taking
you downtown for additional questioning, *but* you need to

understand that may happen. You shouldn't plan any out of town trips without letting us know. More importantly, if you remember anything else or decide there are things we should know, you need to call me immediately. Do you understand?" She handed her a business card.

Janet Davidson accepted the card, studied it carefully, and nodded. "Yes, I understand, Detective. I didn't have anything to do with my husband's death; I'm sure my daughter didn't either."

Lee Anne replied rather sharply, "I hope for both your sakes you're telling the truth. We'll show ourselves out." We walked quickly away and retraced our path to the door.

Outside, I told Lee Anne I'd start re-contacting people in the oil and gas business. It would mean retracing some steps, but I had a little more information now: Jennifer Davidson knew Nate Plum; Jennifer had met with Rachel Bender; Rachel had met with a guy named Adams who knew Klein's business; Sol Klein and Manny Greene were in the mix. Something was up with all those meetings and it wasn't something good.

CHAPTER

TWENTY-TWO

I called Freddie Pearlman's office at Big East and left a message asking him to call me back. I wanted to know which one of his geologists had come up with the original prospect leading to Trumpet Creek. I still had nagging thoughts concerning jealousy over who was receiving credit for the discovery of a giant oilfield; jealousy could be a powerful motive. But was it enough for murder?

Ken Iverson had told me Wildcat Oil's geologist, Gord Levitt, was being taken care of through the company's override program. I believed Ken would reform Wildcat Oil's override program and also give Levitt credit for the discovery.

Conditions at Wildcat Oil would change for the better under Ken.

"Hey, Cort, you still working on the murder?" Fred Pearlman was returning my call.

"Yeah, thanks for calling back, Freddie. I've found out a few things, although it's still one hell of a mystery. Can you tell me which one of your guys came up with the Trumpet Creek Prospect? I know that a Canadian by the name of Gord Levitt developed the idea for Wildcat Oil; I wondered about your shop?"

"Why would my prospect generator be of interest?"

"I'm just trying to figure out who all the players are."

Pearlman hesitated before answering. "Okay, I get it. I just don't want to think you're trying to set somebody up for a murder charge."

I exploded, "C'mon, Freddie! You know me better than that! I wouldn't 'set somebody up' for anything."

"Sorry, I know you wouldn't. This damned murder has everybody jumpy. Our prospect was called Big Powder. Almost every prospect name in southeastern Montana has some kind of connection to the Custer Battlefield, the Little Big Horn. Unfortunately for us, the discovering company gets to name new fields and Wildcat wanted Trumpet Creek.

"We'd had the idea around here for several months. Hell, I personally put some of the leases together based on overhearing some bar talk about the area. I gave the idea to our Powder River Basin guy, Troy Adams. He did some mapping which confirmed what I'd heard and we picked up a bunch more acreage. Too damn bad everything we leased was a little too far east and up in the gas cap."

My pulse rate jumped several beats when Pearlman said 'Troy Adams.' "How's this Adams feeling about how things turned out?"

Freddie took his time before replying. "Apparently, not too good. He quit a few weeks ago; said he was tired of the whole business. He took it personally that Wildcat Oil claimed credit for the field. Of course, so did I!"

"Jesus, Freddie! Why didn't you tell me this the last time we talked? Adams sounds like a guy with a possible motive!"

"Dammit, there you go again! I don't believe that; he was just burned out. He told me he was going to try his hand at investment banking and get out of oil exploration."

"Is he still in Denver? Did he find a job here?"

"No, actually he made a complete break. He moved to New York and, as I understand it, found a job with some Wall Street outfit specializing in energy investments."

My pulse rate increased several more notches; the connections were starting to fall into place. I had an off-the-wall thought, "Was he active in the Denver social or charity scenes?"

Again, he took his time answering, "Yeah, he was involved in lots of stuff; he even belonged to some environmental groups. We gave him a lot of grief about that, but he was good about not bringing it into the office. Basically, I think he was just a concerned citizen, which is probably something we all should be."

"One more thing: do you know Jennifer Davidson, Wildcat Willie's daughter?"

"Sure, anybody who's ever been on the society page or in the charity scene knows Jennifer. She's a good person; nothing like her old man. Why would you even ask?"

"Oh, no reason, I'm just clutching at straws here. Thanks, Freddie. I appreciate your time and the information. I just wish you'd told me about Adams earlier."

As I hung up, I thought no reason, my *ASS!* Troy Adams had just made the leap from an unknown to near the top of my 'person of interest' list. He hadn't received credit for Trumpet Creek and was pissed off; he was involved in charity and social events where he *might* have met Jennifer Davidson; he had connections to environmental groups where he *might* have met Vincent Freeman and maybe even Nate Plum; now he was in New York. New York's a big place, but it's also where Sol Klein was located. It kept coming up: Jennifer was the common denominator.

***

I called Lee Anne. "I don't know what all of this means, but I found out about a geologist who worked for Big East, Wildcat Oil's main competitor. He *might* know Jennifer, Vincent, Nate Plum, and even Sol Klein. He was pissed off about not getting credit for the discovery of Trumpet Creek Field; pissed off enough to quit the business. Guess what his name is--Troy Adams!"

"You're kidding me! Oh my God! This is huge!"

"It's the connection we've been waiting for, Lee Anne! Adams quit Big East several weeks ago and is working in the investment business in New York. I know this is still another leg on the octopus, but it's a damn big one! This guy had motive, *plus* he knows virtually all the players."

She was silent for a moment. "We need to question Adams and Jennifer. We know she's back, you saw her with Plum, so I'll *ask* her to come downtown. How are we going to get a handle on Adams?"

"I'd suggest you call NYPD, see if they'll help. In the meantime, I'll call my friend, Ed Giles, in New York. If Adams is working in the investment business there, Ed can probably find him in a hurry."

***

To try and make sense of what we'd found as well as the number of people on our persons-of-interest list, I began to put together an outline to categorize the suspects by motive.

For Jennifer Davidson, the only obvious motivation was revenge for the death of her mother. She already had plenty of income and obviously lived well. If she *wasn't* involved, she'd probably become even richer from Davidson's estate, but I doubted money would have motivated her. However, she damned sure was involved someway.

Vincent Freeman had several possible motives: his mother's rape, although Vada said she hadn't told him; his environmental concerns, real or not; possible money from the estate; a chance to really monkey wrench Wildcat Oil. He was a hard one to figure.

Nate Plum had the background and maybe disposition to be a killer. Any motive he had would be strictly money. But from whom? He didn't have the brains or intuition to murder someone by himself. Somebody would have had to tell him to do it, and paid to have it done.

Vada Benson had had a damn good motive twenty eight years ago, but she'd taken her own form of revenge by keeping her mouth shut and making herself rich. She probably had bigger reasons for having Wildcat Willie alive than dead.

Janet Davidson would undoubtedly benefit from the estate, but she didn't seem like the type to be involved in plotting a murder.

Rachel Bender was a total wild card at this point. She'd met with both Jennifer and Troy Adams which was suspicious as hell, but I didn't have a clue as to how everything connected.

Troy Adams had been professionally jealous, but was it enough to drive him to murder? He knew, or at least we suspected he knew, nearly all the persons of interest.

That brought me to Sol Klein and his knuckle-headed strong-arm man, Manny Greene. Anybody who would carry a grudge for forty years and who'd been in contact immediately before and after the murder *had* to be a suspect.

Fred Pearlman was too nice a guy and had an ironclad alibi for the time of the murder. J.D. Pierce may not be a nice guy, but he also had a strong alibi and, like him or not, I believed his story.

The cops had found over two hundred dollars in Willie's wallet, so it probably hadn't been a simple robbery gone wrong. What was I missing in all this?

***

Lindsey walked onto the deck. "Hi, sleuth. You look deep in thought; what's going on?"

I kissed her as she bent over me. "Hey, babe, I guess I was a million miles away. This case is driving me nuts. Everything is hurry up and wait. I don't know how you cops can stand doing everything by the book: waiting for warrants and court orders and crap like that. I need something to break so we can get on with it."

"Wow, frustration rears its ugly head! How do you think my boss George Albins, your good buddy, feels most of the time? You sound like a man in serious need of some R and R! You need to get away for a couple of days and quit obsessing with the case. C'mon, it's Friday night and we've got a whole weekend ahead of us. Why don't we pack a bag and take off?"

I started to decline, but thought better of it. "You know what? I think you're right; we need a break. What would you like to do? Where should we go?"

She adopted a pensive look, put her index finger to her chin, and considered her answer. "Let's do something totally off the wall. What about going up to Black Hawk, having a big steak, and gambling the night away? When we get tired or run out of money we'll get a room, sleep in tomorrow, and then leisurely drive home."

I bolted out of the chair. "If you're waitin' on me, you're backing up." I could hear the delicious tinkle of her laughter as I sprinted through the living room headed toward our closet and my overnight bag.

***

It was a lovely evening for the ninety-minute drive from Parker to the Black Hawk-Central City gambling zone. In the early nineties, Colorado's voters had overwhelmingly passed legislation to allow "limited stakes" gambling in the two old mining towns. Unfortunately, the area had been dying a lingering death, with no prospects of rejuvenated mining or other sources of revenue on the horizon. Now, Black Hawk was booming with mega-sized Las Vegas style casinos and hotels. Black Hawk's success had effectively choked off

Central City's life-support system. Visitors from Denver had to pass through Black Hawk first and most stopped to stay and play without driving the additional two miles up the hill to Central City.

We drove up the ramp into the Ameristar Casino and Hotel parking structure. I handed the Corvette keys to a valet and cringed as his eyes lit up. We grabbed our overnight bags out of the trunk and headed to reception. The Wi-Fi connection in the car had paid off as Linds had jumped on her iPad during the trip up the mountain and managed to score a late cancellation suite for the night. We checked in, took our own bags to the room which turned out to be a penthouse, and freshened up before heading for the steakhouse on the second floor. Typical of Colorado's gambling clientele, the restaurant was nearly deserted as the craps shooters and poker players didn't want to waste a minute of their time on eating. We had our choice of tables and selected a balcony spot overlooking the casino floor.

When we were seated, the waiter delivered menus and asked if we wanted to see the wine list. I grinned at Linds, "Absolutely, but why don't you start us with a couple of Three Olives vodka martinis, straight up with a twist?" He nodded and left the menus and wine list.

"Holy Cow! You're taking this break seriously, aren't you? I don't think I've ever seen you drink hard liquor." Lindsey looked stunning in metallic copper-colored slacks and a gold silk blouse. She'd pulled her hair back into a short pony tail and was wearing a ton of bling.

"It was your idea, girl, and a damn good one! I plan on making the most of it. If we're having a steak, what kind of wine are you in the mood for?"

She gave me her most knowing smile and said, "You're the sommelier. You choose."

I opened the voluminous wine list and thumbed directly to the two pages of American reds. They were arranged in ascending order by price, so I snuck a peak at the last entry: a 1972 Heitz "Martha's Vineyard" cabernet for $1,298. I raised an eyebrow and back up a page where I spotted a bottle of 2009 Silver Oak for $94. When the waiter returned with the martinis, I asked for the wine to be opened immediately. It would need at least thirty minutes to breathe.

We ordered our steaks: a rare petit filet for Lindsey and a medium rare Porterhouse for me. She selected sautéed mushrooms, asparagus, and cauliflower as sides and we decided to split a Caesar salad for a starter. We sipped the drinks and I proposed a toast, "Here's to total relaxation,

Linds. Thanks for thinking of this; you were absolutely right--
I need the break."

The salad arrived as we finished the drinks and the waiter
poured our first glasses of the Silver Oak. I had tasted it
earlier and knew it would be a hit. I was right. Lindsey's
smile broadened into a grin as she carefully tasted, savored,
and swallowed. "You did good, babe. This is outstanding!"

The sizzling steaks were placed in front of us and we
tucked in, hardly speaking for the first few bites as we enjoyed
the food. I topped up our glasses and leaned back. Lindsey
glanced at the casino. Our location provided a good view of
the casino entrance as well as the Texas-Hold-'Em poker
tables directly below us. Suddenly she straightened and began
staring intently at the entrance.

I caught her look and asked, "What's up?"

She continued staring for a few seconds and then said,
"Isn't that Tom? Tom Montgomery?"

I leaned forward and followed her line of sight. I was
astounded to see Tom standing at the top of the steps leading
from the hotel lobby into the casino. He was hand-in-hand
with Lee Anne LeBlanc.

I pulled back from the balcony railing. "Holy Shit! It's
him all right. And that's Lee Anne with him."

Lindsey's jaw dropped and she made the "O" sign with her mouth. "Oh my God! Aren't there rules in DPD about dating people you work with? There sure are in our office!"

We both moved our chairs back into the shadows. It took me a moment to process what I was seeing. "I'm sure Denver has the same rules. Good grief, she works *for* him. They've gotta be nuts!"

Although there was no way they could hear our conversation, Linds used a stage whisper, "How do you want to handle this? Should we attract their attention, go meet up with them, or what?"

This was tough; I had to think for a moment. "No, I don't think we should. It would embarrass both of them and make my part of the investigation even tougher than it is now. Let's signal the waiter, get some carry-out boxes and our check, and go to our room. We can finish our dinner, stretch out on the bed, and, you know…see what happens. That is, unless you're dying to gamble?"

Lindsey gave me "the look" and said, "I already know what's going to happen, and I would much rather bet on a sure thing. I just didn't know it would happen this early!"

I laughed out loud. "Nothing I like better than a sure thing. Let's go."

I caught the waiter's attention and told him what we needed. He gave us a knowing, raised-eyebrow look, but smiled and took care of everything just as we asked. I signed the tab and gave the waiter a twenty. We snuck a look over the railing and saw Tom and Lee Anne seated at a Black Jack table with their backs to us. We collected our boxes, exited the restaurant, and took the penthouse elevator to our room. Inside, we set everything on the round dining table, pulled up two chairs, and finished our dinner.

Lindsey said, "Judging from your reaction, I gather you didn't know Tom and Lee Anne were seeing each other?"

"You've got that right! I've seen her a lot more than him, and she never let on at all. I don't think Tom's seen *anyone* since his wife left, and that's been almost four years."

"How come his wife left? You've never talked about it at all. Is he officially divorced?"

"I don't know all the reasons; I think she just got tired of being a cop's wife. She was a worrier anyway and after Tom was transferred into Homicide, she hated it. He told me once whenever he got called out in the middle of the night, she'd get up and sit in the kitchen smoking cigarettes and drinking coffee until he came home. She actually wanted him to quit the force and go into private security or something. Then, to make things even worse, she started drinking vodka instead of coffee whenever he was working."

Lindsey frowned and asked, "How long did that last?"

"I'm not sure; at least a couple years or so. I *do* know Tom was pretty unhappy for a long time."

"How'd she leave?"

"He was working a regular day shift, met me for a beer at Andy's after work, and when he got home, she was gone. Took her clothes, jewelry, half the money in their joint checking account, and left him a note saying her lawyer would be in touch. She left the key under the welcome mat and vanished. He found out later she'd packed everything the moment he'd left for work, called a cab, stopped by the bank to make the withdrawal, and caught Amtrak to Chicago. That's where she was from; she moved in with a cousin. She'd already talked to a lawyer and had the paperwork going before she took off. Tom never had a clue."

Lindsey sipped her wine. "Did she have a job here in Denver?"

I had to think back. "Yeah, she did some freelance stuff as a copy writer for an advertising agency. She worked out of their house though, so she didn't go to an office or anything."

"They didn't have any kids, did they?"

"No, that's about the only 'good' news in the whole deal. Plus, she didn't fight him for a big settlement; said she wanted half of the cash assets including the house, but didn't want any alimony. She didn't make him sell their cars or anything. It only took him about four months to sell the house and it closed before the divorce hearing, so he just wrote her a check."

Lindsey finished her wine, took a drink of water, and said, "Sounds kinda typical of a lot of cops' marriages. First ones rarely last. I can understand the strain; I worry about you when you're working a case—and we're not even married and you're not a cop."

I nodded and gave her an air toast with the last of my wine.

Afterward, we got naked, crawled under a single sheet, turned on the flat screen, and watched a very suggestive French movie with subtitles that weren't needed to understand the action.

Lindsey had been right about knowing what was going to happen. In fact, it happened twice, although her attempt at a French accent nearly broke my concentration.

CHAPTER
TWENTY-THREE

We got up early, threw our stuff in the overnight bags, and checked out via the room internet. Deciding to take the scenic route, we DROVE the Peak-to-Peak Highway through Nederland and Boulder Canyon. It was another glorious Colorado day. We got back to Parker at 1:30 p.m., a full half-day earlier than our original plan. Even though our little break was foreshortened, it had been effective: I felt refreshed and ready to step back into the case.

In the early evening, we were enjoying margaritas on the deck when the phone rang. I was surprised to see Tom's name on caller ID. "Hey, Tom, what's up?"

"We need to talk. You going to be home for a while?"

"Hadn't planned on going anywhere; you wanna swing by?"

"Yeah, I'll be out in a half hour or so."

I closed the call and looked at Linds. "Well, as you could hear, that was Tom. He wants to come by and *talk* about something. I wonder if he spotted us after all?"

Lindsey shook her head in slight disbelief. "I can't imagine how. It must be something to do with the case."

"Could be, although we could handle that over the phone. I'll make another batch of margaritas."

When the doorbell chimed, I glanced out the dining room window and saw Tom's personal car, a bright red Ford F-150 pickup, parked in my driveway. At the front door, I could see two people through the distorted view water glass. One of them was a woman.

I opened the door to Tom and Lee Anne LeBlanc. I tried not to let what I was feeling register on my face. "Hey, what's up, guys? What a surprise! Come on in." Lindsey was standing behind me in the entry way. There was an awkward moment of silence before I said, "Well, let's see…Lee Anne, I know you've talked to Lindsey, but I don't think you've met. This is my girlfriend, Lindsey Collins. Linds, this is Lee Anne

LeBlanc." The women shook hands and Tom gave Lindsey a hug.

Tom hesitated a moment before saying, "Look guys, it's probably pretty obvious this isn't police business, but we thought you needed to know about us being an, uh...an *item* or whatever they call it, before it becomes police business. We thought we'd better tell you in person before some rumor got out."

I put my hand over my heart, faked a backward stagger, and exclaimed, "Holy shit, buddy--that's a bombshell! Well, come in and tell us the story. Luckily, you're both off duty because I've made a pitcher of margaritas and it's a fabulous evening out on the deck." I closed the door and Lindsey led the way to the kitchen. I got out glasses, salted the rims, and poured drinks for everyone. Outside, Tom and Lee Anne sat in the two-person glider and Linds and I took the lounge chairs.

I raised my glass toward the couple and said, "Here's to an interesting story. I guess congratulations are in order. I'm happy for you both."

Lindsey was closest to Tom and clinked glasses with him. "I'll echo that. Good to see you smiling, Tom."

He was displaying the broadest smile I'd ever seen. "Thanks. I hoped you'd understand, both of you. Everything happened so quickly that we almost didn't recognize what was going on. We sure as hell didn't have time to think it through. If we had, I doubt if we'd have ended up where we are." He turned to look at Lee Anne. "Would you agree with that?"

She sipped her drink, probably stalling her answer, "Sounds about right, I guess. Like he said, 'It just *happened.*' We know we can't continue to work the same cases, or even in the same division, but we wanted to fill you in and see if you have an objection to trying to close this one out before we let DPD know. When we do, I'll ask for a transfer out of Homicide. There are no rules against cops being married, *except* they can't work in the same division. Not that there are marriage plans or anything." She laughed self-consciously and took Tom's hand.

I replied, "I don't have a problem with it. And besides, I'd hate to bring someone new up to speed anyway. Plus, this way I'll only have to 'report' to one of you, right?"

Tom shook his head and rolled his eyes, "You can make a joke out of anything. But, thanks for understanding. This is a good margarita by the way. You got any more?" It was Lee Anne's turn to shake her head.

Lindsey jumped up, "C'mon, Lee Anne, you might as well get used to waiting on these slobs. It's the *little woman's place* you know." She laughed as she led the way back to the kitchen.

Tom looked at me quizzically. "Are you really all right with everything?"

"Absolutely. I hope she can smooth off some of your rough edges. You're such a prick most of the time that her influence will be good for everyone." Tom glanced over his shoulder and flipped me the bird.

After they returned with the fresh drinks, Tom's demeanor changed and he returned to being a cop. "Probably not the best time to bring it up, but where are we going with the case? Lee Anne says you guys are developing more suspects, but there's not much concrete about any of 'em."

I nodded. "We've got way too many suspects all right, but I'm thinking Troy Adams is going to be the answer to a lot of questions. There are just too many things having to do with him to be coincidences. Jennifer Davidson is in the mix too, but figuring out how is going to be tough. We've got to start bearing down with our questions." I turned to Lee Anne, "When are you bringing her in?"

"Tomorrow, first thing--can you make it?"

"Wouldn't miss it for anything; I can't wait to ask her about Plum."

Tom said, "From everything you've told me, I'd say she's involved. I guess it'll have to wait for tomorrow though." He rose from the glider, drained his drink, and put the glass on the table. "Thanks for understanding. It means a lot to both of us." I stood and we did the "man hug" thing with back slaps. Lee Anne and Lindsey watched awkwardly, laughed self-consciously, and also embraced. The four of us completed the dance by switching partners.

We showed them out and returned to the deck. Lindsey enthused, "She's great! I haven't seen Tom smile like that *ever*. I sure hope everything works out for them."

"Me, too. Tom helped me through a lot back when Gerri was murdered. I'd like to see him find some happiness in his life."

***

Sunday night, after Tom and Lee Anne left, I called Ed Giles to reiterate how important it was to locate Troy Adams. He said he was working on it.

Monday morning, I was finishing the paper and a second cup of coffee when the phone rang at 8:23 a.m. It was Ed. I was glad New York was two hours ahead of Denver."

"Hey, sport, you outta bed yet?" Ed and I had been
friends since his days as an investment banker in Denver,
when I'd been doing an initial public offering for The Crude
Company, my start-up oil and gas exploration outfit. We were
both early risers and runners back then. A lot of the
information needed to fill the offering prospectus had been
developed during those early morning runs.

"You know I am, man. What've you got for me? I
assume there's something or you wouldn't be calling so soon."

"Wasn't hard to find Adams; I did a search of investment
bankers and found him with Northeast and Central
Investments. It's a boutique outfit specializing in energy
companies. I checked it out by giving him a call. I gave him a
story about being from Denver, being in the same biz, maybe
knowing some people in common, and how we should get
together for a drink sometime. I think he bought it all; he even
said he'd heard my name--and yours--before."

I laughed. "It's no wonder you're a success at pushing
stocks. You're as full of shit as a Christmas goose! How far
did you take it?"

"Not far: I asked him about his background; how long
he'd been in New York; where he was living; what he was

doing; if there was anything I could do to help him, you know, bullshit stuff like that."

"Where *does* he live?"

"In Greenwich Village. I looked up the address, and if you're going to live in The Village, it's pretty well located, close to everything."

"What's he like?"

"Arrogant son-of-a-bitch, at least over the phone. A real 'me-me-me' type. He kept talking about how successful he'd been; about all the oil he'd found. He's one of those guys who think he's the smartest person in the room."

"Maybe we can use that if he thinks he's smart enough to fool the cops--and me. It's going to be tough getting him back to Denver for questioning though; there isn't enough evidence to arrest him for anything."

Ed was silent for a couple beats, then said, "You interested in a suggestion? I think this guy is such an egotist he might just come if you ask him. I think he'd take it on as a challenge to prove he *is* smarter than everyone."

I laughed. "Remind you of anyone?"

Ed laughed harder. "Yeah, you about ten years ago."

I closed the call and hit speed dial for Lee Anne. "Can you hold off on bringing Jennifer downtown? My friend from New York just got back to me."

"What's he got?"

"Adams' address and phone numbers for starters."

"Super! Did he find out anything about what Adams is up to?"

"He's not a cop, Lee Anne."

"You're right, of course. That's our job."

"*But* he talked to Adams and has a scheme for getting him to come to Denver voluntarily."

"How does that work?"

"Ed said Adams is so arrogant that he might just agree to come here for questioning, just to prove he's smarter than we are."

"I thought you said this guy wasn't a cop? Sounds to me like he's acting like one."

"What the hell? Same thing applies to me!"

"That's what Tom says! Why do you want to hold off on Jennifer?"

"I think we'd learn more if we see them in a room together."

"I like it. It sounds like a real plan for a change, so let's go for it. I'll fill Tom in; I imagine he'll want to be the one to call Adams." Her voice had a happy lilt to it. I had to wonder if she was happy about my news or because of Tom.

"Hey Cort, I want to go off the record for a minute. I want to thank you for the way you and Lindsey treated me, or I should say, *us*. It's been worrying both of us, especially Tom, so, uh, it was nice."

CHAPTER
TWENTY-FOUR

Over the next few days, I checked in regularly with Tom
and Lee Anne. I was getting extremely tired hearing that
nothing was happening. I spent a lot of time researching
Trumpet Creek oilfield, and everything I read indicated it was
going to be even bigger than the early reports had suggested. I
kept thinking about Vada Benson's share and what this was
going to mean to her.

Thursday afternoon, Lee Anne finally called and
exclaimed, "I can't believe it, but your friend was right about
Adams. Tom called and gave him a story about how we were
stalled and running out of ideas on the investigation. He told
Adams his name had come up as someone who knew a

number of the people involved: Davidson, Fred Pearlman, and possibly, even Jennifer Davidson. Tom asked him, nicely I might add, if he'd consider returning to Denver to be 'interviewed.'"

Her excitement was contagious; I asked, "How'd he react?"

"At first, he started asking a lot of questions about what we wanted: who we wanted to talk about, how long it would take; things like that. I think he's trying to figure out how much we know. Tom was really good at dodging most of it; kept talking about how we were stymied and needed a break. I think Adams bought it because he agreed to come! Can you believe it? Your friend had him figured to a 'T' when he called him a super egotist."

"Ed's a smart guy. When's Adams coming?"

"He's arriving at 11:48 a.m. tomorrow on a Jet Blue flight. Tom's going to meet him at DIA and haul him downtown."

"'Haul him downtown?' This isn't an arrest is it? He's not bringing a lawyer is he?"

"Not that we know of, and no, it's not an arrest…at least not yet. Unless he outright incriminates himself or confesses to something, we don't have enough."

"I'd place a fairly large bet he's not going to do something stupid--except for agreeing to come here; when do you expect to be downtown?"

"1:00 p.m. I'm picking Jennifer up at noon; I called her after we'd talked to Adams and she agreed to come in. Also, like you suggested, I didn't say anything about Adams. I assume you'll be there?"

I laughed loudly, "Whadda you think? Incidentally, what did Jennifer have to say for herself? Did you ask her where she's been?"

"Not yet, I just read her the riot act about leaving town without telling us. She, of course, knew we'd been in her house; we had to leave a posted notice, plus she saw the finger print powder. She didn't seem too upset, said she understood and 'appreciated our concern.' She's either one of the best actresses and coolest customers I've ever seen, or she really doesn't have anything to hide. I'm anxious to see her reaction when we hit her with Plum."

"No more than I am. See you tomorrow."

***

I checked in on the main floor of the Justice Center, and found Lee Anne had left a message to come to the third floor where the interrogation rooms were located. The civilian on the desk sent a police auxiliary officer, a retiree from the looks of her, to escort me. Surprisingly, the third floor also had a "reception desk", except this one was manned by a police sergeant. His name tag read "Boyle" and, from the looks of him, I began thinking his first name might be "Hard." I gave him my best "I'm here to help" smile and said, "Afternoon, I'm Cort Scott, here to see Detective LeBlanc. She's expecting me."

Sergeant Boyle gave me a slow once over, "Lawyer?"

"No, private investigator; I'm working for the DA's office on the Wildcat Willie Davidson murder."

"Got some ID, Mr. Scott?"

I handed him my PI card. He scrutinized it carefully and said, "Nice, and now how about a driver's license?" So much for professional courtesy. I dug out my license and handed it over. He took copies of both and gave them back. "Okay, *PI* Scott, good enough. Detective LeBlanc is in room four, straight down the hall, last door on the left."

There were four numbered rooms on each side of the hall. Between each numbered door was another door marked "Police and Authorized Personnel Only." Obviously, they were observation rooms, the ones with one-way windows and mirrors. I hoped I wouldn't be relegated to them; I wanted to be involved in the questioning.

The door to room four was ajar and I could hear voices. I knocked softly as I pushed the door open. Jennifer Davidson was sitting on the far side of a polished metal table that sported a prominent hasp for a handcuff chain. She wasn't handcuffed, but seemed to be fixated on the table, the hasp, and the surroundings. Lee Anne was standing on the near side of the table.

Lee Anne said, "Hi, Mr. Scott, thanks for coming in." She was being formal again. She turned back to Jennifer, "You'll remember Cort Scott, I'm sure? He's a special investigator for the DA's office and is helping with the investigation of your father's murder."

Jennifer smiled, "Yes, certainly. It's nice to see you again, Mr. Scott." I wondered how happy she'd be in a couple hours.

"Jennifer. Thanks for coming in." I noticed one change: she was wearing brown slacks and a beige, loose-knit sweater instead of her usual jeans and DU sweatshirt.

We heard voices and footsteps approaching, and a thirty-something man preceded Tom into the room. Adams was medium height, five-ten or eleven and looked like an athlete.

He was wearing gray slacks, a blue striped shirt, open at the neck, and a navy blue blazer. Everything looked expensive.

Closely observing Jennifer for a reaction, I was disappointed. At best, a look of recognition crossed her face; her eyebrows rose slightly and a slight smile tugged at the corners of her mouth.

Adams' reaction was more animated, but not much. His jaw slackened and his eyes reflected a little confusion. "Well, this is a surprise, Lieutenant. You didn't say Jenn would be here. Is this some kind of set up?" His tone was not accusatory or harsh, but he wasn't happy. "Hi Jenn; are you part of this?" He crossed the small room and embraced Jennifer. One question answered: they knew each other and were probably more than casual friends.

Tom maintained his "just looking for help" demeanor. "I don't know what you mean by 'set up', Mr. Adams. Like I've told you, we're at somewhat of a dead end in our investigation of Ms. Davidson's father's murder. We simply thought getting you two together to answers some of our questions might be helpful. Obviously, you already know one another." Tom extended his hand across the table to Jennifer, "Good afternoon, Ms. Davidson. I'm Tom Montgomery, homicide. I'm the lead detective on this case--your father's murder."

Jennifer took his hand, "Yes, Lee Anne has mentioned you. I'm disappointed to hear you're having trouble with the case. I hope we can help."

Tom turned his attention back to Troy Adams. "Mr. Adams, this is Detective Lee Anne LeBlanc who's been doing most of the leg work on the investigation, and this is Cort Scott. He's a special investigator for the DA's office. Thank you for coming in. Would anyone care for something to drink: coffee, tea, soda, water? How about you, Lee Anne? Cort?" Everyone declined. I was hard pressed to stifle a smile; I'd never heard such a conciliatory tone from my rough-edged friend.

Adams took the seat beside Jennifer and also stared at the handcuff ring for a moment before looking at me. "Well, I've certainly heard your name, Scott, recently in fact. I believe we have a mutual acquaintance in New York. Is my newfound friend, Ed Giles, part of the investigation team, also?"

It wasn't something I wanted to hear. I didn't want Ed involved. I tried a puzzled look, "There's no 'team' I know of, but how do you know Ed? He is a friend of mine, and used to be in Denver."

"Probably just a coincidence then; he contacted me recently and we talked about Denver and people we knew. I, of course, knew of you when I was here; we're both geologists I believe." Adams voice dripped with sarcasm. He had a smirking grin on his face that I wanted to wipe off, or better yet, knock off.

Instead, I put on my best look of surprise. "Oh really? How come I was under the impression you're an investment banker?"

Adams' eyes sparked and he looked impatient. "Ahh, come on now, that's very disingenuous. I suspect you've been talking to several people in the oil and gas business here and surely you know I worked for Big East?

"I think we'd best be getting on with this, uh, 'friendly' question and answer session. Lieutenant, it's your move." Ed had been right; arrogant wasn't a strong enough term for this prick. He glanced around the room again, studied the mirror which, of course, was supposed to camouflage the observation room. "All this looks quite official and quite intimidating, just as I'm sure you intended. Lieutenant, are you sure we shouldn't have a lawyer here?"

Another word we didn't want to hear. Tom replied, "You're not under arrest, Mr. Adams; nor is Ms. Davidson. Obviously, if you feel a need to have a lawyer present, it's your right. Frankly, we'd like to keep this friendly and informal. When lawyers get involved, it seldom stays that way, but it's your call." I knew Tom was taking a big chance. He was betting Adams' arrogance and desire to know what we knew would override his inclination to lawyer up.

Tom won his bet. Adams took Jennifer's hand and said, "Sure, let's keep it 'friendly.' How can I, or *we*, help you?"

***

Tom and Lee Anne took the chairs across the table from the couple. I remained standing inside the closed door. Tom asked if they agreed to have the interview recorded and they both said, "Yes." He flicked the switches on the equipment, and recited the time, place, and who was present.

Lee Anne opened with, "Jennifer, we've been trying to contact you and have a number of questions. We were getting very concerned about you. Where were you, and why didn't you tell us you were leaving town?"

Jennifer flinched and hesitated a couple of seconds before saying, "I didn't know I had to tell you; I didn't think about it. It just seemed like everything was closing in on me and I wanted to get away. I, uh…I went to see Troy in New York."

Lee Anne raised her voice slightly. "You didn't think about a lot of things, did you? You didn't think to tell us you knew Mr. Adams here--or Sol Klein for that matter. What the hell's going on with you? Are you *trying* to make yourself look like a suspect in your father's murder?"

Jennifer's shoulders sagged and she dropped her head slightly, staring at the table top for a moment. She raised her head and whispered, "I didn't kill my father. I've already told you I'm not surprised he's dead, but I didn't kill him. Yes, I've met Sol Klein." A tear slid down her right cheek; I saw another drop form at the end of her nose, which she sniffed back. "I met Troy at a charity function several months ago; we've been seeing each other since. With everything that's happened, I just made a quick decision to go see him in New York. I needed a 'friend' and, frankly, I don't have any here. I probably should have told you; I'm sorry."

Lee Anne snorted, "Sorry doesn't cut it. As I said, we were *very* concerned about you; enough so we obtained the search warrant and entered your house. We were afraid something might have happened to you."

"I don't think you had the right to do that! Enter my house, I mean." It was the most animated I'd seen Jennifer.

Lee Anne kept up the pressure. "We had every right. Your father had been murdered and you were missing. We had no way of knowing what was going on. But more important than any of that, why did you meet with Nate Plum at a bar in Broomfield?"

Jennifer snapped her head up. "How did you know about that? About Plum?"

"It doesn't matter *how* we know--we know. What were you talking to Plum about?"

"I wanted to talk to him about Vince Freeman."

"What about Vince Freeman? What were you trying to find out?"

"I guess I wanted to know if he had killed my father."

"Why didn't you ask him? Why would you go to Plum? How did you contact Plum? You told us you'd never met Freeman and weren't involved with him in any way."

Jennifer started to answer, but was interrupted by Troy Adams who cleared his throat and said, "I gave Jenn Plum's cell phone number."

I'd been silent until now. "How do you know Plum?"

Adams' tone was still sarcastic, "As you *well* know, I used to be in the oil and gas business here. I knew your name before your buddy, Giles, started snooping around. Jenn had already told me you are working with the police. You must be a thrill junkie or something; ratting out people is a big comedown from starting companies and drilling oil fields isn't it?"

It took some doing, but I didn't rise to the bait. He continued, but with a little less attitude, "Anyway, strange as it may seem, I'm also active in environmental causes. I knew Freeman was involved in protests and demonstrations targeting oil and gas operations and Wildcat Oil in particular. Since I didn't care for Wildcat Oil or Davidson, I thought there could be an opportunity to double down and screw him up by slipping Freeman some information.

"I kept seeing Plum and Freeman at protests but couldn't seem to get close to Freeman. It was like he had body guards or something, so I spoke to Plum. As soon as I began talking, he started seeing dollar signs and intentionally kept me away from Freeman with a cock-and-bull story about Freeman needing to keep his hands clean. Anyway, I ended up giving Plum some information about oil and gas lease auctions and what they could do to stall environmental impact studies. I never did meet Freeman. I always dealt with Plum.

"As soon as I saw the news reports of the murder, I called Jenn. She was shaken up, almost hysterical, and kept asking me who I thought might have done it. Then she said she thought you guys, the police, suspected her, and she wanted to know if I had any ideas about how to clear her name."

Lee Anne interrupted and asked Jennifer, "Why should you think we suspected you? Could it be because you hadn't told us about knowing Klein or meeting with Rachel Bender?"

Again, Jennifer's body seemed to shrink; she paused several moments before answering. "I guess so, although everything was completely innocent. I tried calling Vincent Freeman several times, but he never took or returned my calls. I mentioned it to Troy and he told me about Plum. I decided to ask him if he thought Vincent could be responsible."

Lee Anne practically shouted, "Damn it Jennifer, if you want us to believe you, you've got to start telling us the whole story, the whole truth! Start with Klein and Greene. We'll get back to Plum later."

Jennifer Davidson nearly tipped over backwards when Lee Anne raised her voice. Tom, apparently playing the "good cop" part, put his hand on Lee Anne's arm. "Remember, Detective, Ms. Davidson is here voluntarily. We're trying to keep this informal."

Jennifer regained her composure, raised her gaze, and slowly began to speak. "Sol Klein called me not long after my mother died. He was awfully crude and boorish, but, at first, he seemed genuinely sorry about her passing. He told me stories from when she and my father had first married and about being in business with my father. He mentioned a 'falling out' on the business side but didn't elaborate, at least not then.

"I was still grieving and made a huge mistake when I told him I wasn't close to my father and blamed him for my mother's death. A few weeks later, Klein called again and said he was coming to Denver and wanted to meet me. He said he'd been thinking about what I'd said, how he had 'a score to settle' with my father, and how we could both 'get even' with him. I tried to tell him I wasn't interested, but he was insistent about coming.

"Three days later he called. He was in Denver and asked to meet me at Elway's restaurant in the Four Seasons downtown. I tried to beg off, but he kept bringing up my mother, how much he'd liked her, and how many more stories he could tell me. I finally agreed to meet him that evening-- another mistake.

"When I arrived at Elway's and asked for 'Mr. Klein's' table, the maître de' smiled and acted like Klein was an old friend. Turns out, Klein had paid given him $100 to put on the act. It was for my benefit, I guess, although I don't know why.

"There was another man at the table, and Klein introduced him as Manny Greene. He described Greene as his 'business associate,' but Greene didn't say twenty words while I was there. It was apparent he wasn't a *businessman*; I figured out he was probably some kind of bodyguard.

"Klein asked me if I wanted a drink, but I declined. He was a repugnant, ugly little man whom I took an immediate dislike to. His grammar was terrible, far worse than I remembered from the telephone. He was almost, I don't know, 'dirty' or something. I wanted to leave immediately, but he started talking about Mother, at least at the beginning. Obviously, he *had* known her. He talked about where she grew up, where she'd gone to school, and their 'old neighborhood.' He kept telling me how mad it made him that she *had* to divorce my father.

"He soon switched to how he'd never understood why she'd married in the first place and how he'd never liked my father. Then he launched into how my father had cheated him out of lots of money. Before I could stop him, he was talking about a plan for getting even and how I could help to get 'revenge' for my mother. He said he knew something from the past, something my father had kept hidden for over twenty-five years and would pay almost anything to keep quiet.

"I didn't want to hear any more and started to stand. Manny Greene grabbed my arm and told me to sit down. He actually pulled me down. Klein got real quiet for a minute and then said, 'Let her go. I don't think she's going to help us; maybe the less she knows the better.' Greene took his hand off my arm, so I got up and started to walk away when Klein said, 'There are other members of your so-called *family* who might be more interested in seeing your fucking father get what's coming to him.'"

It was the first time I'd heard Jennifer Davidson swear, and even quoting the F-bomb shocked me. I said, "Who did you think he was talking about?"

"The only person who made sense was Vincent Freeman. That's when I started trying to contact him, and how I ended up talking with Plum.

"But I also thought about Janet, the woman my father married after divorcing my mother. I even considered her daughter, Rachel. I was just clutching at straws though. I kept coming back to Vincent."

I asked, "So you couldn't contact Freeman; did Plum give you any answers?"

Jennifer shook her head. "Not really, he just kept asking if I was going to help Klein bring '*bigger than life*, Wildcat Willie Davidson' down. It didn't seem like he wanted to talk about Vincent at all."

Tom jerked upright. "So Plum knew Klein? Is that what you're saying?"

Troy Adams had been listening carefully to the conversation. "I may have something to add." Everyone turned toward him. "Nate Plum asked me if I'd ever heard of Sol Klein. He said Klein had contacted Vincent Freeman and told him he had a plan to 'get to' Davidson. Klein said there'd be a lot of money in it if Vincent would help him. Plum said Vincent got all pissed off, blew the guy off, and told him he wasn't in this for money. But Nate overheard Vincent's end of the conversation, so the first chance he got he grabbed Freeman's phone, checked the calls, and took down the number. He said just because Freeman wasn't interested in money didn't mean he wasn't. I'm sure Plum contacted Klein."

Lee Anne went back to Jennifer, "Why did you meet with Rachel? And why did you wait so long after you saw Klein?"

Jennifer shrugged before she replied, "I brooded over what he'd said, you know, about my father's 'big secret.' I continued to think it had to have something to do with Vincent, but I wanted to find out if she might know about it being anything else. She'd lived in the house with Janet and my father while I lived with my mom.

"I hadn't seen Rachel since we were little kids and decided to make contact, see if she would even meet me. She reluctantly agreed, so I flew to San Francisco and we had lunch together. Surprisingly enough, we sort of hit it off. I told her what Klein had said about 'other members of the family' and asked if she had any idea what he was talking about. She didn't, but that opened the flood gates and we both started talking about our mutual dislike of my father, her step-father."

Something occurred to me, "Why should Rachel hate him? Hadn't he provided her and her mother with pretty fabulous life styles?"

"He provided plenty of money if that's what you mean. But, according to Rachel, it wasn't a good *life*. There was no love in the house and he treated Janet badly. Rachel thinks he was cheating on her like he did my mother, and he was really mean to Rachel. She couldn't wait to move out and get as far away as she could. But mostly, I'd say, she hated the way he treated Janet. Pretty similar to my story, isn't it?"

I interjected, "So, did she want revenge? Did she want to see him dead?"

Jennifer reeled back with a horrified look. "*No, no, no*...she wasn't anything like that! She wouldn't have been involved in something like murder!"

Tom took over. "Okay, Troy, your turn. When did you leave Denver for New York?"

Adams replied, "Several months ago, almost a year now."

"Why did you leave?"

"Oh, many reasons, I suppose. 'Burnout', if you need a good one. Ask your buddy, Scott, here, about burnout. I understand it's why he decided to become a PI." He smirked in my direction as he said it. Again, I didn't react to the jibe.

Tom paused before saying, "You had a good job with Big East Oil before leaving, didn't you?"

"It was all right, but nothing special--just eight-to-five stuff."

"But you were well paid and received credit for what you did?"

Adams scooted his chair back a few inches before replying. "Look, why don't you cut to the chase, Lieutenant.

You want to know if I was mad about not being credited with the discovery of Trumpet Creek Field; that's the bottom line, isn't it? If I was pissed off enough to want Wildcat Willie Davidson dead, right?"

"Well, were you?"

Adams laughed, "I was mad for sure, but kill somebody? C'mon, you can't be serious!"

Tom stood, "I'm serious as a heart attack, Adams. Someone wanted him dead and, so far, you've got as much motive as anyone."

Adams bristled, "I think we're done here. I don't think we want to be part of your little dog and pony show anymore. C'mon Jenn, let's get out of here."

Lee Anne said, "Would you mind stay for a few more minutes while we discuss something?"

Adams took Jennifer Davidson by the arm and said, "No, we've cooperated all we're going to. We've had enough. If you want to charge us with something, go ahead, but we'll have our lawyers here before the ink's dry on the warrants." They stepped from behind the table and walked to the door. Adams stopped to look at me. "This is bullshit, Scott. You and your cop friends had better get off my back…and Jenn's too. This is the first and last time we're doing anything to *'cooperate'* with your so-called investigation. And, tell Ed Giles not to bother trying to chat me up about anything; he's just as much a prick as you." Adams jerked the door open and sped into the hall, guiding Jennifer in front of him with his hand on the back of her arm.

CHAPTER
TWENTY-FIVE

"That went well, don't you think?" We had gone upstairs to Tom's office after leaving the interrogation level.

"Not so's you'd notice." Tom looked and sounded pissed.

Lee Anne sipped tea. "Interesting reactions, I think. Jennifer looks more like an innocent bystander and Adams more like a guy who gets off on manipulating people, along with maybe arranging things, like a murder."

I asked, "Do you have enough to arrest him, at least on suspicion?"

Tom said, "Probably not, but we'll take what we have to the DA. We need Adams to make a mistake, or tie him more closely to Klein, or possibly to Plum. It's even tougher because he's in New York. We need to keep him under tight surveillance. Her too." He looked at Lee Anne, "Set all that up will you, for Adams, Davidson, and Plum? You'll have to work with NYPD on Adams, so see if they'll give us a hand with Klein and Greene too, okay?"

She nodded and said, "Jennifer told me she didn't need a ride home; her limo is picking her up. I arranged a tail because I'm betting she'll take Adams with her. I'll call New York right now about Klein and Greene. See you later, Cort."

As soon as she left, Tom said, "I know I'm biased, but goddamnit, she's a good cop, a good detective. She's got great instincts. If we keep our 'thing' going, I'm going to hate to lose her from homicide."

I shot him a sly look as I stood up, "You could leave her in homicide and *you* could request reassignment…go back to school patrol or truancy."

Tom flipped me off.

***

The surveillance on Jennifer and Adams didn't yield anything. They went directly from the justice center to her house and spent the rest of the day there. The following evening, a limo picked them up and delivered them to the

Denver Art Museum for a charity event honoring two major contributors. One of the honorees was Freddie Pearlman. Tom managed to get a female undercover officer into the event who kept an eye on everyone under suspicion. She reported Adams and Pearlman had a short conversation early in the evening but no other contact. Nothing could be gleaned from that, since Adams had worked for Freddie at Big East. The policewoman said Pearlman appeared "distracted" for much of the event and left as soon as he had received a congratulatory champagne toast. Adams and Jennifer returned to her house shortly before midnight and there was no further activity.

At noon the next day, a cab picked up Adams and took him to DIA where he boarded a 3:17 p.m. flight for New York. Tom called ten minutes after wheels up to say NYPD was ready to sit on Adams when he arrived there.

***

ADA Brenda Gatlin called as Lindsey and I were sitting down to dinner. "I thought you'd like to know Nate Plum is up to something. We've been keeping a close eye on him since you and I talked. He's changed his pattern; something is happening."

"What makes you think that, Bren?"

"Couple of things: he bought a new truck two days ago and today he went to Wal-Mart and bought luggage and clothes."

"That doesn't sound good; sounds like someone getting ready to take off. Was he alone?"

"Yeah, and that's unusual too. He usually runs around with somebody else from the rat pack living in Freeman's house."

"I wouldn't have thought he had the money for a new rig. Did you guys check out the truck purchase?"

"Yep, and get this, he wrote a check for the full purchase price--twenty-nine thousand and change. It's a last year's model, but brand new Chevy Silverado."

"Where the hell does a scumbag like Plum come up with that kind of money?"

Brenda chuckled, "Funny you should ask! We checked with the bank and found out he opened an account thirteen days ago, which, incidentally, was three days after the murder. The bank said he did everything by email and wire transfer, except for the signature card. Apparently, he took care of that a day or so before we started tailing him."

"Did you trace the wire transfer?"

"Tried, but we don't have a subpoena and officially can't request that kind of information. Luckily, I know somebody-- don't ask! The wire came from a numbered account in the Cayman Islands. That's as far as we can take it."

"What was the total amount?"

"Fifty large."

I whistled. "Raise any eyebrows around your shop?"

"Whadda you think wise-ass? Nate Plum's never made more than twenty bucks an hour in anything he's ever done. He probably made some big money dealin' drugs but it was all cash, so I don't know if he's ever even had a checking account before. You got any ideas on who has that kind of money and who might utilize an offshore bank account?"

I considered her question, "Unfortunately, several people we're looking at could. This isn't going to narrow the field much. Do you guys have anything you can grab Plum for? Can you put him in the slam for a few days so we can grill his ass?"

"That'd be a big 'No'; we don't have probable cause for anything. The best we can do is keep watching him."

"Well, that's something at least. This damn case is making me crazy, Bren. Thanks for the info, and keep in touch. I'll do the same."

Lindsey had been picking at her plate while I was on the phone. "You still frustrated, sleuth?"

"I'm way past being frustrated. We're not much closer to figuring out who offed Willie than we were two hours after somebody flipped his switch."

"It's only been three weeks; something will happen soon."

"I wish I could believe that. The TV 'real crime' shows always say the first forty-eight hours are critical and we're a long ways past that. Tom's catching a lot of heat, everybody from the mayor on down. It can't be helping his frame of mind to be involved with Lee Anne right now either, although that's a good thing."

***

Tuesday morning I had finished a short run and was about to step into the shower when the phone rang. It was Ed Giles. "Hey, Ed, what's up?"

"I'm not sure. Something weird as hell, so I thought I'd better give you a call. Adams called me and I met him for a drink last night."

That was a hell of a surprise after what Adams had said about Ed, and a surprise I wasn't happy about. I pulled my running shorts back on and walked to my office to sit at the desk. "Yeah? What'd he want?"

"First things first, somebody beat the shit out of him. He's all bruised up, black eye, the whole nine yards. He started off on a big-time rant about me, or really about you, 'setting him up.' I damned near walked out because I was thinking he was after *me,* and then it seemed like he got over it and just started to ramble. I got the feeling he seemed nervous as a whore in church, and he was pretty blasted. He'd start talking about one thing and then jump to something else with no continuity at all. He's not nearly as cocky as he was the first time I talked to him. I tried asking him about what happened but all he said was 'troubles.'

"I finally tried something else, asking what he was doing at work. That's when it got interesting. He told me it was mostly finding 'alternative' banking arrangements for clients. You know what that means don't you? He's putting money into offshore or overseas accounts."

I sat bolt upright. "*Holy shit*, Ed! The DA's office in Boulder discovered a fifty grand wire transfer from a Cayman Islands account to a lowlife who is in the mix. Did Adams mention the Caymans?"

"Not specifically, but anyone working that side of the street *has* to include the Caymans. They have nearly as much secrecy as the Swiss, but fewer rules. Here's something else, Adams said most of his work is still coming out of Denver. According to him, he's got two or three deep-pocket clients who back him. They set up investment accounts, let him trade freely and apparently, don't ask many questions.

"That's an unusual arrangement. If I were to guess, I'd say it's a way to channel cash in the form of commissions directly to Adams. He, in turn, is probably hiding cash for his *clients* in overseas accounts."

That brought me all the way to my feet. "He didn't mention any names, did he?"

Ed laughed, "He wasn't *that* drunk! That's something you could make some inquiries about in the oil community, though. After all, those are the people Adams would have known best."

"This is big, Ed. I'll get right on it. Thanks!"

"You're welcome, but I've got a question: Did you tell Adams I was helping you?"

"No, absolutely not. In fact, it worries the hell out of me he's making the connection. Whoever pounded his ass could be tailing him, and meeting with him could have put you on the radar. NYPD is supposed to have him under surveillance too, but they won't be babysitting you. Look, buddy, you've been a huge help, but you're not a cop. It's time for you to clear off. Don't contact him anymore and don't meet with him even if he calls you, okay? And, Ed, keep an eye out, all right?"

***

I didn't think it would work to start asking people directly if they had a numbered account in Switzerland or the Caymans. I needed to make it look like a general question related to the investigation.

I decided to call Vada Benson on the chance Wildcat Willie Davidson had numbered accounts and that she knew about them. "We're spinning our wheels, Vada. We're opening some new lines of investigation and I'm hoping you can help."

Fortunately, Benson was sober, different than the last time we'd talked, and surprisingly cooperative. "I'll do what I can. What do you need?"

"Do you know if Davidson had any overseas banking accounts, you know, like Cayman Islands or Swiss numbered accounts?"

She answered immediately. "Yes, he had Swiss accounts. I don't know much more than that, but I know he had them. How is that important in figuring out who killed him?"

"I don't know, it's just something that has come up-- another line of investigation. I'm trying to figure out if the Denver oil community had access to those kinds of deals. Do you know how he set them up or who he worked with?"

"No. It was something he handled on his own."

"Did you ever hear of anybody else, either in Wildcat Oil or Denver, with those kinds of accounts?"

"You mean other than me?" She said with a laugh.

It caught me off guard. I sputtered, "*You* have one?"

"Not that it's any of your business, but yeah, I've got an account in the Caymans."

I nearly swallowed my teeth. Nate Plum's wire transfer had originated in the Caymans. "Let me ask you something else then, do you know a guy named Troy Adams?

"No, never heard of him, who is he?"

I didn't know how much I should tell her, but decided this was too good to back off. "He was a geologist for Freddie Pearlman, but now he's an investment banker in New York.

I continued, "What about Nate Plum? Ever hear of him?"

"Same answer, 'No'; who's he?"

"A scumbag who runs around with Vincent."

Vada sighed, "I've told you before I don't know anything about Vincent or his friends or operation. Why is this Plum important?"

"Because he's advanced to the front of the line with respect to the murder."

"Oh shit! You're not trying to tie him to Vincent are you? Vincent didn't have anything to do with it!"

"I'm not *trying* to do anything. Like I said, we're spinning our wheels. Plum has lots of loose ends associated with him and we *are* trying to tie some of them together."

***

No putting it off anymore, I needed to talk to Freddie Pearlman face-to-face. I parked in my garage, three blocks from Big East's offices in the 17th Street Plaza building. It was going to be another hot one; Denver's downtown building canyons and miles of streets kept the heat concentrated. I kept thinking about people always saying, "Yeah, but it's a dry heat." Once it reached a hundred degrees, it was just hot, dry or not. As my old friend, Hedges, would've said, "I was sweating like a peach orchard boar" by the time I got to Pearlman's. Like this one, not every saying Hedges used made sense (after all, pigs don't sweat) but they were always funny. The ultra-light windbreaker I'd worn to cover my shoulder holster wasn't helping with the heat.

Big East's receptionist looked skeptical when I told her I didn't have an appointment, but was an "old friend" of Mr. Pearlman's. She dialed his private secretary--more likely an "administrative assistant" according to Vada Benson--gave my name, and then mouthed the words "just a moment" at me. Thirty seconds later, she nodded at me, and closed the call. "Okay, Mr. Scott, Mr. Pearlman will see you. Go through to the hall and turn left, Mr. Pearlman's office is at the end."

I thanked her and followed directions. Approaching the double glass doors near the end of the hall, I saw another reception area. It was small but nicely appointed. A woman who resembled the actress Amy Adams sat behind the desk. She stood as I entered and said, "Good morning, Mr. Scott. Mr. Pearlman is waiting for you. Would you like coffee or water or anything?"

"Coffee would be nice, with just a splash of cream, please." She motioned towards the closed door and I entered Freddie Pearlman's inner sanctum.

He stepped from behind his desk as I entered, stuck out his hand, and said, "Well, well, well, Cort Scott! How are you? It's been a long time, too long, since I've seen you!"

Freddie's face had aged a little since whenever that last time had been. He was a small man, probably five-seven and a hundred and fifty pounds. I immediately thought of the contrast to Wildcat Willie who'd been over six feet and close to three hundred pounds. Always an impeccable dresser, Freddie was wearing light-brown, muted plaid, summer-weight suit pants, a white shirt, and a pearlescent tan tie with a light blue diamond pattern. His suit jacket was draped over a free standing valet stand in the corner of his office.

As we shook hands, I said, "Can't complain, Fred. Of course it wouldn't do any good anyway, no one listens."

Pearlman laughed. "You've got that right." He motioned toward the chairs arranged on three sides of an ornate coffee table, and we sat down. "What can I do for you? More questions about the murder?"

Amy Adams walked in behind me with cups and saucers on a serving tray, crossed to the coffee table, and placed the cups on paper coasters. "Your coffee, Mr. Scott; your tea, Mr. Pearlman."

We both thanked her.

I second-guessed my drink selection considering the outside temperature, but tried the coffee; it was just right. "Yeah, I'm still working the murder, trying to pull some things together. I've been getting some troublesome information and am hoping you can shed some light."

Freddie Pearlman looked at me carefully across the top of his cup. He seemed to be considering what I'd said before replying. "I've told you everything I know, Cort. What kind of 'troublesome information' have you received?"

CHAPTER

TWENTY-SIX

I decided to go for broke. "Here's a whole list for you, Freddie: some people have been establishing Cayman Islands accounts through your guy, Troy Adams; Adams and Jennifer Davidson are seeing each other; both of them have met with a lowlife creep named Nate Plum who works for Vincent Freeman; Freeman is Wildcat Willie's bastard son; and the most notable thing of all, we know Nate Plum received a wire transfer of fifty grand from the Cayman Islands. That's a shitload of what the cops and DA call 'circumstantial evidence,' Freddie."

He didn't speak, but raised both hands, palms up in supplicant fashion, as if saying, "What's that got to do with me?"

"The real problem is you seem to be a common denominator for most of these *circumstances*. I think you know a hell of lot more than you've told me."

Pearlman held the saucer in his left hand and sipped from the tea cup in his right. "Are you accusing me of murder, Cort?"

I placed my coffee on the table, and said, as coldly as I could, "Not yet; but you need to clear up a lot of shit, and you need to tell me all you know. Are you one of the guys with a Caymans' account?"

He put his cup and saucer next to mine. "That is absolutely none of your business."

I was really winging it now and decided to push the issue. "Goddamn it, Freddie! The cops, including the Feds, have started issuing subpoenas; they're looking at Adams and Plum. If your name comes up on any of this, they're going to tie you to the murder. If it plays out the way I think, you could be indicted for a whole raft of big-time felonies. I'm talking about conspiracy to commit murder, murder for hire, money laundering, and I could go on. And, what's worse, you'd be

just as guilty as whoever pulled the trigger. The state will be
piping sunlight to you for the rest of your life. I can't offer
you any deals, but I can guarantee it will go better for you if
you cooperate." Most of that was BS; I didn't know anything
for sure.

I saw a flicker of fear pass across Pearlman's eyes and he
paused before answering. "You don't know what you're
asking--

I shouted, "*DAMN IT, FREDDIE*, I'm not *asking*
anything! I didn't like Wildcat Willie either, no one did.
Nevertheless, he didn't deserve to be murdered! If you
bankrolled it, then you're fucking responsible! Get off the
dime, Freddie, man up and answer the questions!"

Pearlman reacted like I'd slapped him. He fell back in his
chair and gathered himself. "Sol Klein and some ape named
Greene came to see me about six months ago. I remembered
Klein from when I was a kid in New York. I didn't know him
personally, but everybody in the neighborhood knew *of* him,
and that he was a loan shark. I hadn't heard his name in years.
Anyway, he started talking about what a shithead Davidson
was, and how he, Klein, knew *I'd* been the one who
discovered Trumpet Creek and that Davidson and Wildcat Oil
had stolen the credit. He went on and on about how Davidson

had treated his first wife, divorcing her and driving her to drink. He said it killed her; not too far from the truth, according to Jennifer.

"Anyway, Klein segues right into how Willie had cheated him, how he'd put up the seed money to get Wildcat Oil started and then got cut out when they started finding oil. He said he was finally going to collect and, if I'd help him, I'd get my revenge too."

Pearlman got up, turned to the south-facing window framing Pikes Peak sixty miles away, and continued his story with his back to me. "I must've had my head up my ass to even listen to the seedy, old bastard. I *knew* he was a goddamned mobster, *knew* it was stupid, but I can't tell you how much it bothered me that Wildcat Oil was getting credit for Trumpet Creek. Damn it all, I'd worked on that prospect for years and then fucking Wildcat Willie slipped in and got all the glory!

"I told you Adams worked on Trumpet Creek for me. I don't know why, but he took it personally when *he* wasn't credited for the discovery. In my opinion, that was kind of stupid because *I* put him onto it in the first place. But, for whatever reason, he quit the oil business and moved to New York. Somehow Klein ran into him and got the story. I don't know how they hooked up, but Adams must have told one hell of a tale.

"I knew Jennifer Davidson and Adams had met before he left Denver. I assume she must've told Adams about Vincent Freeman and his monkey-wrenching operation and Troy passed that along to Klein. I didn't know Jennifer talked to Klein, but the old son-of-a-bitch sure as hell did his goddamn homework. He even tracked down Davidson's wife and the step-daughter and tried to enlist them; they were smart enough to tell him to go to hell. I shoulda done the same."

Freddie returned to his chair, opened a drawer in the table, and extracted a long, green cigar. He motioned at me, said, "La Flor Dominicana Double Claro?" I shook my head. He used a gold clipper to nip the end and lit up with a lighter that could've doubled for a cutting torch. After several puffs to get it going, he continued from behind a smoke cloud. "Klein said he had a way to squeeze Davidson until he'd be forced to pay, but that wouldn't be the end of it. After he got *his* money, he planned to keep squeezing; he wanted to run Wildcat Willie out of the business. That was supposed to be my 'revenge.'"

I interrupted, "I don't get it. What the hell did Klein have for leverage? It'd been nearly thirty years since Davidson ripped him off."

Pearlman considered his answer. "Apparently, several things: he was going to start by dropping hints about Davidson getting his start with mob money; about money laundering; about selling more than a hundred percent of his deals, which is fraud. And the biggie, he said he had evidence Willie had raped some woman and Vincent Freeman was the result."

I studied Freddie and wondered if he knew the whole story. "Do you know who the woman was?"

"No. And I don't know what kind of 'evidence' Klein had or where he got it. Like I said, I must have been crazy to ever get wrapped up in this! I mean, I knew what Klein was planning was blackmail and extortion. I guess I must have thought Davidson would just rollover and I'd be shut of him once and for all."

I couldn't stop myself. "You know, for a smart guy you're the dumbest bastard I've ever met, Freddie." He nodded in reluctant agreement. "How did Adams figure into it and what was the plan?"

"Klein said we'd each put fifty thousand into a Caymans' account Adams would set up. All three of us would have access, but Adams would be the money man. He'd start feeding money to Vincent Freeman and Freeman would really start to ratchet up the pressure on Wildcat Oil. He'd sabotage

their operations, bring frivolous lawsuits, and maybe even
surreptitiously threaten their personnel. After they started
getting the message, Klein would have Manny Greene 'call'
on Davidson. Greene would tell him that Klein wanted a
million bucks to keep quiet or he was going to start tipping the
Feds. If Willie balked at all, Greene was going to immediately
mention the rape stuff *and* that the price had just gone to two
million."

It was my turn to start pacing around Pearlman's office.
"How far did they take it? When did everything go
sideways?"

"The whole damn plan almost turned to shit before it even
got started. When Klein contacted Freeman to tell him what
he wanted, Freeman told him to get stuffed. He said he wasn't
in it for money; he was trying to make a difference. But right
after that talk, Nate Plum called Klein back and said he could
do it, and that Freeman hated Davidson so much he'd come
around. Plum wanted some money to be the middle man and
Klein agreed."

"It took a couple of weeks before Freeman called Klein
and said he was in. After that, Adams started giving Freeman
money. The first thing they did was arrange for a flim-flam
operation at a state oil and gas lease sale in Wyoming.

Freeman sent some guy to buy a lease Wildcat Oil had
nominated. They were going to bid whatever it took, but had
no intention of paying off the bid. You know the winner has
several days to pay up, but if he doesn't pay, it takes months to
go through the process of getting a tract re-nominated and put
back up for auction. They just wanted to gum up the process
for as long as they could.

"Next, they paid some wild-ass environmental lawyer to
file suits against several of Wildcat's operations scattered all
over the Rockies. There was other stuff too; I'm pretty sure
some gathering systems were blown up, some pump engines
were wrecked, and some containment dikes were destroyed.

"But the shit hit the fan when Greene got to Davidson
and told him what Klein wanted. Instead of paying off,
Davidson went ballistic, threatened to call the cops on them
for extortion, said the statute of limitations had run out on
everything, and he'd quit worrying about any of it years ago.
He said he was just like JP Morgan or General Electric--he
was too big to fail. Sounded just like the prick."

I fixed him with a stare, "What happened then?"

"I never heard another word until Davidson got whacked.
Since then, I've been too scared to do anything. I think you
can see why. What's going to happen now?"

"We're going to police headquarters and you're going to tell all of this to Tom Montgomery and the DA. Call your lawyer and tell him to meet us there, but tell him you're doing this completely voluntarily, and you don't want him trying to stop you."

I called Lee Anne and told her I was bringing Fred Pearlman over immediately; he *wanted* to make a statement. She said she'd let Tom know and get someone from the DA's office over.

I waited while Fred called his lawyer and then asked his secretary, that's what he called her, to come in. He told her he would be out the rest of the day, to cancel any appointments, and he'd call her as soon as he knew his schedule. She asked if everything was all right, or if there was anything she could do. He told her No, but he'd be in touch.

He gathered up a few papers for his briefcase, pulled on his suit jacket, and we left. Freddie said he was parked in the building's lot and I could ride with him. It was ten blocks to the justice center and over ninety degrees outside, so I agreed. We entered the parking elevator; he pushed "P3" for the third level. I would have liked to say something but couldn't think of anything. Freddie stared silently at the floor.

CHAPTER
TWENTY-SEVEN

Lindsey and I were having dinner on the deck when Lee Anne called. "Do you have time to talk?"

"We're just starting dinner, but it'll keep. What's up?"

"We spent all afternoon with Pearlman. You did a great job getting him tuned up; he told the story exactly as you described, and he told his attorney to sit there and keep his mouth shut. He's scared to death. When we turned him loose about five o'clock, the DA told him--

I exclaimed, "*You cut him loose?*"

"Had to; we didn't have anything to charge him with."

"Jesus Christ, Lee Anne! Couldn't you guys think of *anything?* At the very least, Pearlman is part of a conspiracy to, uh, well… "

"Exactly, a conspiracy to do *something*, but not much of a basis for an arrest warrant. If we could prove somebody paid for Davidson's murder from the Caymans' account, we can arrest him. But until we can prove something, he's on his own."

"Goddamnit, he's a--what do you call it--a material witness? You could have at least put him in protective custody! You guys are screwing up! If these assholes get wind he's been talking to the cops, they'll cancel his ticket!"

"I'm sorry, Cort. We don't have any choice."

"That's bullshit! There have to be choices. Can't you at least put a tail on him? It's not enough, but it might give him a little protection."

"I don't know, maybe. I'll check into it. It'll have to wait until tomorrow though, because we'll have to talk to the DA."

"This *sucks,* Lee Anne! Look, if it's a question of manpower, I'll do it. I'm working for the DA's office, aren't I? Freddie's a friend, or at least he was. I don't want to see him snuffed, regardless of what he's done."

Lee Anne sighed, "Okay, I'll pass it all on in the morning. But Cort, don't do anything on your own."

I couldn't hide my impatience and frustration, "So what's going on right now?"

"Hopefully, the NYPD surveillance on Klein, Greene, and Adams is continuing, and the DA's office is researching whether we've got enough for arrest warrants on conspiracy to commit extortion and suspicion of murder. I talked to your friend, Brenda Gatlin, and Boulder issued an arrest warrant for Plum on a parole violation: I saw him smoking that torpedo, remember? We want to get him in custody so we can sweat him."

I wished I'd thought about the marijuana when *I'd* talked to Brenda. "Good to know. I gotta tell you though, none of this seems like enough." I closed the call and went back to the table.

Lindsey poured more wine. "You don't sound happy. What's going on?" I told her and she thought for a moment, "I can understand why you're worried. From what you've said, Pearlman isn't like Klein or Greene, you know, some kind of gangster. He's a businessman who got pissed off and jealous; he got caught up in a scheme to get even and made some stupid mistakes. He doesn't sound like a killer."

I said, "I think that's true, but from what he told me, the stupid bastard got into it up to his eyeballs. He could've put a stop to it as soon as Klein talked to him. I know he didn't pull the trigger, but he sure as hell helped greased the slide for whoever did. I hope it doesn't get him killed."

We finished dinner, cleared the table, and took the wine, a 2009 Rodney Strong Russian River pinot noir, to the glider. A nice forked-horn buck was munching on chokecherry leaves behind the house. He looked up at us, insolently dropped his pellets on my lawn, and returned to his browsing.

Lindsey took my hand. "What would you say to a soak in the hot tub, sleuth? We haven't had much 'together' time since you started on this case. I'm feeling a little needy."

That got my attention. She was right. We hadn't been intimate since our trip to Black Hawk. "I'd say 'Let's go for it.' I'll bet I can find another bottle to put us in the right frame of mind."

She gave me her lascivious look. "Right frame of mind is okay, but don't overdo it. I don't want you being 'overmedicated' if you catch my drift." She laughed, picked up her glass, and headed back inside. As it turned out, we each consumed the absolute correct dosage.

CHAPTER

TWENTY-EIGHT

Mack Groves, my ADA friend and "official" employer, called about protecting Fred Pearlman. It wasn't what I wanted to hear. He said they'd agree to put a car outside his house dark to dawn, but that's as far as they could go. They weren't going to sit on him at work or try to tail him. I raised hell, but Mack said that's the way it was.

Two days passed with no developments. I was driving Lindsey crazy when she was at the house, and I was afraid she was going to need some "me" time at her place. That would have made things even worse. I needed to make something happen.

It was almost noon in Denver, 2:00 p.m. in New York.

"Adams? This is Cort Scott calling."

Adams was slow answering. "What the hell do you want? You've got some balls calling me after that bullshit 'meeting' last week!"

"We've discovered Nate Plum received a wire transfer of a large amount of money from a Cayman Islands account. We know you've opened accounts for various people, possibly including Klein. I need a list of those people."

Adams replied angrily, "Get a fucking warrant, Scott. I'm not giving you anything! That's totally protected, private information and you have no right to it for another goddamned fishing expedition. I'm warning you to get off my back on this. I told you, I don't know anything about Davidson's murder. You're not even a cop for chrissakes; I don't have to answer to you."

"Listen up, Adams! You may not know it, but you're in *way* over your head. Klein has been 'arranging' things like this for fifty years; he'll arrange another killing if he figures you're a weak link."

The call disconnected.

***

It was 7:48 a.m. I was sitting on the deck, reading the paper, and having a cup of coffee when my cell rang. My ring tone, a barking dog, frightened a big mule deer doe eating my day lilies. The screen said Tom Montgomery. "Hey Tom, you're up and around early. What's up?"

"Somebody popped Pearlman. Lee Anne and I are headed downtown now. We'll be there in thirty minutes. Can you meet us?"

"*GODDAMN IT! Son-of-a-bitch!* I fucking *told* you!" I paused, took a deep breath to absorb the bad news, and said, "Yeah, I'll come. Where?"

"Third level of the 17th Street Plaza parking garage. Park out on the street; we've got the entrance blocked."

"I'm leaving right now." My heart sank and my stomach rolled. Forcing Freddie Pearlman to talk to the police had gotten him killed--*I'd* gotten him killed by poking at Adams. Klein or Adams must've had eyes on Pearlman and murdered him. They were the only ones with motives. Freddie could have sent them to prison...or worse.

I didn't exactly obey the speed limits and made the trip in forty minutes. I parked in a lot at Eighteenth and Larimer and ran to the 17th Street Plaza building. The parking entrance and exit were draped in yellow crime scene tape. A uniformed cop was standing between the two driveways. I walked up, gave him my name, and said Lt. Montgomery was expecting me.

The cop asked for ID, looked it over carefully, and said, "Go ahead; the lieutenant's down on the third level."

I ducked under the tape and sprinted down the exit ramp to the third floor. There were only three cars parked on this side of the garage including a white BMW SUV. I slowed when I saw the uniforms, plain clothes, and suited-up crime techs milling around the BMW near the elevator entrance. I saw a body in a business suit crumpled in the door of the elevator.

I approached the group and spotted Tom near the center. He nodded in my direction and held up one finger to indicate I should stay back until he was done issuing instructions. I followed orders. Lee Anne walked from behind the crowd near where I was standing. She stopped a few feet away, nodded her head, but wouldn't make eye contact and didn't say anything.

Tom spoke to the cops for another minute, turned, and walked slowly over. Lee Anne joined us. Tom's face looked like someone with bad acid reflux and one hell of a headache. His voice was raw with emotion when he spoke, "What a colossal fuck-up! We finally catch a goddamn break when you pried this guy loose and now he's a corpse. We should've trumped up something to hold him. He'd still be alive if he'd spent the time in a cell. God *DAMN* it! This fucking case is going to end up costing me my job!"

I didn't know what to say so just asked, "You got anything yet?"

Tom shot me an incredulous look. "I just got here for Christ sake! We don't know shit yet--looks like he took one or more right in the head as he was stepping in the elevator."

"Any idea when?"

Tom pointed at the BMW, "That's his SUV. He uses a pass card for monthly parking...it was still in his hand. We've had a car outside his house the last couple of nights, but it leaves at 5:30 a.m. We'll check the card reader, but I'm guessing he got here right around six a.m., before most people start showing up. Some gung-ho stock broker getting to work early found him and called 9 1 1 at 6:17 a.m. We had a car out front and a patrolman down here in three minutes."

"What happens now?"

"Same shit as before; we work the scene, start talking to people, and try to find a lead."

"Goddamn it, Tom! You've got all the leads you need: Adams, Klein, Greene, Plum!"

Tom yelled, "We don't have shit! Maybe we've got a head start with those names, but we've still gotta work the case."

"So what do you want me to do?"

"Just like before, I need you to work the oil and gas business angle. Start running your traps to find out who had it in for him; who might have wanted him dead. You know the drill."

This time, I exploded. "That's *bullshit* and a fucking waste of time, Tom! Klein or Adams killed him or had him killed. They're the only ones with motives. They must've been watching him--or maybe me; saw us going to police headquarters and put two and two together."

Tom bristled. He was fighting to keep from lashing out. His face turned red, the veins in his neck and temples swelled, and he clenched and unclenched his hands. He had to be wondering who the hell I was to question how he was running the case. Finally, he took a deep breath and let it out slowly. I watched him regain control. "I hate it when you're right, but you are. You were right about the danger to Pearlman. This is on me. Come back to the office with us and we'll start working the phones. We need to see if Boulder has a handle on Plum because they haven't picked him up. We need to know about the surveillances on Klein and Adams.

"We probably should also check on Jennifer Davidson and even Vada Benson. Would you do that for me? Tom's face had softened and he was breathing almost normally. "Cort, I'm sorry I jumped at you. This case has me fucked up. I'm literally 'fighting City Hall' with everybody from the mayor on down bugging me for answers I don't have. It was bad enough with just Davidson; it's going to get worse now."

He turned away from the crowd of cops and lowered his voice. "Trying to handle this case *and* be with Lee Anne at the same time may be more than I can manage. I don't want to screw up with her; I haven't felt this way about anybody in a long, long time, if ever. But I've *got* to get these murders cleared too."

I felt for my friend. "You don't have a problem with me, Tom. I hope you can work it out with the job and Lee Anne. I'm going to my own office to make the calls; I can concentrate better there than police headquarters."

I walked back to my car and drove the three blocks to my regular garage. I parked on the fifth floor, because I always parked as far away from other cars as possible hoping to avoid dinging my doors. The fiber glass bodies on Corvettes weren't made for dings.

***

I called Brenda Gatlin. "Hey Bren, we've got big trouble. There's been another murder and it's connected to the Davidson case."

"Oh man! That's terrible! What's going on? Who's dead?"

"Freddie Pearlman, another Denver oil guy. He gave us some information we think ties Plum to a wise guy from New York *and* to a Cayman Islands' bank account. The cops just found Pearlman dead in his office parking lot. Somebody was probably tagging him and must've spotted him talking to the police. They decided to shut him up. The worst part is, I got him to go to the cops in the first place. I probably got him killed."

"That sucks, Cort, I'm sorry. But there probably wasn't anything you could've done."

"I coulda kept an eye on him myself; I coulda *not* forced him to go to the cops. Don't try to make me feel better, Bren. It isn't gonna happen. Now all I want to do is catch his killers, which is why I'm calling. Did you have eyes on Plum last night and early this morning?"

"Yes and no; we saw him drive his truck into Freeman's place late yesterday afternoon. About nine last night, two vehicles left at the same time, but Plum's truck wasn't one of them. They headed toward the Rock Bar, split up at the intersection, and one went to Broomfield. We only had one guy on the stakeout; he had to make a decision, so he followed the one into Broomfield. That turned out to be Freeman and one of his other creeps, not Plum."

"Crap! So we don't know if Plum was in the other car, or left Freeman's later, or what?"

"That's about the size of it. We had an unmarked car back out there at 6:00 a.m., but there hasn't been any activity. We put out a BOLO on Plum's truck but---

"What's a BOLO?"

"Aw, c'mon, Cort…you're supposed to be working with the cops! It means 'Be on the Look Out,' like an APB--an All Points Bulletin. Plum doesn't have plates on his truck yet, just a temporary, but it'll show up if he uses any of the toll roads with plate readers. It won't give us real time, but it might put him in an area."

"Better than nothing, I guess, and if it's all you've got, it's all you've got. Keep an eye on Freeman's place, will you? And, let us know if you sight Plum."

"We'll try. You do the same from your end, okay?"

"I'll try.

***

I called Vada Benson next. "Vada? Cort Scott."

"You sound like hell! What do you want? It's awfully early."

"Somebody killed Freddie Pearlman this morning and we think it's related to Wildcat Willie's murder."

"*Oh My God!* Freddie Pearlman? What do you mean 'related'?"

I decided to tell her what I suspected. "I think Freddie got sucked into a scheme with some mobbed up guys from New York. They were going to extort Davidson for what they figured he'd cheated them out of, plus interest. Freddie was a lot more pissed off about Trumpet Creek than he ever let on, and he went along with these assholes to get some payback. They were using Vincent's outfit to turn up the heat on Wildcat Oil, and they were threatening to expose Davidson's past…including the rape."

Vada gasped, "How in the hell could they know about that?"

"That's what I need to know, Vada. Are you *absolutely* sure you never told Vincent about it? Did you tell *anyone*?"

"*NO*, never! I swear I've never told a soul!"

I believed her. "How did Klein find out then?"

"Who did you say? Klein? Are you talking about Sol Klein?"

"Yes, do you know him?

"I know *of* him; when I started working for Davidson, he used to call all the time. He knew Davidson and his first wife. He was always talking about how well he knew Rhonda from the 'old neighborhood;' said he'd met her before Davidson. The way he said '*knew*' was really dirty sounding. A couple of times, he mentioned how he still called her now and then. I used to suffer through those conversations until I could pass him on to Davidson."

"How long did that go on?"

"Not too long, just until they divorced. He still called after that, but was always pissed off and only wanted to talk to Davidson. I know the two of them argued a lot, but I never put it together.

"I swear to God, I never told anyone about the rape; Davidson was the only one who knew. But now I'm wondering if he dropped the ball with his wife before the divorce. I mean, I *know* he told her about fathering Vincent, which was the reason for the divorce. But I'm positive she never knew I was Vincent's mother. I doubt if she even knew who he was, his name or anything. She knew Davidson was a bully; knew what he was like even around people he supposedly cared for, like her. I wouldn't have been surprised if he raped her too. Maybe she figured it out on her own and told Klein what she thought."

I pondered what she'd said, "It would help explain a lot of things. Listen, Vada, in case we're completely wrong about everything, you need to be careful for a while. It might be something totally different from what we think, but it's also possible other people are being targeted."

She sighed, "To tell you the truth, I haven't left the condo since the day you and the cops were here. I've been having my groceries and booze delivered; the concierge brings them up. I'm not going anywhere until you guys make some arrests."

***

"Jennifer, it's Cort Scott."

"Oh. Hello." Her voice was cold.

"I'm calling to tell you Freddie Pearlman was murdered early this morning. We---

I heard Jennifer catch a deep breath and gasp into the phone, "NO! This can't be happening! Not Freddie

Pearlman! My God! Who's going to be next? Please tell me it isn't true!" The anguish in her voice seemed real. I had a quick thought, I might have been wrong about her.

"I'm afraid it is. The other bad news is we think Sol Klein, Manny Greene, and possibly your friend, Adams, may be involved. When was the last time you spoke with him?"

Again, she paused before answering, "I'm sure Troy is not involved, not in murder. I spoke with him this morning. He called before going into his office. He apologized for calling so early; said he just wanted to say 'hi' before starting the day."

Adams was establishing an alibi. "Has he ever called you like that before?"

"Well, no, not that I remember. Why?"

I ignored her question. "Are you sure he was calling from New York?"

"I assumed so. It was from his cell phone."

"Jennifer, I don't want to scare you anymore than you already are, but you need to be careful. Keep your doors locked and don't open them unless you're sure of who is there. Let your calls go to voice messaging before returning any. And one more thing, call me if Adams phones again. Will you do that?"

She ignored my question. "Do you think Troy is involved in this? Is that what you're implying?"

"Yes."

CHAPTER

TWENTY-NINE

Friday morning, at 6:15 a.m., Lindsey answered the phone, listened a moment, and handed it to me.

Lee Anne was breathless. "We've got problems; NYPD can't find Adams."

I sighed loudly, "This is getting to be old news, first Plum and now Adams. What did they say?'

"I just got off the phone with them. They said they actually haven't had eyes on him since Wednesday night and--
-

It wasn't Lee Anne's fault, but I yelled into the phone, *"Wednesday! Goddamn. And they're just calling you now?* What the hell is going on?"

"I don't know. They put the tail on him as soon as he landed at La Guardia last Sunday tracked him home, and then to work each day. On Wednesday, he left work as soon as the markets closed, hit a bar with a couple of guys, and then ducked into the subway. Their tail lost him for a moment, but assumed he got on his regular train. The cop watching his apartment never saw him. They should have alerted us right then, but apparently they thought he'd show up like usual on Thursday morning--except he didn't.

"To make it worse, the cops thought they could run a scam, call his office and ask for him. Somebody answered his phone, said he was on another line, and asked if they wanted his voice mail. They assumed--there's that word again--it meant he was there, so they said, 'No,' they would call back later. When he didn't show up, they called his apartment and got his voice mail. I have no earthly idea why they didn't call us then, but they made some lame excuse about 'he wasn't a high priority' for them. Tom's so mad he can't talk."

I wanted to throw the phone as far as I could, or break a window, or scream. "I can't believe this shit, Lee Anne! He could be in Denver for Christ sake! He could've shot Freddie Pearlman himself!"

"I know. It's a bad situation."

"That's not the half of it! What are you guys doing?"

"It's probably too little/too late, but we're putting people at DIA and I got NYPD to do the same at La Guardia and JFK. We had dropped the tail on Jennifer Davidson, but we'll have someone back on her within the next hour. I've already called Boulder; they said no one's spotted Plum's truck in days. He's either bugged out or he's holing up at Freeman's."

"I'm not kidding you, Lee Anne, and I hate to say it, but this is a total cluster fuck!" I regretted using the profanity, but not that much.

"I know."

"What about Klein and Greene? Has NYPD lost them too?"

"That's another story---

"Shit, you've gotta be kidding me! Not more! I can't take it!"

"NYPD was never able to establish a tail on Greene, but they said you could set a clock by Klein. They started watching him Monday. He left his office at 5:30 p.m., walked two blocks to his apartment building, never left, and reappeared at 8:30 a.m. Tuesday morning. He walks to his office, stays until noon, and goes to lunch at a delicatessen around the corner. He's back in the office by 1:00 p.m., stays until 5:30 p.m. and repeats.

"He's working hard at establishing an alibi."

"Sounds about right. Klein is the only one we can say for sure wasn't in Denver early yesterday morning. You know we can't watch all the general aviation airports here *or* in New York, and this bunch has access to plenty of money; they could be using private jets. Nobody has the time or resources to check out every private flight between Colorado and New York. Hang on, Tom just walked in. I'm going to put you on speaker."

Tom's voice was strained. "You got anything?"

"Less than you, if that's possible."

He ignored my jab, "I wish we had eyes on some of these assholes. I keep thinking there are more shoes getting ready to fall. What are you going to do now?"

"Go for my run and try not to think about the NYPD."

***

Everyone had disappeared. Tom called Saturday, and Lee Anne on Sunday to report no sightings of Adams. Brenda gave me the same good news about Plum. We all decided to meet in Tom's office first thing Monday to come up with some kind of plan. I didn't harbor a lot of hope.

Our "taskforce" included Tom, Lee Anne, Brenda, Mack Groves, and me, and we filled Tom's office. Tom looked like he'd aged five years: his face was lined and drawn, dark circles were evident under his eyes, and I thought I might not be imagining gray in his hair.

Everything we covered was old ground; no one had any news or, more importantly, any brilliant ideas of how to proceed. We finally agreed to exercise the search warrant on Freeman's place and, hopefully, grab Plum at the same time. At least it would be something. We'd meet at Freeman's gate at 6:45 a.m. tomorrow.

***

I went to my office to catch up on the drilling reports from some wells I was interested in when my cell phone barked. "Mr. Scott? Cort? This is Jennifer Davidson."

I stifled my surprise. "Hello Jennifer. What can I do for you?"

"You asked me to call if Troy contacted me. He just did."

"Where is he? Do you know?"

"Yes. He's here, I mean, he's in Denver. He's coming to my house. Since your call, I've been thinking about what you said regarding Troy being involved in my father's death. When he called, he seemed, I don't know, nervous or distracted or something. He kept saying we needed to talk and there were some things he needed to tell me. I tried to ask him some questions, but he didn't want to discuss anything over the phone. He seemed so nervous and distressed I decided to ask if he'd be willing to talk to you too. He said he would, but only you. No police, at least not yet. Could you come to my house?"

"Of course, Jenn. When is Troy coming?"

"He said he'd be here just past noon, about an hour."

"Okay, I'm downtown at the moment; I can be at your place in forty-five minutes."

"Thank you so much, I'll be watching for you."

I would have to hustle. I locked up and ran to the parking garage, wishing it was closer than three blocks. I lucked out on the midday traffic and, by only slightly exceeding the speed limits, made the trip in forty minutes. After checking through the gated entrance, I stopped in front of Jennifer's house, thought better of it, pulled forward, and made a U turn. I parked on the opposite side, half a block away, near a large willow whose low hanging fronds would partially hide my car.

I crossed the street and stepped up on Jennifer's small front porch. She opened the door before I could ring the bell. She was back to her 'uniform' of jeans and a sweatshirt, although this one said, "Colorful Colorado." "Come in, and thanks so much for coming! I stepped inside.

"Hello again, asshole! Put your hands on top of your head." Nate Plum stepped out from behind the door. He was holding a cheap but lethal-looking Cobra automatic. "Turn around." I did as he said. He lifted the back of my jacket, pulled my gun, and handed it to Jennifer.

Troy Adams stepped into the entryway from the small office to the left. He was holding a Sig Sauer P250, probably a 9 millimeter. He smirked, "Well, how cozy, the gang's all here! How wonderful."

CHAPTER

THIRTY

Jennifer Davidson led the way to the family room. I noticed the sliding door to the patio and garden was open and a gentle breeze was ruffling the partially drawn sheer curtains. Three chairs were drawn up to the patio table; two beer bottles, a water glass, and an ashtray were on the table.

Adams told me to sit in the tall, straight-backed chair facing the fireplace at the end of the room. He and Jennifer took seats on the couch, and Plum sat across from me. Jennifer handed Adams my Beretta and they traded guns. I couldn't figure that out.

Everyone jumped as my cellphone ring tone barked. Plum growled, "Give it to me!" I dug the phone out of my

jacket pocket as slowly as possible, glanced at the caller ID--
Tom Montgomery--and handed it to Plum face down. I was
hoping he wouldn't catch it within the four ring limit I had set.
He grabbed it and looked at the screen as the last ringtone
sounded. "Who's Tom Montgomery?"

Jennifer's eyes widened, "He's Scott's cop buddy, the
DPD homicide guy." She looked at me and said, "Did you
call him? You tell him where you were going?'

I shook my head, and immediately realized I'd just made
two mistakes. First, I should have called Tom; second, I
should have lied and told Jennifer I had.

If anything, Plum looked even more disreputable than
when I'd seen him at Freeman's place. His orange hair had
grown out, showing a half-inch of brown at the roots, he was
unshaven, and his clothes were wrinkled and dirty. The acrid
scent of pot trailed in his wake. Adams looked like he had just
stepped from the front page of GQ: tan slacks, white starched
shirt, dark green blazer, burgundy Bass Weejuns.

"Jennifer, you might want to put a plastic sheet down for
your boy, Nate. He's going to leave a spot and probably an
odor on your chair." I hoped they had a tight choke collar on
the thug. I wanted to get him riled up enough to gain
advantage, but not enough to get shot.

Jennifer's demeanor had changed dramatically. "Shut up, Scott. We don't have time for your bullshit." She turned to Adams, "The plane's going to be ready at 2:00 p.m., and it takes about twenty minutes to get to Centennial. You guys need to leave by 1:30."

Adams looked at her closely, "You sure you're ready for this?"

Jennifer went steely-eyed and paused before answering, "I'm as ready as I'm going to be. How the hell do you get ready to be shot?"

Her answer gave me pause; I began to see what they were planning. I was going to die here as part of an elaborate escape. They were going to kill me and Jennifer was going to be a wounded "witness;" probably shot with my gun. After Plum and Adams made their escape, she would call 9-1-1 and tell the cops some story about how Plum had forced her to call me, and how a shootout had taken place in her house. I'd been killed and she'd been wounded by a stray round from my gun. I hadn't quite figured how Adams fit in, maybe he didn't. Maybe she wouldn't even mention him. "How come, Jennifer? I can sort of understand about Wildcat Willie--understand, not justify--but why Freddie Pearlman, and now me?"

She smiled slightly, "Maybe you can't justify my father's death, but it's not hard for many of us. I would think your 'suspect' list is pretty long; a lot of people truly *hated* him.

"If Pearlman had just kept quiet, stonewalled, and, you know, denied, denied, denied, he probably could have ridden it out. But you're responsible for him. You scared him and he folded.

"As for you, you're just too smart for your own good. I don't think your buddy, Tom Montgomery, or his little southern belle detective, Lee Anne, would've figured anything out if you hadn't led them to the oil and gas community. You got to Pearlman and through him to Troy. Again, it's your fault. If we get rid of you, I still don't think they're smart enough to put it together without you."

I slowly shook my head, "I gave you way too much credit. In fact, you pretty much had everyone fooled, but not after this. It's not going to take the cops long, with or without me." I looked at Plum, "There must be a lot of money in this for you, and it must be nice to have somebody do all the thinking for you. Of course, you're the only one who's going to end up with a needle in the arm. With three murders for hire, you've written your own death warrant, while these two

skate. And where the hell are you going to spend all that
money? You sure as hell can't stay in the States!"

Adams jabbed my gun at me and yelled, "Shut the hell up,
will you? You're a fucking dead man walking!"

Plum began to laugh. "What's it to you? I don't give a
shit where I go. Somewhere warm where there's no
extradition treaty and plenty of weed; there are lots of places
for me!

Again, Jennifer spoke sharply, "You shut up too, Nate!
C'mon, let's get this done. If I sit around much longer, I'll
chicken out." When she stood, she jacked the slide of Adams'
gun. I knew there was a round in the chamber.

Plum jumped up, pointed his Cobra at me, and said,
"Let's go, Scott. Out front!"

I'd have to make some kind of move before we got to the
entryway. That's where they needed the cops to find me--shot
as I entered. Plum brandished the gun, motioning towards the
hall. I led, with Plum behind me, then Adams and Jennifer
trailing.

Three steps into the hall, Adams yelled, "*HEY, NATE!*"
The gunshot was deafening as Adams shot Plum just over the
right eye. He had turned enough reacting to Adams' yell to
take the bullet from the front.

Before Plum's body had hit the floor, I spun to the left
and charged Adams. He pulled the trigger as I smashed into
him. My left hip felt like I'd been branded, like it had caught
on fire. My rush carried Adams backwards into Jennifer, who
caromed back into the family room. Adams crashed into the
wall and I grabbed his right wrist. We bounced off the wall to
the floor. He tried to roll, but was too close to the wall and
only managed to pin his own arm beneath him. I tried to
punch his head, but had no leverage. I got my open hand to
his jaw and pushed his head up and into the baseboard.

He tried to raise his gun hand, but I had his wrist. He did
manage to pull the trigger. The report was incredibly loud.
The bullet must have hit the wall--at least I wasn't shot again.
I pushed off with my toes trying to wedge his arm even more.
I slammed his head into the baseboard. He grunted, tried to
knee me, and bite my fingers. I slammed his head into the
baseboard again, hard this time. He moaned and went slack.

I felt the burning in my hip and smelled cordite. As I
started to move, Jennifer Davidson spoke quietly, "Stay down;
if you move, I'll shoot you."

I slowly turned my head toward her voice. At first, I
could only see her feet and legs to the knees. As I continued
to turn, my field of vision expanded to where I could see

Adams' Sig Sauer held in a military-approved, two-handed grip. A thought passed through my mind: someone who could plan three murders and was willing to take a bullet in the arm would probably not hesitate to pull the trigger.

I heard the hall bathroom door open and someone--a man--reached across me from behind and took my Beretta from Adams' hand. Jennifer said, "Okay Scott, roll toward me, but stay on your back." I did as she instructed.

Ken Iverson shot Troy Adams through the heart.

348 Lee Mossel

CHAPTER

THIRTY-ONE

Adams' body bucked with the impact, and his body convulsed violently. It sounded like he sighed loudly. I don't know why, but a random thought occurred to me: he'd been lucky to have been unconscious. Iverson aimed the gun at my head and said, "Get up, Cort. Move slowly."

I was probably slipping into shock. Iverson's voice sounded as if it was coming from a barrel a thousand miles away. I couldn't seem to respond. I made feeble pawing motions with my hands. Iverson raised his voice to a shout, "Snap out of it! You're not shot. Get up." My eyes were blurring and my ears were ringing from the gunshot. I realized my left hip burned like hell, but the pain was actually a benefit. I began to focus.

I managed another half turn onto my stomach, gathered my knees and elbows under me, and lurched to a kneeling position. Jennifer said, "I think he *is* shot. There's blood soaking through his pants." She walked around me toward Iverson and they exchanged guns: she now had mine; Iverson had the Cobra.

"Too bad, but things like that happen when you get in a gunfight. We'll have to think about which one shot him, Plum or Adams. Plus, we'll have to be careful how we stage the scene; make sure we put the right guns in the right hands; good thing the bullet didn't stay in him since it was his gun. Get the rest of the way up, Cort. We're going to need you out front, closer to the door."

I got to my feet; the pain was subsiding. "Got to admit, I didn't figure on this, Ken." That was an understatement. The shock of the past two minutes was nearly incomprehensible.

The corner of his mouth twitched. "Maybe not, but you were getting too close. We had to move to 'Plan B.' If you would've just taken the bait on some of the other 'suspects' we led you to, it wouldn't have come to this. We thought for sure you'd go after Plum, I mean, what the hell, he *did* kill

Davidson for chrissake! We even thought you'd probably tie
him to Vincent and take 'em both down. If you'd have done
your job, you'd be a hero: solved the murders, caught a killer,
taken down a New York mobster, and even cleaned up some
co-conspirators. You're still going to end up a hero, but now
you'll be a dead one."

I needed to stall for time, maybe get a chance to jump
Iverson. If this was going to be it, at least I wanted to go
down fighting. "I've got to admit you had me headed in that
direction. How'd I miss on you? Why not tell me the story?"

"You missed on me, or rather on *us,* because you're not as
smart as you think you are. In some ways you're a lot like
Adams, always thinking you're the brightest and the best.
Sure, I'll tell you the story; no one's going anywhere for a
while. But walk out to the entryway; I don't want any more of
your blood back here." He looked back at Jennifer and asked,
"How much time do we have?"

She looked at him carefully before answering. "We're
not on a schedule except for a time of death for these two; I'm
certainly not in a hurry to be shot." It surprised me when she
offered, "We basically let Troy make the arrangements for a
jet back to New York. It kept him from being suspicious at
all, almost like it was his idea. He was the one who convinced

Plum he'd be flying to some dumb ass 'exotic locale.' Nate actually thought Manny Greene was sitting in a jet out at Centennial waiting for him." A look of concern crossed her face, and she studied Iverson again before saying, "Are you sure we should be telling him anything?"

Iverson laughed, "Why not? I'm proud of the way we had this worked out. Besides, he isn't going to get the chance to tell anyone." He pointed toward the front door and I limped that way, hoping he wasn't just going to shoot me as soon as I got there.

When we reached the entry and I'd stepped onto the accent rug, Iverson said, "Okay, that's far enough." I tensed for what would come next, and was relieved when he said, "Like I told you, I worked for Mr., --ah, forget that crap, I don't have to call him that anymore--Wildcat Willie Davidson for over fifteen years. It was fifteen years of undiluted hell. He was the worst son-of-a-bitch ever, far worse than anything you've heard or imagined. By the time I figured out I actually *hated* the bastard, I was gut-hooked on the money. That's how he kept people he wanted; with the money. There was just so damned much of it! It's like dope, you're addicted to it.

"At first, I was like his other geologists. You know how it is; you gripe about working Saturday mornings, but you buy into his bullshit about 'who knows which Saturday you're going to find the big one;' the prospect that works, the one to make you rich. I was luckier than some because I found a pretty good field only six months or so after starting work for Wildcat Oil. I learned pretty quickly about his damned bookkeeper overrides, and all the horror stories of guys wanting to leave. But Davidson was crafty; he delivered my first override check personally, hand carried it into my office, closed the door, and started talking.

"He said Mitch Griggs, who was exploration manager at the time, was planning to quit and would probably sue for his overrides. Davidson already had a plan to 'negotiate' with Griggs and then 'reluctantly' agree to make the assignments, *but* only on the prospects he'd actually generated--not the exploration manager's traditional cut of the other geologists' prospects. It was a 'carrot and stick' approach: Mitch would get an override assignment on what he'd personally found, but would lose out on the rest. We were in a bit of a lull right then, with low crude prices it was tough to sell deals, but things were changing, and we were going to get super busy in the next few months. Davidson said if I'd agree to become exploration manager, he'd increase the override on my prospects, *plus* cut me in on everybody else's. After what he'd just said about Mitch Griggs, I asked him if he'd give me direct assignments, but he just laughed, and said, 'I'd have to trust him.' He also wanted me to sign a contract barring me from ever suing. He even showed me a printout of how much everything would be worth if the company was only as successful as it had been over the past five years. The numbers were so goddamned big! I knew at the time, I was being a fool, but I agreed and signed the contract."

He glanced at Jennifer who didn't seem to be listening. "Jenn's heard all this before. But she already knew what a terrible person her father was."

He continued, "We kept increasing our activity level, hiring more guys, drilling more wells, and making more discoveries. It was like a giant snowball, rolling down hill, picking up speed, and getting bigger. The thing hanging over my head, though, was that damn agreement.

"To make matters worse, he kept getting meaner and meaner. He'd come into my office, close the door, and start talking about how he was screwing around on his wife, and how he'd done the same on his first wife, Jenn's mother. He literally tried to get me to pimp for him, always asking about

the secretaries and sales women working for the service
companies.

"And then about a year ago, he called me up to his office
late on a Friday. That wasn't unusual; it usually meant he
wanted to fire somebody or talk about how we could rip off
our partners. But that time, he was drunk as a monkey and
just wanted to bullshit. I don't know if he thought he had me
tied up so tight I couldn't, or wouldn't, say anything, but the
first thing you know, he started telling me about how he used
to screw Vada Benson.

"He talked about seducing her, how much she liked it,
would do anything for him, and keep quiet. I don't know if he
was trying to make some kind of Jewish confession, doing a
guilt trip, or what, but he said he'd gone stupid once and
forced himself on her. He actually used the word 'rape.' He
complained he'd been paying for it ever since and in more
ways than one: the deal he'd made with Vada, Vincent
Freeman, and everything else.

"I filed it away; one more reason to figure a way out, and
keep my money. But I had a problem too; I had culpability in
some of the deals we'd done. Remember when you asked me
about selling more than a hundred percent of deals? I told you
I'd heard rumors about it, but not on my watch. That was

bullshit. I helped him do it all along, right up to the present day. When we came up with a prospect and then something changed and we knew it would be a dry hole, we'd go ahead and put it together, promote the hell out of it, sell as much interest as we could, drill the dry hole, pocket the money, and laugh all the way to the bank.

"Anyway, when Klein showed up, it got me thinking about how to get the best of Davidson, and how to get out from underneath the bastard. A few days after Klein and Greene showed up in my office, I got back in contact and told them I had a plan.

"We'd threaten to expose everything in Davidson's past, force him to pay Klein off, and eventually drive him out of his own company. I would take over running Wildcat Oil including Davidson's interests, which are worth millions. I'd cut Klein in with a sweetheart deal so he could launder all the money he wanted, but this time with an upside: we'd be finding oil. I also figured that once I was in control, I could cut Vada off. I mean, what's she going to say? She already has more money than God, plus her own dirty laundry. Believe it or not, I actually planned to clean up the company and the operations."

I took a chance, "How did Freddie Pearlman and Adams get involved?"

Iverson sighed, "It was probably a mistake, but I told Klein about Freeman and how, if we played our cards right, we could use him to help put the squeeze on, and maybe even get him to put up some money. I knew Pearlman was bent outta shape over Trumpet Creek; Adams too. I'd heard about Adams going to New York, so I told Klein to look him up. Adams jumped at the chance to ruin Davidson, and the two of them made the contact with Pearlman. Klein laid out the scheme and Pearlman went for it. He never had a clue that I was behind the whole deal."

Jennifer was paying attention now. "That's where I come in."

I started to shift my weight to ease my hip, but Iverson waved the gun at me. "Stay put, Cort! You're right where we need you for the endgame, so if you want to hear the rest, stay still." He looked at her, "You don't have to say anything, Jenn."

She seemed determined to join in, "Like you said, what difference does it make? It'll all be over in a little while." Miss Goody Two Shoes didn't sound so innocent now. "You see, I'd met Troy Adams not too long before he quit Big East and moved to New York. We had a fling I guess you'd call it, but frankly, he was a smug, conceited, dull tool; not really my type. We continued seeing each other, though, and I must have said more than I should about my feelings toward my father. Out of the clear blue, Troy started dropping hints about a plan to ruin him. He basically asked me if I wanted to be part of it-- I did.

"That's when I met Ken, told him I'd talked to Troy, and knew what was going to happen. At first he was so mad at Troy for saying anything that he wouldn't return calls or speak to me." She smiled at Iverson and it wasn't a platonic smile. "I had to seduce him, which I did. It didn't take long for us to recognize our 'common interests', so to speak. We both wanted to be out from under my father, we both wanted the money, and we both wanted some form of revenge. And then the strangest thing happened--we fell in love."

That was a lightning bolt; not something I had expected.

"It was a little complicated, but, like I said, Troy's not the sharpest knife in the drawer. He never figured it out. I kept playing him along; we thought we might need someone to take a fall. As it turns out, this is perfect. You and Troy killing each other in a heroic effort to rescue me solves a lot of problems."

I had to keep this going. "Was it part of the plan from the
start to kill Davidson? You keep talking about getting him out
of the business, then taking over?"

If there's such a thing as "a look of remorse", one crossed
Iverson's face. "I hadn't gauged how much Klein hated him,
but no, neither of *us* planned it.

"Apparently, way back when in New York, and before
Davidson came on the scene, Klein and Jenn's mother had
started seeing each other. Her family put a stop to it because
Klein was already mobbed up. In their eyes, Davidson was
'respectable;' going into the suit business with his parents and
all that. Klein was furious and stayed that way. He held a
grudge and finally figured out a way to force his way into
Wildcat Oil--and then Davidson screwed him again."

Jennifer looked slightly ashen and softly said, "I don't
think my mother made very good choices."

Iverson continued, "Looking back, I think Klein planned
on having him killed right from the start. He jumped on my
plan, said he'd finance it with or without Pearlman, and he
made some kind of side deal with Adams to start laundering
big time bucks for him."

Jennifer interjected, "Adams was on board with the murder from the start; he told me so. I think he floated the idea to see if it would shock me."

Iverson gave her a look of surprise, "Did it?"

"Not after you told me about the rape, about Vincent, and the other women who came later."

I thought Iverson's look became more reflective. I asked, "So how'd it go down?"

They exchanged glances and Iverson spoke, "Basically things changed when Vincent Freeman told Klein he wasn't interested in the idea; told him to get the hell away from him. But then Plum called Klein right back and said *he'd* do whatever they wanted if the money was big enough. That played right into Klein's hands, so Greene came out from New York and he and Plum set it up.

"I started feeding ideas to Adams, who'd pass 'em on to Plum, who'd make 'suggestions' to Freeman about upping the ante on Davidson. Freeman didn't even know he was being played. According to Plum, Vincent seemed 'real happy' Plum was doing more and getting 'involved'. They did all kinds of shit: sabotaging well sites, screwing-up equipment, interfering with lease sales, and even filing law suits.

"Greene flew out to Denver again and I made sure he 'slipped' past all our security and got in to see Davidson. That's when things really turned sour: Davidson threw Greene out, laughed at him, and told him to tell Klein to get fucked. He said he wasn't afraid of them and wasn't going to pay a 'goddamn cent.' He even threatened to turn it around by calling the cops and getting them charged with extortion."

"Greene delivered the message and Klein freaked out. He put out a contract on Wildcat Willie, gave it to Greene, and Greene subbed it to Plum. Three days later, Davidson was murdered. I didn't know it was going to happen. And, Jenn didn't either."

Jennifer softly spoke, "It was a bit of a shock because it happened so fast, but it didn't take me long to get over it. I was telling the truth when I said I wasn't surprised. He was a bastard!

"I was also telling the truth about caring for Freddie Pearlman. He got in over his head and didn't even know it. Klein thought he was the weak link all along. After you got Troy to come to Denver by prodding him with your phone call, he put two and two together and started getting worried about Pearlman. Troy told Klein that Freddie was a risk, so Klein got somebody to tail Freddie. He was already being tailed when the two of you went to the police, and whoever was watching him also spotted the police stakeout at Freddie's house. It only took them two days to map out the schedule, see the cops take-off in the morning, and figure out he went to his office early.

"Troy still had access to Big East's office building; he let Greene in and Greene did the killing. Troy liked to act tough, and even though he knew what was going down, it shook him. He wasn't the same afterwards. *He* became the weak link."

Iverson picked up the story. "There were just too many moving parts at that part; we had to find a way to take Adams out."

All I could do was shake my head. I couldn't believe the things I was hearing. I also didn't know how long I could keep stalling and waiting for some kind of opening. "So, what was the real reason for you meeting Plum at the Rock Bar then? Obviously, you weren't trying to find out if Vincent had been involved."

She looked at me for a while probably trying to decide whether to answer or not. Finally, she made up her mind. I didn't know whether that was good news or bad. She said, "Plum called it actually. He said neither Klein nor Greene would answer his phone calls and he wanted more money. He

said if he didn't get it right away, he'd start incriminating
Troy.

"I sort of talked him down; told him we had a plan that
would wrap everything up and he'd get another fifty grand. I
told him he'd get a chance to kill you, *plus* get the money; he
got all excited and agreed. That's how we got him here today.

"Like I said, although Troy wasn't as tough as he made
out to be, it was easy to convince him to take Plum out when I
said Plum was threatening to talk. In the end, they were both
too greedy and too dumb for their own good." She looked at
Iverson, "Let's get this over with."

I had to try something, "Damn it, Ken, Jennifer hasn't
killed anybody. I can tell the cops you blundered into this
mess; ended up with my gun after Adams had shot Plum and
wounded me. I'd say you saved my life when you shot
Adams. You can still get out; you can put a stop to this,
this...insanity! You two could cut a deal with the DA, tell
what you know about Klein and Greene and Troy Adams, and
probably walk away." I was grasping at straws. I knew it was
all bullshit; they would never walk, and I wouldn't let them.

Iverson shook his head, "Don't beg, Cort. It's not your
style--and neither is the bullshit. You know we're not going
to walk. As far as the cops are concerned, we're just as guilty

as Plum and Greene. Our only chance is to take you out of the investigation and get the cops zeroed in on Klein and Greene. Without you, the cops aren't going to make all the connections.

"This is going to make a good story: you and Adams and Plum kill each other when you came charging in trying to rescue Jenn. She is the only witness and she'll be wounded and hysterical. She'll say Adams and Plum forced her to call you, and you must have been suspicious because you smashed in the door the second she unlocked it. When you crashed in, it surprised Plum and he only managed to wound you in the hip. You killed him, but then Adams and you traded shots and both connected. Sometime during the fight, a stray slug creased Jenn's arm.

"She'll call 9-1-1, hysterical, and barely coherent. She can't believe what's happened. When she's able to be questioned, she'll 'confess' to knowing about Adams' and Klein's plan to extort money from her father, and how it was okay with her because he was such a cruel bastard. But she had no idea it was headed toward murder. After that happened, she tried to split with Adams over his involvement, which, in her words, 'probably led to everything that happened here.' She never knew Pearlman was mixed up in any way.

"After the dust clears, the cops will have to concentrate on Klein and Greene and that's a dead end--no proof and ironclad alibis. They'll conclude Plum killed Davidson, which he did, and either he or Adams killed Pearlman. Without you, there's nobody pointing fingers at us; I don't even exist. I'll be running Wildcat Oil, so Jenn and I will have business matters to discuss. When enough time passes, nature will take its course."

CHAPTER

THIRTY-TWO

The front window shattered; a flash-bang grenade exploded in the small dining room adjacent to the entryway; the door burst off its hinges. I dove sideways, away from the explosion toward the office. Iverson staggered backwards; Jennifer, who'd been partially shielded from the dining room explosion, ran toward the family room. S.W.A.T. team members in full combat gear rushed inside and covered Iverson with assault rifles. My ears were ringing and my vision was blurry from the flash. I could barely hear an officer screaming, *"DROP IT, ASSHOLE! DROP IT!"*

Iverson, who'd been facing the blast, was shaking, his mouth was opening and closing and his eyes were bugged out.

The gun he was holding pointed to the floor at a forty-five degree angle. I don't know if he could hear or understand the S.W.A.T. warrior's words, but he slowly lowered the muzzle and allowed the gun to slide from his fingers.

Additional men rushed in through the door: two more S.W.A.T. team members, followed by Tom Montgomery in a combat vest, with an H & K 45 Tactical in his right hand. It looked like an artillery piece compared to the Cobra that Iverson had dropped. My senses were coming back; I heard a shout from the back of the house. Tom yelled, "Cuff this shithead!" and started cautiously down the hall. I regained my footing and followed. Every part of me hurt.

As we emerged from the hall into the family room, I saw Jennifer Davidson racing across the patio toward the garage. She was carrying my gun. Suddenly, Lee Anne appeared and executed a perfect blindside shoulder tackle. Jennifer dropped the gun as they smashed to the ground at the edge of the patio. They both scrambled to their feet; Jennifer adopted a martial arts stance that looked like she knew what she was doing. Lee Anne did the same. Jennifer bounced forward, set up, and tried a sweep kick. Lee Anne jumped away from the kick negating its force, moved inside, grabbed an arm, and pulled her opponent over her shoulder in a perfect takedown. She didn't release the arm; instead, she stepped over, put her foot on Jennifer's shoulder blade, wrenched the arm to full extension, and twisted. Jennifer screamed in pain.

Tom sprinted out of the house to the combatants, his .45 still in hand, and yelled, *"THAT'S IT!"* Lee Anne dropped Jennifer's arm, waited until she got to her knees, and roughly jerked her erect. Jennifer reached for her shoulder and began massaging it. Her face was contorted in pain.

Tom said, "Cuff her ass and take her back inside. Mirandize her and the one in the house and we'll haul 'em downtown." Lee Anne pulled polished-steel handcuffs from the back pouch of her vest and brusquely cuffed Jennifer. Two of the S.W.A.T. team guys frog-marched her toward the house.

Tom looked me over and said, "Looks like you've had a rough day, buddy." He pointed at my blood-soaked pants, "You seem to be leaking a little oil; you okay?"

"Kinda burns, but I'll make it. Couple of inches left and I'd need the meat wagon and probably a year to rehab a hip."

"Six inches left and you'd be talking with a higher voice."

I didn't feel like laughing at his joke. "I'm damn glad to see you, Tom. I thought they were going to cancel my ticket.

I kept stalling as best I could; asking questions, getting the story, but I'd about run out of time. How'd you find me?"

"Pinged your cell. Why the hell didn't you call and tell us what you were doing?"

"I didn't have time; Jennifer called and sounded pretty frantic about Adams coming to her house. I hauled ass to get here."

Tom snorted and gave me a disgusted look. "That's BS! You had a goddamn half-hour drive to here; you've got a cellphone, so you could have phoned easy. That was just plain stupid; typical you, though…going cowboy!"

He was right of course. I could have called. It just hadn't occurred to me. It *had* been stupid. "Yeah, you're right, sorry. How'd you pull off the silent approach and entry?"

"When we pinged your phone, the closest tower showed Belleview and I-25; Lee Anne and I both figured you were here. It was a hell of a decision to scramble a S.W.A.T. team, but you weren't answering your cell. I tried your office too, same deal--so I did it."

"How'd you get to the house so quietly?"

"We parked the truck around the corner, ran down behind the houses across the street, cut through the buildings, and came out right by your car. That way we could approach from the side without windows. We were just taking up positions when we heard a shot. We moved as fast as we could, but it took a few minutes to get the grenade launcher. I was scared we were too late. What the hell was going on?"

A wave of dizziness hit me and I needed to sit down, so I pulled one of the patio chairs close and sat. "It was pretty wild in here; they grabbed me as soon as Jennifer answered the door. Turns out, there were two double crosses going on: Plum thought he was going to kill me and wound Jennifer with my gun, then he and Adams were going to Centennial Airport and fly off in a charter Sol Klein had arranged.

"Instead, Adams shot Plum with my gun--double cross number one. Adams believed he and Jennifer were going to stage it like Plum and I had killed each other and go ahead with the rest of the plan. I changed their plan when I managed to tackle Adams, but then Iverson jumped out of the hall bathroom and killed Adams--double cross number two.

"I didn't have an inkling that Iverson was involved. They were still going to do the 'wounded Jennifer' thing to remove any suspicion from her."

Lee Anne interrupted, "Do you mean they actually thought we'd believe *three* of you killed each other? That's

fucking crazy!" She was pumped up from the fight with
Jennifer. Tom winced at the F-bomb.

I nodded, but said, "Well, Jennifer would have been the
only 'witness;' they had all the guns and bullet trajectories
figured out. You'd have to prove she was lying."

Lee Anne scoffed, "We'd have done it! No one would
believe that story."

Since I would have been dead regardless of whether my
friends had figured it out or not, I shrugged.

CHAPTER
THIRTY-THREE

The first touches of a Colorado fall were noticeable: a little cooler in the mornings, the sky was a deeper blue; I could see a slight yellowing of the scrub oak behind the house. The daytime temperatures were still in the seventies and it was a perfect Sunday afternoon as Tom, Lee Anne, Lindsey, and I settled in on my deck. I poured everyone a glass of 2007 Eberle Estate Cabernet I had opened forty-five minutes earlier.

Raising my glass, I said, "Well, here's to you guys! I understand your transfer came through, Lee Anne; you're moving into the airport division, right?"

A broad smile spread across her face. Tom was smiling also. She said, "Yep, it came through Friday. Airport division is about as far as it gets from Homicide, but I guess that's good."

I sipped the wine. "How's your pulse, buddy?"

"Couldn't be happier! I went directly to the chief and laid the cards on the table…well, most of 'em anyway. I was as honest as I felt I could be; he didn't even blink, although I'm pretty sure he had us figured out. I'd already talked to the commander at the airport; he's a good friend and knows the score. All told, it went pretty smoothly."

Lindsey chimed in, "I'm so happy for you guys! That must have been rough, hiding your lives that way."

Lee Anne nodded and said, "Yes, a little; not all bad though. I think we were able to function okay."

I asked, "Have you been able to decompress since the Davidson murder case?"

Tom nodded, "I think so. We've taken a couple of long weekend trips just to get away from everything." He smiled at Lee Anne, "Believe it or not, we travel pretty well together." He drained half his glass, swallowed, smacked his lips, and said, "Hey, that's pretty good. What'd it cost?"

Lee Anne shook her head, sighed, and said, "Oh God, Tom, you don't ask something like that!" She took a sip, rolled the wine across her tongue, and smiled, "Wow, it really is good, Cort!" She grinned mischievously, winked at me, and said, "How much *did* it cost?"

"Less than you'd expect, but more than Tom probably spends." I laughed and Lee Anne joined me. Tom scowled and pointedly changed the subject, "How's the hip? Still bothering you?"

"Not really, but it took a couple months. It sure gave me a new appreciation for the term 'flesh wound.' You know, it took eighteen stitches to close the tear and it's right where the muscles bunch up every time you move your leg."

Linds hopped up, "I can see we're going to need more wine. I'll get the other bottles you've opened. Incidentally, Tom, he's been milking that damn hip for everything it's worth since he got shot. Ever hear of sympathy sex?" She shot me her best, most lascivious grin and disappeared into the house. Tom laughed; Lee Anne smiled and looked away.

I topped up Tom's glass, which finished the bottle. Lindsey returned with two more Eberle bottles: another '07 Cab and a 2011 Cab-Shiraz. I said, "So, have you wrapped up the case? You guys have been awfully quiet since the arrests; what's transpired? Everything in the DA's hands now?"

Tom and Lee Anne exchanged glances; he gave a hand gesture indicating she should answer. "It was complicated, but I think we've tied up all the loose ends. We used your statement as a template for interrogating Jennifer Davidson and Ken Iverson. With your stuff, it went fairly smoothly. She was a little uncooperative at first, but it changed when she realized we already had everything we needed. We think she's resigned to her fate and decided to tell it all; maybe it'll get her some consideration when it comes to sentencing. She didn't physically kill anyone which will work in her favor, but being part of four murders, no matter how you cut it, is going to land her in prison for a long, long time.

"Iverson, on the other hand, quietly answered every question. Remember what you told us about his saying the money was like a drug and he became addicted? I think the same thing applied to Jennifer. He talked a lot about his divorce, how unhappy he'd been for years, how much he despised Davidson, and how meeting Jennifer had changed everything. He said she made him feel 'young' again. He became 'addicted' to her."

I said, "That's sad in so many ways; Ken was a good guy, or at least he used to be. I never had a clue he was behind the whole deal until the instant he walked out of that bathroom and killed Adams. Talk about a shock to my system! Did their stories agree?"

Tom spoke, "Yeah, pretty much. He filled in a few details."

"Like what?"

"Mostly about Klein and Greene, although the most interesting thing was the fact Vincent Freeman didn't have anything to do with the murders, the extortion plot, anything. He was being set up as a fall guy through the whole thing. They really thought we'd go after him, based only on things like his association with Plum and his targeting of Wildcat Oil."

I said, "Coulda happened, I guess. They were leaving a pretty good trail."

Lee Anne shook her head, "No way! There was never anything solid implicating Freeman. It was just like them believing we'd bite on having three guys shoot each other to death. How stupid was that?"

I thought about it. "I admit it all sounds stupid now, but I would've been dead if you guys hadn't busted in when you did. Stupid wouldn't have mattered to me. You're right about Vincent though; I guess I just disliked him so much I thought he had to be involved."

Lee Anne acknowledged, "That's what they were counting on."

"So how'd it go catching up with Klein and Greene?"

Lee Anne continued, "Klein wasn't a problem. We contacted NYPD within three hours of questioning Iverson and Jennifer. NYPD still had a tail on him, lucky for us considering their recent screw-ups, and when we gave 'em the word, they just knocked on his door. They told him he was under arrest on a warrant from Colorado and was being charged with conspiracy to commit murder in the death of William Davidson. The detective said Klein looked at him kinda funny and said, 'That fucking Davidson's done it to me again.'" A look of disapproval crossed Tom's face at the profanity even if it was a quote. "They sent us a mug shot when he was booked into jail; he looks a hundred years old."

I chuckled and said, "He might be; the old bastard has been a crook for over half a century. I'm betting shutting him down will close out a bunch of crimes; ironic that it'll happen in Colorado."

Lee Anne nodded, "He had some slick-suited New York criminal attorney on the same damn commercial flight the marshals used to bring him here. Shyster had the audacity to ask for bail at his arraignment. It was denied and his lawyer launched into a speech about kangaroo courts and lynch-mob justice. The judge listened for about a minute, banged her gavel, and said, 'I've already ruled, counselor. Now sit down and shut-up before I find you in contempt. We like to administer justice quickly out here in the Wild West, releasing your client on bail would practically guarantee that won't happen.' Klein's mouthpiece looked at old Sol, shrugged, and packed up his briefcase. We heard he literally caught the next flight back to New York."

Tom said, "Greene, however, is a different story. You know, we never have figured out who their 'eyes' were in Denver, but whoever it was must've seen what went down at Jennifer's and got the word to him. When the cops got to his place--he lived in some kind of rat-hole townhouse or condo or something--he'd already bugged out.

"After they ran his rap sheet, they found out he has a brother who owns a cabin in the Pocono Mountains in upstate New York. NYPD contacted the county sheriff who sent a deputy there to check it out. The sheriff walked in a mile or so through the woods and staked the place out. Sure enough, he spotted Greene, radioed it in, and they got a team out there. When they were organized, the sheriff used a bullhorn to demand he come out, but the dumb shit started shooting.

"Turned out, he had a whole arsenal inside: several automatic pistols, couple of assault rifles, and a shotgun. The firefight lasted for twenty or thirty minutes. He wasn't showing any signs of giving up so the sheriff fired a couple of tear gas canisters through the window. That did the trick. Greene literally waved a white flag and yelled he was coming out with his hands up. He begged them not to shoot him."

I asked, "Do you have him back here yet?"

"Yep, got him last week. He's a mean son-of-a-bitch, but dumber than a box of hair. He keeps saying he doesn't know anything about anything; claims he's never heard of Wildcat Willie Davidson or Fred Pearlman or even Klein. His lawyer is also from New York, same as Klein's, so it'll be interesting when he's had a chance to see what we've got. The DA says there aren't going to be any plea bargains for any of 'em, Jennifer Davidson included."

Lindsey had been rather quiet, she yelled, "*Good!* So let me see if I understand: Plum killed Davidson, Greene killed Fred Pearlman, Adams killed Plum, and Iverson killed Adams. Is that right?"

Tom and Lee Anne both nodded and spoke as one, "Yes."

Lindsey said, "Good grief, equal opportunity killers! Jennifer and Klein were the only ones who didn't murder someone."

Lee Anne slowly shook her head almost despairingly, "That'll probably end up keeping both of them from getting life without parole. It helps Jennifer, but Klein's so old, conspiracy to commit murder charges will probably keep him in 'til he dies. I hope so!"

I asked, "Any idea of when the trials will start?"

Tom replied, "You know how these damn things work; it'll take forever…probably be close to a year. I talked to your ADA buddy, Mack Groves, about it yesterday. He's personally going to handle the prosecutions on Greene and Klein: Greene on first degree murder for Pearlman; Klein will get two counts of conspiracy to commit, for Davidson and Pearlman.

"The DA's office has asked for a special prosecutor for Jennifer Davidson--guess who? Your other friend, Brenda Gatlin. Iverson will be last; they're *still* sorting out charges on him. But at the very least, it'll be first degree murder for Adams, and conspiracy to commit for Davidson, Pearlman, and maybe Plum. There's a lot of other stuff if they want to pile on: extortion, fraud, money laundering…you name it, these guys did it!"

Lindsey asked, "What do you think the chances for convictions are?"

Lee Anne lifted the Cab-Shiraz bottle, read the back label, nodded approvingly, and poured a generous glass before answering. "The prosecutors think we've got ironclad cases against every one of them. Like we said, no plea bargains, we're going for the max. We're expecting life with no possibility of parole for Greene and Iverson; life for Klein and Jennifer. Like I said, that's a death sentence for Klein and Jennifer will be an old woman *if* she ever gets out."

I raised my glass in salute, "Considering those sentences, here's to Wildcat Willie selling more than 100% percent of his last deal."

EPILOGUE

Vada Benson poured three jiggers of Three Olives
vodka over a couple of ice cubes, picked up the glass of
Silver Oak cabernet, and walked back to the couch. She
handed the wine to Vincent Freeman, held out her drink,
and they touched glasses. "So, are you going to keep
targeting Wildcat Oil after all this?"

Freeman grinned, tasted the wine, and said,
"Hopefully, I won't need to with you taking over. If I
can't trust my own mother to change things, who can I
trust? How in the *hell* did you pull everything off?"

Vada sipped the vodka, set her glass on a coaster,
and leaned back in the corner of the couch. "It wasn't
all that hard, really. I approached Janet Davidson and
her daughter, Rachel, right after all the arrests came
down. I knew they didn't have any interest whatsoever
in the company, although they owned it. I told them
with Davidson dead and Ken Iverson gone, unless
someone stepped in immediately, the whole company
would fall into disarray, which is true, by the way. I
said no one knew more about the company and how it

works than me; that I felt comfortable in taking over and making decisions so that things could continue.

"Their primary interest was in how much money they would receive if that happened. I said they would get all of Davidson's share, and could split it any way they wanted, *less* five percent to me for taking over as CEO. They didn't even want time to think about it! They agreed on the spot."

"So what's it worth to you?"

"*BIG* numbers--that's what it's worth! Wildcat Oil produces about twenty million barrels a year; after you figure all the partners' shares, the land and mineral owners' royalties, the overrides, and everything, Wildcat Oil probably nets about a third of that, or about three and half million barrels. Crude price is about ninety bucks a barrel currently, so that calculates to approximately six hundred million dollars a year in gross income. Davidson, himself, owned sixty-seven percent of the company, so he was taking in around four hundred million. Of course, all the drilling expenses, operating costs, leasing, and hell, even the office space and salaries have to come out of that. Still, to answer your question, if I take five percent, I should get ten or twelve million a year."

Freeman choked on his wine and sputtered, "I had no idea! But, wait a minute, didn't you tell me that the one percent you were already getting was worth fifteen million or so? That doesn't make sense."

"My one percent is different. It's out of 100% of every barrel the company produces. Plus, that's after Davidson paid all the costs. Understand?"

"Not entirely, but it doesn't make any difference. It's a lot of money. But what about my end of it--the concerns I have about the environment and such? What about that?"

Vada picked up her glass and took a drink. "I'll make some changes in how we do business. I'm not saying I'm going to do everything you ask, but things will be better...a lot better. But, Vincent, let me give you some advice, 'Don't bite the hand that feeds you.'"

Vincent Freeman looked carefully at his mother, the mother he'd never really known, and said, "I'm going to ask, although I don't know if I want to hear the answer...Did you have anything to do with what happened?"

Vada smiled over the rim of her glass, "Like *you* said, 'you don't really want to know.'"

ACKNOWLEDGEMENTS

For me, writing a book is hard work. This one, with a subtle shift from "crime thriller" to "mystery", seemed particularly difficult. I gratefully acknowledge the constant support and encouragement of many people including, first and foremost, my wife, Jan, for her continued support, suggestions, edits, corrections, and help.

Donna Chase, who completed her superb editing work with the pressure of my arbitrary publication date looming.

I owe additional thanks to Bob Ragsdale; Bill and Judy Walker, Ben and Linnea Peterson, Bob and Tina Buente, Ann Padilla and Bob Grabowski, Dave Chew, Bob Lent, and Mary Caughey.

Cortlandt Scott's character borrows heavily from several of my author idols' protagonists including: CJ

Box (Joe Pickett), James Lee Burke (Dave Robicheaux), Robert Crais (Elvis Cole), Michael Connelly (Harry Bosch), Elizabeth George (Thomas Linley), Robert B Parker (Spenser and Jesse Stone). My thanks to all of them for creating vivid, interesting characters.

About the author:

Lee Mossel was born in Eugene, Oregon, and raised in the small logging and lumber mill town of Noti about twenty miles west.

He attended the University of Oregon, graduating with bachelors and masters degrees in geology, and spent thirty-five years as a petroleum geologist in Denver, Colorado, working for several oil companies. He also cofounded and managed two independent petroleum exploration companies.

Since retiring, he has served on various boards of directors, written numerous op-ed pieces and newspaper columns, given talks on the oil and gas business, and generally enjoyed life.

Beginning with *The Murder Prospect* in 2012; *The Talus Slope* in 2013, he has begun a career as an author of crime thrillers and mysteries. *More Than 100% Dead* is his third Cort Scott novel.

He enjoys world travel, sports, fine wines, good food, and golf...not necessarily in that order. He lives in Parker, Colorado, a place featured in the Cort Scott series.

The Cortlandt Scott Series

The Murder Prospect

The Talus Slope

More Than 100% Dead

E-books for all electronic devices at:

Smashwords.com

Paperbacks at: **amazon.com**

Connect with me online:

http://www.leemossel.com

lee@leemossel.com

Made in the USA
Charleston, SC
10 October 2015